FANGS & FENNEL

ALSO BY SHANNON MAYER

The Venom Trilogy

Venom and Vanilla (Book 1)

The Rylee Adamson Series

Priceless (Book 1)
Immune (Book 2)
Raising Innocence (Book 3)
Shadowed Threads (Book 4)
Blind Salvage (Book 5)
Tracker (Book 6)
Veiled Threat (Book 7)
Wounded (Book 8)
Rising Darkness (Book 9)
Blood of the Lost (Book 10)
Elementally Priceless (A Rylee Adamson Novella 0.5)
Alex (A Rylee Adamson Short Story)
Tracking Magic (A Rylee Adamson Novella)
Guardian (A Rylee Adamson Novella 6.5)
Stitched (A Rylee Adamson Novella 8.5)
RYLEE (The Rylee Adamson Epilogues Book 1)

The Elemental Series

Recurve (Book 1)
Breakwater (Book 2)

Firestorm (Book 3)
Windburn (Book 4)
Rootbound (Book 5)
Ash (Book 6)

The Blood Borne Series

(coauthored with Denise Grover Swank)
Recombinant
Replica

The Nevermore Trilogy

Sundered
Bound
Dauntless

A Celtic Legacy

Dark Waters
Dark Isle
Dark Fae

Contemporary Romance

High Risk Love
Of the Heart

FANGS & FENNEL

THE VENOM TRILOGY BOOK 2

SHANNON MAYER

47N⬤RTH

Published by 47North, Seattle

www.apub.com

Amazon, the Amazon logo, and 47North are trademarks of Amazon.com, Inc., or its affiliates.

ISBN-13: 9781503942103
ISBN-10: 1503942104

Cover design by Jason Blackburn

Printed in the United States of America

CHAPTER 1

"Alena, sister of mine, no matter what you think, no matter how much I love you, this is a damn bad idea you have. I think it's stupid." Tad slowed his steps as we approached the King County Courthouse and put a hand under one of my elbows. I wobbled in my heels as I glared at my brother, but I said nothing. What was there to say? We both knew the court system would be against me from the get-go—me being a Super Duper was all it would take to have the judge ignore me. But I had to try. I couldn't just hand over all I'd worked for to a rotten apple of a man—Roger the Cheater. Never mind that we were technically still married; Roger didn't deserve a single piece of my pie.

I tightened my hold on the stack of papers I'd put together over the last week. Sheet after sheet of proof that I existed, that I hadn't died. To dispute a death record fabricated for the convenience of a government that didn't want to deal with the messy reality of Super Dupers on the fringes of society. The fake death certificate floated out there in the sea of excessive—duplicate, triplicate—paperwork, and no doubt there was a notarized copy in Roger's clammy, weak hands. I stared hard at the folder, and peeking out from the top edge was a piece of paper with my full name on it, barely legible in the dying light of the day. All my government papers, signature comparisons, affidavits from my father and grandmother that I was who I said I was. Not from my mother, though; that was too much to ask from a woman who clung to her hard-core beliefs even now that both of her children were quite literally on the other side of the fence.

As a Firstamentalist, my mom believed I was a monster, and if I was being honest, I couldn't totally disagree with her. I mean, I was able to turn into a giant snake at will, and I packed enough punch in my fangs to kill with only a few drops of venom. Not exactly what I would call normal, even on a good day. But being a Firstamentalist meant that, for my mom, there were no shades of gray; you couldn't love your own family members if they were turned into Super Dupers. You were either a good person who attended church—Firstamentalist church, to be clear—or you were going to hell. And if you were a Super Duper like me, you weren't just going to hell—your soul was corrupted beyond repair and would corrupt anyone you were around. To say that the situation made family dinners awkward was a bit of an understatement.

The sun dipped low behind us, the cloudy winter day sucking it below the Seattle skyline with a single gulp. January was speeding by, but I barely felt the cold. A small perk to being my particular brand of Super Duper. I still shivered, but it had nothing to do with the weather.

Even with all the papers I'd so carefully put together, I knew it was going to be a huge challenge to prove that I existed—harder to do than making a ten-egg soufflé. Because the world didn't see supernaturals as people. We didn't exist, not in the eyes of the government, and that meant we didn't need to have rights.

Which was going to make proving I needed a proper divorce and deserved half of everything from my jerk of a two-timing husband difficult, to say the least.

But I had to believe I could do this, that I could show the judge I was really here, and that it didn't matter that I wasn't technically human any longer. I refused to let Roger and his scheming girlfriend, Barbie, walk away with everything I'd worked so hard to build.

So I put on a brave face and straightened my back. I would not be the doormat my mother wanted me to be; I would not be someone Roger could just mow down so he could go on with his life as if I'd never existed. If he thought he was going to benefit not just from my death, but also from all my hard work and years at my bakery, Vanilla and Honey, he was about to see he was sorely mistaken.

"Tad, there is no way the judge can say I don't exist, that I'm not alive, when I'm standing right in front of him." I shot a quick glance at him as I navigated the steps.

"Yes, he can, because it's the law, and you know it. And this is the human courthouse. We could start a riot just by being here." Tad shoved his hands into his jeans' pockets and hunched his head in his dark-gray hoodie, pretty much mumbling the last of his sentence. I snuck a glance around us at the humans flowing in and out of the large H-shaped building. No one looked our way; no one even paused at Tad's words.

No one noticed they were walking next to two supernaturals. If they did, I knew pandemonium would ensue, and not for the reason most people would think. I mean, humans knew supernaturals existed. But that didn't mean they truly *knew*. Vampires, werewolves, warlocks, and Greek gods walked next to them daily. The humans would panic if they knew just how many of us interacted with them on a daily basis. If they knew . . . I could only imagine just how fast they'd be pushing the government to permanently put us on our side of the Wall.

The thing that frightened them, though, wasn't the idea of claws and teeth, or shape-shifting and blood drinking. No, the thing that we represented more than any of that was a slow, painful death cut off from your family. The Aegrus virus had originated and spread via Super Dupers. To a Supe, the virus was a cold, a flu at worst. But to a human, contracting it was certain death.

The Aegrus virus was brutally efficient in its ability to kill a person within weeks. Your body slowly turned on itself, shriveling into a husk of what you once were, muscles atrophying; hair, teeth, and nails falling out; and all the while your mind staying as sharp as ever while you died in a shell of your own body.

Worse, the virus cut people off from those they loved. The quarantine protocols were such that uninfected humans were encouraged not to visit their sick family members. If they did manage to get through the red tape, they were required to wear hazmat suits and allowed only short visits. The infected were kept away from the rest of the city at a specially built hospital on Whidbey Island. Cut off by water and disease.

There was no cure, no way around the disease once you had it. Unless you made the choice that both Tad and I had, and you were willing to be turned into one of the monsters. That wasn't common knowledge, though. Most humans didn't even realize there was a possible cure—if you called being made a Super Duper a cure. Really we'd just traded one disease for another. I shivered at the direction of my thoughts.

Only a few short weeks ago I'd been human, or so I thought, and then I'd contracted the Aegrus virus. I'd learned that the only people who could actually contract the virus were those who had a little bit of supernatural blood in their genetics. Enough to make them susceptible but not enough to help them survive the virus. Which meant there was something hiding in my family tree. The virus had me on death's doorstep in no time, and the only way to save myself was to make a deal with the devil. A deal that involved turning me into what Dahlia, my roommate at the hospital, called a Super Duper.

Long story short, I'd done it to live, and I ended up with more than I'd bargained for. Now I was like . . . a *super* Super Duper. As in supersize. As in superpowerful. I brushed a strand of long dark hair out of my face, exasperation flowing through me once more at the thought of what Merlin had made me. A Drakaina, of all things, a woman siren who could shift into a giant, venomous snake at will. That's what I got for being prideful and subverting God's will. At least, that's what my mother and the Firstamentalists would say. My jaw tightened as irritation flowed through me.

"We aren't infectious," I said under my breath as I clutched my paperwork harder. I mean, I wasn't coughing, I didn't have a fever—two signs a Super Duper had the virus. Tad grunted and glanced at me, jet-black hair falling over his eyes, giving me just a flash of green before he turned away again.

"You don't know that for sure, and worse, neither do they. I mean, I didn't know I had it when I infected you. If they find out—"

"They won't," I snapped, my nerves already strung as tight as they'd ever been. Like frosting a giant wedding cake while the bridezilla leaned over my shoulder. And yes, that had happened. Okay, this was worse than that, but it was close. "I just have to get them to sign the divorce papers. Once it's done, then everything is legal and they can't reverse things. They can't deny me my rights then." I drew in a breath and tried to push the fear and anxiety out of my belly. That was what I was hoping for anyway. Sure, it was a bit sneaky, but I didn't have much of a choice as far as I could see. Once the signatures were on the paper, it would be a done deal. Again, I was hoping, but hope was all I had left.

"They'll throw us back behind the Wall, and that's if we're lucky," Tad grumbled, bringing my attention back to him. I let out a sigh and shook my head.

"Who exactly is going to do that? The Supe Squad is in shambles and can barely lace up their boots, even *with* orders. And with Oberfluffel missing, there is no one to give said orders. The human police aren't really interested in dealing with Super Dupers unless they absolutely have to."

Tad pulled a face as if he'd swallowed a lemon. "*Oberfall* is not missing. He's on hiatus, according to Dahlia."

I grinned at him and took advantage of his mention of Dahlia to change the conversation. "Pillow talk again?"

His face flushed bright red and he looked away. "I'm just saying he isn't missing. Don't make more of it than you have to."

"I'd have thought you'd be happy he's gone," I said.

My brother tugged at the edges of his hoodie. "Smithy is in charge while he is away. Oberfall is a dick, but Smithy is a complete hard-ass. He can't be reasoned with. When it comes to being straitlaced, he's as straight as they come. Problem is, the rest of the SDMP don't see him as the leader yet; he has to prove to them that he's worth following. Until that happens, they'll be all over the map."

I shifted my arms as my paperwork slid. "My point is the Supe Squad isn't doing anything. They shut down, and with Remo and his vampires taking out the chip-monitoring machine, you and I are probably safer here than on the north side of the Wall."

When you lived on the north side of the Wall, you were surgically implanted with a chip that allowed the local police to keep all Super Dupers under their thumbs. Said chips also had the ability to shock their recipients, furthering that ability to keep them in line. With the machine that monitored and controlled those chips no longer functioning, it meant the Super Dupers could just about do as they pleased. I wasn't fully certain that was a good thing.

A man walking close to us in a dark-blue suit and a bright-red tie paused and glanced at me, his eyes worried.

"Wall Street," I lied. "We were talking about Wall Street."

His eyes swept me up and down, and a slow grin spread across his face. "Are you one of the new secretaries? I am in the market for one since my last secretary quit."

"Oh." I glanced down at the papers in my arms and the short black skirt I wore. "No, I'm here to finalize my divorce."

"Really?" The man in the suit perked up even more and held out his hand. "Name is Bradley Froat, lawyer, specializing in divorce. I could help you be free of your husband in no time at all. I could *open* you up to move on to . . . other things." He winked at me and made a not-so-subtle kissing motion with his lips.

I glanced at his hand and took a step back, thoroughly disgusted. Did he really think that his attempt at smooth talk and a kissy face was a turn-on? "Well, I'd say it was nice to meet you, Mr. Froat, but that would be a lie."

"You aren't even going to shake my hand? Didn't your mother tell you it isn't polite to walk away when someone else is talking?" He raised both eyebrows at me, as if I'd insulted him. Well, okay, I had, but that wasn't the point. He'd started this.

I pinched my lips together, irritation sharp and zinging through my blood. The old Alena would have apologized and begged forgiveness. Probably would have given him a coupon for her bakery.

Not anymore.

"Three things, Mr. Froat: one, I am going to be late if I don't hurry; two, my mother is the last person you should bring up in conversation with me; and three, I am not the nice girl you think I am, so *don't* irritate me, and don't make kissy faces at me." I turned away from him. "May I also point out you're as big a jerk as my brother for not even offering to help a lady who has her arms full of papers before you try and make a move on her."

"Hey," Tad barked, "you'd say no if I did ask."

I rolled my eyes. "And this is why you were single for so long, and why if you aren't careful, Dahlia will dump you. You have to ask, even if you know I'm going to say no. Give me the option."

I hurried toward the courthouse, already putting Mr. Froat and his rude come-on from my mind. Tad, though, wasn't moving on so easily.

"You are still the nice girl, Alena, even I know that," he said softly.

"I'm not." Too much had happened in the last couple of weeks for me to believe I was a nice girl anymore.

For starters, I'd killed people. Bad people, to be sure, people who would have killed me, but the thing is, nice girls don't kill people. Ever.

And I'd kissed someone other than my husband before the divorce was final, which in some ways was worse. Because I'd wanted to kiss those lips that still hovered in my thoughts. I hadn't wanted to kill anyone—that had been sheer self-defense. Even my mother couldn't completely deny that I'd been fighting for my life.

Thoughts of said kiss warmed me from my toes right up to the tips of my ears in a flash of heat that had me struggling to breathe normally. I drew in three long breaths as I tried to cool my body and my thoughts down. But the remembered touch of Remo's lips on mine was hard to banish. I fanned a few papers at my face, trying to cool myself.

"How can you be hot in this miserable weather?" Tad asked as we hurried through the building's main doors.

I was not about to tell him that my face was flushed from my memories of a kiss that would have melted the ironclad panties off a nun.

Finally breathing at a more usual pace, I managed to get my heart rate and mind back to some semblance of normal. I needed to focus, not fantasize.

Ahead of us was a swell of bodies, people coming and going in the wide hallway and lined up against the walls, whatever chairs there were filled to the brim. Everyone was here for some form of justice, just like me.

I paused and shivered. The smell of body odor lingered heavily in the air along with stale smoke, bad breath, and too much cologne and deodorant applied in an attempt to cover it all up. I coughed and Tad shot a look at me, his eyes wide as he grabbed one of my arms.

He dropped his head so it was close to mine. "Are you sick?"

"No." I coughed again, wishing I could cover my mouth with something, anything. With my arms full of paperwork, it was all I could do to tuck my face against the sheets. "It's the smell. This many bodies stink."

A grunt at my shoulder spun me around. The faint musk of bear rolled up my nose, making the Drakaina in me tighten in prep for a strike. The bear shifter nodded at me. "Humans do stink in large numbers. You'll get used to it, though. Just don't breathe deep."

I nodded. "Thanks. I'll try that."

Normally finding any Super Dupers on this side of the Wall was rare, never mind all in one place like the courthouse. But with Oberfluffel gone and his team of enforcers in shambles, any serious cases were being shipped to the local human courthouses. Of course, no one had told the humans.

Two more Super Dupers passed us, their eyes carefully averted. One was a vampire I didn't recognize, and I overheard him thank the court registrar for scheduling his date for after dark. I glanced at my watch. It was closing in on five in the afternoon, the end of the day for the court, the end of the sun for fourteen hours, and the start of a vampire's day. Which of course made me think of Remo and that smile of his. Dang, I had to get that man out of my head.

Tad relaxed his hold on me, and his words brought me back once more to the here and stinky now. "The smell isn't too bad. Can't be worse than family dinners with Auntie Janice and her crew."

I grimaced and then slowed my pace so we stopped by a small alcove, a little bit separate from the rest of the petitioners. "That awful lavender perfume she wears. It never covers up the smell of mold. You'd think they'd notice it on their clothes."

He nodded and laughed. "It's like they roll around in it, all four of them."

I grimaced. "Mom wouldn't like us bad-mouthing them."

Tad pointed at me. "Mom's not here. Unless you want her role of Judgy McJudger Pants today?"

My lips twitched and I laughed. "No, thanks. I'll pass."

My brother leaned back. "You know that Everett lit Uncle Robert's hair on fire? On purpose while he slept in his chair. I watched him do it, couldn't believe what I was seeing."

Shannon Mayer

I spluttered, "He did not." Then I amended, "When?"

"When he was about fifteen. Would have made me twelve." Tad laughed. "That's why Uncle Robert wears his hair long; it covers the burn mark on the back of his neck. After Everett lit his dad up, he tried to blow out the flames, but that only made it worse. Of course that lavender perfume shit acted like an accelerant."

I couldn't help the laughter; I could just see Everett frantic with his big bug eyes as he tried to put the fire out while Uncle Robert yelled at him. Dad's side of the family was . . . well, it was hardly straitlaced. "You think that . . . with Dad being a Super Duper that Uncle Robert is too?"

Tad shrugged. "No, I doubt it. They had different fathers."

That they did. But a part of me wanted to believe that Uncle Robert was a Super Duper too. Mostly because I didn't want to be the only black sheep in the family. Okay, me and Tad, since Dad was in denial, but still the numbers were against us.

"Maybe we should go visit them." I shifted my hands on the stack of papers.

"Alena, what the hell are you doing here?" Roger's voice whipped me around so fast I slipped on the false tile floor. A few papers fell from my file folders and fluttered to the ground in between my husband and me. Soon to be ex-husband, if I had anything to say about it.

Roger had brown hair and soft brown eyes, and there had been a time when I'd thought he was the love of my life. Of course, that was before he'd turned out to be a total—

"Asshole," Tad snarled, stepping between us. "You brought your girlfriend with you to your divorce proceedings? Really? How much of a douche canoe are you? Never mind, no need to answer that."

I blinked and looked around my brother, recognizing the woman behind Roger. Bottle-blond hair and blue eyes, tiny waist and too-long nails, and a rack the size of my biggest mixing bowls. She was pretty, I would give her that. If you liked three layers of makeup and clothes that were tight enough to make you think they were likely painted on in places.

I smiled and kept my tone sweet, though it was a struggle. "Hello, Barbie, how am I not surprised you're here? Making sure the money comes through to you? I mean, that is the only reason you're with him, isn't it?" Oh, there was more than a little sting in seeing her. Even though I wasn't the mousy church girl I'd once been, the pain of knowing he'd chosen her over me—even before I'd gotten sick—still lingered.

Barbie's baby-blue eyes narrowed so far I thought she might have closed them. "You're a freak, and you're going to get nothing. Because it's the law, and Rog is in the right."

A tiny piece of me cracked, and words escaped me before I could filter them.

"And you're a whore who is sleeping with Roger to get *my* money and my house."

Her eyes popped wide and Roger sucked in a sharp breath. Tad laughed. "Oh yeah, let her have it, sis. Both barrels—and go."

I immediately regretted the words. Not because they weren't true, but because they were mean. "I'm sorry, I shouldn't have—"

Roger grabbed at Barbie, clinging to her hand. "She loves me, Alena. I know because we were together long before you got sick, and she's with me now when I'm in the fight for my life and future against a woman who obviously never really loved me."

The hypocrisy of his words was not lost on me, but that he couldn't even hear what he'd just said . . . how could anyone be so blind?

Tad's jaw dropped, which was saying something, since he could unhinge it. I glared at him, and he pulled it together. "He . . . he . . ."

They stormed away as Tad spluttered for words. I stepped in front of Tad, blocking his way so he couldn't go after them. When it came down to it, he would defend me, and I loved him even more for it. But this wasn't the time or place.

"Let it go, Tad. This will be dealt with in court. Where a judge will see how much of a fool he is and how he doesn't deserve anything, never mind everything." I held my head high, even though I knew what I was saying was a long shot. No matter how ready Roger was to admit his infidelity, Super Dupers didn't have the same rights as humans.

Hence the Wall between us, and usually the two separate justice systems. If it hadn't been for the shambles of the Supernatural Division of Mounted Police at the moment, I wasn't sure I'd even have this chance. So I was going to take it and run with it for all I was worth.

The sound of boots clattering on the floor turned everyone around, silenced the low buzz of chatter, and drew more than a few gasps. Four police officers walked in with a single figure between them, and while the officers looked good in their crisp uniforms, they weren't the ones who drew the gasps, I was sure of it.

The detainee stood taller than my six-foot height and his dark-brown hair was a simple buzz cut that made the sharp angles of his jaw that much more pronounced. Dark eyes, the irises rimmed in violet, flicked over me, sparkling as if he'd seen a candy he couldn't wait to gobble up. Two piercings rested in his jaw, fake fangs that mimicked the real fangs I knew he had hidden behind his lips. There was a faint ghost of stubble over his face that made him even more luscious than before.

Sure, I was still married, but I wasn't dead. I could look. And fantasize.

"Remo, what are you doing here?" I managed to say without completely stumbling over the words. I'd not seen the vampire mob boss since he'd slept—only slept—in my bed after the battle with Achilles. To be crystal clear, I hadn't slept with Remo. He'd stayed with me, to protect me, I think. At least that's what I told myself. I also told myself I hadn't missed him at all.

Liar.

According to Remo and the rest of the Super Dupers, there was no cross-species dating. Even Tad and Dahlia were treading a dangerous line by seeing each other.

I swallowed hard as Remo slowed next to me, and my heart went into double time, tripping over itself.

"Here, let me take these," Remo said, scooping the paperwork from my arms and handing the whole pile to Tad.

I couldn't look away from him as he slid his arm around my waist and tugged me close enough that I could smell the cinnamon on his breath. My eyelids fluttered, and I battled the urge to moan.

"I heard you were in court today. I had them move up my hearing so I could be here. In case you needed help. And . . . I've missed you," he said.

He'd missed me. If I thought my heart was pounding before, it was nothing to the runaway beat of it now. Like a mixer whipping at full speed.

"Excuse me, my *wife* and I were having a discussion," Roger snapped suddenly, cutting through the moment. Damn, where had he come from? I thought he'd disappeared farther into the courthouse.

Roger grabbed my hand and tried to tug me away from Remo.

Remo's eyebrows shot up, and he tightened his hold on my waist, easily keeping me at his side. "You must be Roger, yes?"

I jerked my hand out of Roger's, and he glared at me. Like I'd done something wrong.

He turned his stink eyes on us both. "Yeah, I'm Roger."

Remo smiled at him, not quite wide enough to show off his fangs. "Then I have to give you my thanks for being fool enough to set her free. I must say, you *are* an idiot of extraordinary proportions."

I had to fight the smile. Mother always said it wasn't polite to act smug. Of course, Roger had made sure I had my ego smacked down more than a few notches. Maybe all the notches.

"She didn't always look like this, you know. She was a fun sponge: brown hair, brown eyes, boring. In *every* aspect of her life. And she went out of her way to make sure no one else had fun." He snorted. "*Every* aspect, even the bedroom."

As if we didn't all get the implication the first time around.

I couldn't help myself from shrinking away from Remo, while anger began a slow, burning build inside of me. Roger was right; when I'd been turned into a Super Duper, there was no doubt my looks became a hundred times what they'd been.

Remo didn't let me go. "Her beauty is only an added bonus to the woman she is. Like I said, you are a fool to not have seen it, no matter how she appeared to you."

One of the escorting officers tapped Remo on the shoulder, and I recognized Officer Jensen. Funny I'd not even seen him with Remo in the room. But I wasn't surprised that he was here with Remo. He was Remo's inside man on the human police force, and I had no doubt the vampire mob boss had arranged the situation to his benefit. No doubt at all. I mean, he'd changed his court date to line up with mine. As far as I could see, there was no end to Remo's reach.

"We have to get you to your hearing, sir," Officer Jensen said, though his eyes flicked from Remo to me. As if questioning what was going on between us.

Now, there was the small matter of me having used my siren abilities on Jensen when I'd needed help battling Achilles. The impression I'd left hadn't yet faded, apparently, and it made his loyalties waver between Remo and me.

Remo nodded. "Of course. I would hate to be the cause of the entire court system being put behind schedule."

Without warning, he pulled me fully into his arms and pressed his lips to mine. I melted, unable to stop myself from snaking my arms around his neck. Cinnamon and honey, his mouth was this delectable concoction that made me want all of him, down to the last drop. Heat rushed through my veins as he held me tight, even as he pulled out of the kiss.

His eyes were wild, filled with unspoken things I wanted very much to hear from his lips. "You undo me," he said softly.

I stared up into his eyes, my breath coming in hitches and gulps. "I know the feeling."

"You two are disgusting, making out in public, a married woman going on with her lover," Roger yelled loud enough that I knew everyone within thirty feet would have heard. Maybe even farther, with the echo.

Remo turned his head without a single hesitation and snarled at Roger, fangs fully exposed. Roger and Barbie squealed in unison and scrambled away from us, falling over each other to get away from him as fast as possible.

Remo's eyes slid back to mine, and he smiled. "Go get him, Alena. You are worth a thousand of him, don't forget it."

One more kiss, gentle and so soft it was like velvet brushing over my skin, and then he stepped away. Claiming territory. I don't know where the thought came from, but I knew it was right the second it crossed the front of my brain.

"You did that on purpose," I blurted out, "to make him think we've slept together." I wanted to slap him, but I could barely move with the languor of the kiss still flowing through my limbs. He flashed a small grin back at me, totally unrepentant, as the officers moved him down the hall.

"I know I did. I want him to know that you are off limits to him. You're mine, Alena. And I don't share."

His words were dark and full of promises my gutter brain was all too ready to dive into. So I said the only thing I could.

"I'm still married."

"Tell that to the judge," he threw back, and then he and his entourage disappeared around the corner.

Someone bumped my shoulder, and I turned to see Tad staring at me. He grimaced. "Here, take your papers. I'm not your assistant."

I grabbed the folders and clutched them to my chest as though they were a shield that would keep Remo away, put Roger in his place, and make everything go back to the way it should be.

"Tad, tell me I can do this. I need one person to believe I can do this. I'm not sure even Remo believes." I stared at him, willing him to support me. He looked down and away, and my heart fell with his gaze.

"Alena, you can't fight the law. Not when you don't exist to them. All they will do is string you up and use you as an example of what not to do. You could actually hurt the rest of us by doing this. But I'm here, right? I'm with you." He slung an arm over my shoulder and guided me down the hall.

I shrugged his arm off and sniffed. "You know, a platitude now and again wouldn't kill you. A little 'rah-rah, go get him' could go a long way to making this day not a total waste."

"Alena Budrene versus Roger Budrene," a voice boomed over the PA system, and I jumped as the vibrations rolled over my skin.

"That's you," Tad said.

I nodded. "Yeah, that's me. But not for long."

At least, I hoped Budrene wouldn't be my name after this.

CHAPTER 2

I hurried into the courtroom, Roger and Barbie ahead of me, Tad behind.

At the front of the room sat the judge, looming over the whole place in his black robe behind a desk that seemed to take up half the length of the chamber.

The woman to his left cleared her throat. "Divorce proceedings for Alena Budrene and Roger Budrene."

The judge shuffled some papers on his desk, and I squinted at the plaque in front of him. Judge Watts.

He let out a tired sigh and peered over the top of his glasses at Roger first, then me. His eyes widened and he blinked several times. Finally he pulled his glasses off, rubbed his eyes, and slid the glasses back on. "Mr. Budrene, you are divorcing your wife, is that correct?"

"Yes, but—"

The judge lifted a hand, then pointed a finger at me while his eyes never left Roger. "And is that her?"

"Yes, but—"

The judge pointed at him. "Not a word more than yes or no until I ask for it, or I will throw you in jail for contempt. I have a migraine and I want this over as soon as possible, as I'm sure you both do too."

A tiny bit of hope flared in my chest. I liked Judge Watts more with each word he spoke. He shuffled his papers and frowned. "Mrs. Budrene, it says here you died? Tell me, how can that be?" He held up what I knew was a death certificate with my name on it.

I swallowed and then cleared my throat. "As you can see, Your Honor, I am very much alive. I have my driver's license"—I dug into the pile of papers—"affidavits, government documentation of every kind to show that I am indeed alive, and I am Alena Budrene." I smiled up at him with that last bit and dared to use a bit of my siren abilities to help things along. Not a lot, just a little push. The monster inside of me snickered.

Judge Watts visibly softened. "I can see that, my dear. Jacob"—he glanced at his clerk—"we need to clear up this young lady's snafu with that death certificate. Put a note in to deal with that."

The clerk nodded and wrote something down.

The judge turned back to me. "Can you explain to me why exactly there is a divorce, then? There are far too many people divorcing because their partner doesn't squeeze the toothpaste tube the way they want." He paused and smiled gently. "What I want to know, Mrs. Budrene, is, what are the grounds for the divorce? And are you both seeking a divorce, or is one party willing to try and make things work?"

I had a feeling he wasn't always so soft with people, particularly when he had a migraine. I placed the stack of papers on the table in front of me and smoothed my top out, tugging the edges of it. "I believe we are both in agreement to the divorce."

Roger nodded and then seemed to catch himself. As if agreeing with me on anything would be a sign of admitting I really existed as a person.

I smiled at the judge. "Well, it started when I got sick, and the doctors thought I might not make it. That's when I found out that Roger was cheating on me. I mean, he'd been cheating on me a long time, I guess, but that's when I found out. And he left me in the hospital to die." I'd practiced this speech in case I was asked, and had the time needed to make an effort to get tears and the right inflection.

Except now that I was actually telling the story, there was no need to pretend to cry. The pain of what Roger had done welled up. I closed my eyes, and a tear trickled down my cheek. "He told me he was taking the inheritance my grandparents had left me, and he was selling the house they left me to my parents—for a premium price, no less. He had already lined up to sell my business to a woman who had no desire to take care of it. She wants it for spite and nothing else."

"Do you have proof that the property in question was deeded to you?" the judge asked.

I nodded and pulled out a thick file. "Everything in here is from my grandparents, stating that I am the legal heir. You can see that the deposit went not into a joint account but an account only in my name set up by my grandparents. The same for the house, which was deeded in my name shortly before I fell ill." I paused, wishing I had similar documentation for the bakery.

Judge Watts stared at me, a look of horror etched on his face. "My dear, what did he plan to do with all the money after he took it from you?"

I held my hands clasped together in front of me. "Open a dog-grooming business with his girlfriend."

"And cats," Roger spit out. "Dogs and cats."

As if that helped.

Judge Watts's eyebrows shot up. "And cats? You think you need all that money for grooming dogs and cats?"

Roger, given free rein to talk, hurried to explain. "Yes, we need to have rent money, and Barbie needs to be situated right. We are going to replace her vehicle and get her proper equipment so she can be the best pet groomer that Seattle has seen."

I wasn't so sure giving that much detail was going to help Roger's case. The perfect reason to keep my mouth shut and let him ramble.

"The grooming business is expensive to get going; we've been talking about it for years."

For years? If I didn't know better, I'd think that maybe Roger had been in on getting me sick in the first place.

The judge rolled his eyes. "You realize you're being taken for a ride? It is beyond me how you landed not one but two beautiful women when you are obviously short more than a few bricks in the load you carry."

Behind me, Tad choked on a laugh, and I wanted to smack him. I didn't want him to distract Judge Watts from his train of thought, a train that was headed in the direction I wanted. The last thing I needed was for him to think I had laughed, that I was being disrespectful to him.

I was going to get a proper divorce, and I wanted to cheer. The system *did* work. I was going to get justice even though I was a Super Duper. Maybe this would mean something to the rest of the supernatural world, but even if it didn't, it meant something to me. Roger wasn't going to be rewarded for being a jerk. Sheer giddiness spooled through me like spun sugar floating in the air, and just as sweet.

"I suspect one truly loved you, and the other is in it for the money. I'll let you guess which one," Judge Watts said with a pointed look at Barbie.

Barbie raised an eyebrow at him, and tipped her chin high, but said nothing.

"And as I see it," he continued, "Mrs. Budrene is entitled to all of her inheritance, which, by these papers here, is hers. The house, the inheritance, and half of all joint marital assets."

Barbie let out a little cry, turned, and stomped from the room. "We're done, Roger, *done!*"

Well, that was that, then. I fought the smile that wanted to steal over my lips.

Judge Watts continued to rifle through the papers, shaking his head at a rather stunned-looking Roger. "Perhaps with your next choice of woman, you'll look for someone who isn't in it for your money."

"Is the bakery half mine?" Roger asked, and I bristled. He would go for the throat.

The judge glanced at me. "The bakery?"

I swallowed and cleared my throat. "Vanilla and Honey is the bakery I opened. I borrowed money from my parents to do so, and I paid it back."

"Did Mr. Budrene work at the bakery?" Judge Watts looked at the papers.

I shook my head. "No."

"Did he do the accounting? The business marketing? The ordering and receiving?"

"No."

"Did he do anything at the bakery?'

I shook my head. "No, he didn't."

The Judge's lips pressed to a thin line. "So he milked you for all you had while he bounced with his girlfriend behind your back?"

The crowd tittered softly. It felt like they were laughing at me, and I struggled not to burst into tears. Or cringe. Or lash out. I looked at the floor; it was all I could do.

"I believe so." I made myself lift my head back up. I was not to blame for this.

The judge nodded. "Taking the length of your marriage into consideration"—he shuffled some papers and peered at something—"you will have to buy him out of the bakery, because from what I see here, this is community property. You acquired the bakery during your marriage. And so as to be fair and equitable, as is the law of our state, I will award you each half of the business. Furthermore, it is my decision therefore to grant the divorce between Alena and Roger, equally splitting those assets that were jointly acquired, along with the debts that were also jointly acquired, and awarding Mrs. Budrene—"

"She had the Aegrus virus," Roger blurted out. "She didn't look like this before, and she's a supernatural now. Some sort of snake thing."

Like watching my ten-egg soufflé fall, the hopes of making the divorce official, of getting my inheritance back, slowly deflated into a puddle at my feet.

Judge Watts snorted. "A snake thing? And do you have proof of this claim, or are you just trying to get more money from your lovely soon-to-be ex-wife?"

Hope glittered. The judge was still on my side.

Roger nodded, and I had no doubt that it was because he was agreeing with both things. The money and the proof.

My heart rate ticked up a notch, and my hands grew clammy against each other as I pressed them tightly together.

"At the stadium ten days ago, that big rumble with the supernaturals was her and some guy with a sword." Roger held up his phone. "I got it on video."

The room spun around me, and I clutched at the table in sheer desperation to keep on my feet. I was going to be sick.

The judge held out his hand. "Let me see this video." He took the phone from the bailiff and pressed play. The noises from the phone were all too clear to my sensitive ears. I heard my own voice call out, "Achilles," and I knew what came next.

If Roger got the shot, the judge would see me shift from the beautiful woman he saw standing in front of him into a giant snake that towered over twenty feet tall when I rose up in an attack stance. Fangs bared, multicolored coils writhing as I swept through the stadium toward Achilles to save my brother and my friends.

From behind me, Tad stepped closer and put his hands on my shoulders. "I know it's too late, but for what it's worth . . . I actually thought you had this."

I had no words. There was nothing to do now but wait for this to play out. Literally.

The judge's eyes widened, and his mouth dropped open. How could I argue with the truth?

"I'm still me," I whispered. "I'm still Alena."

Judge Watts shook his head and handed the phone back to the bailiff, who took it to a rather smug-looking Roger. Then the judge looked at me. Any trace of softness he'd shown me was gone. He leaned forward over his bench, his hands clenched into fists on his desk.

"You are *not* Alena Budrene. You are a wolf in sheep's clothing, and I almost handed you everything you wanted instead of to this hardworking *human* man." He shook his head, heavy jowls trembling.

Tad's grip tightened on my shoulders, and I reached up to clasp my hands over his. He'd been right, all of my friends had been right about this. I'd been foolish enough to believe that with enough proof on my side I could make the system see I really was still me. That even if I looked different, I was still the same woman. Justice was not seen for Super Dupers the same way as it was seen for humans. I was a fool to have thought it would be different for me.

"In light of this new evidence, insofar as I can see, there is no need for a divorce, seeing as the woman who Mr. Budrene was married to is dead—"

A boom like thunder cut Judge Watts off midsentence. The entire courtroom froze. Eyes widened all around us, but nobody moved.

"This is bad, sis," Tad said.

"Has nothing to do with us," I whispered back. Okay, the likelihood was high it *did* have something to do with me. "Just in case, get my papers, would you?"

He nodded and gathered them all, mixing them up horribly.

Maybe the next hero Hera had drummed up to kill me had found us? I tried to swallow and struggled to make it happen. My mouth was as dry as a two-week-old brownie with no frosting.

I cleared my throat. Maybe I could still salvage this. "Your Honor, please, I am still alive. I am still the same woman."

No one looked at me; everyone's eyes were trained on the open doors.

A second boom was followed close on the heels by a third that shook the rafters. Plaster fell from the ceiling, and the lights swayed overhead. The crowd cried out, and Barbie was the loudest of them all as she ran back into the courtroom. One of the bailiffs slammed the doors shut behind her. As if that would keep the shaking out.

"Oh my God, Roger. I could have died." She leapt into his arms, knocking him to the floor.

He let out a grunt as he stumbled and fell under her weight, but I was already looking at the threshold that led to the hallway. The tall framed wooden doors rattled as though something large had walked by. A few weeks ago, I would have said that was not possible. Now I wasn't so sure.

The doors burst inward and Officer Jensen fell in, his eyes searching the crowd. "Alena?"

"I'm here."

"It's Remo; he needs help."

There was no question. I kicked off my heels and ran toward Jensen. "What's happening?"

"The rival gang is making a hit on him. They set him up, knowing he would be here without backup. They must have someone here in the human courts keeping them up to date."

The building shook again, and I grabbed his arm to keep myself steady. "What the hey diddle fiddle are they using? Rocket launchers?"

His eyes widened. "How did you know?"

I groaned. "I didn't. They sound like a rocket launcher off Tad's *Halo* game."

Officer Jensen shook his head, took my hand, and ran down the hall. "He's cornered, nobody can get around the rival vamps, there's too many of them."

"What makes you think I can?"

He skidded to a stop at a T intersection. "Umm, two-story snake ring a bell?"

"I don't know that I can take a rocket launcher!" I spit out. "I'm not a fighter, Officer Jensen, in case you've forgotten."

"Oh, we're way beyond formalities. First name is Ben." He peeked around the hall. "Okay, you're up."

He pulled me hard, and slingshot me around the corner. I squawked as I hit the ground, tumbled once, and ended up flat on my back, my skirt bunched even higher on my thighs. I rolled to my belly and found myself staring at a pair of boots that buckled all the way up to the knees. I slowly lifted myself and my eyes at the same time.

"What have we here?" A deep rumble purred. "Let me guess, this is the new girl, the one we've all been hearing about."

I stared up into a pair of dark eyes partially hidden under a shock of hair almost as dark as my own raven locks. He was all muscle without an ounce of fat on him. His quads looked like they were trying to burst out of his pants like an overfilled muffin tin.

"I doubt anyone has been talking about me," I said.

"Oh, the green eyes give you away. That and the exquisite beauty. Remo always did have exceptional taste." He tipped his chin to one side and gave me a sly smile that bared a single fang to me. Without warning, his hands were at the back of my head and he'd pulled me to him for a hard, demanding kiss.

The shock wore off in under a second, and I slammed my hands into his chest as I braced my legs. The blow threw him back at least ten feet. A low murmur rolled, and I looked around. A dozen vampires, by my count, and none were on Remo's side, if Jensen was right. I stood up and straightened my clothes.

"Remo, are you okay?" I called out.

"Not my best moment." He groaned, and the enemy vampires smiled as they parted so I could see him. He was trussed up between three vampires, and blood poured from wounds all over his chest and neck. Bite marks. They were draining him.

And that was all it took to wake the snake in me up. To be fair, it wasn't really a snake, but a Drakaina, but that's semantics. That side of me was easily riled when it came to blood and wounds on those I cared for.

No matter what I might say to Remo, I did care for him. More than I even wanted to admit to myself.

"I'm ssssorry," I said, the *s* drawn out as I prepared to shift. The vampires tipped their heads as a unit, like nothing more than a group of meerkats wondering what was going on.

"Did she just apologize to me?" The one who'd kissed me stood and raised an eyebrow at me. Something about him tugged at my memories. Like I'd seen him before. But I knew I hadn't.

"No, I'm apologizing to all of you." I didn't smile, just breathed in and loosed the tight coils of snake inside of me. Like unlatching a springform pan, it was just that easy to open myself up to the monster I was now.

Shifting from woman to giant snake was fast and painless. Smoke curled around my body, obscuring my vision for a split second before it cleared and I stared down at the vampires, who took a united step back, their eyes widening like children who'd finally seen the bogeyman, and he was as terrifying as their imagination had whispered in the dark.

I knew what they saw. My scales were purple, blue, and silver, glittering and beautiful, even though they were attached to me. A snake over a hundred feet long with a girth of over six feet and a pair of fangs that were anything but subtle. Raised up, I was easily two stories tall. I know all this because Tad had decided we needed exact measurements.

My head brushed against the ceiling, and I opened my mouth, fangs dropping low as I hissed at the gathered vampires. Maybe I could just scare them away, make them run.

"Shoot her." The vamp in the front snapped his fingers. "Cooked snake for dinner, boys and girls."

So much for making them just go away. I flicked my tail forward and slammed it through the first row of vampires. The blow sent them through the drywall and then pinned them up against the concrete wall of the courthouse hard enough that the concrete cracked. I dropped them and swept my tail back, catching a few more and clearing them off Remo. He lifted his head, his eyes locking on mine, then flicking behind me.

"Duck."

There was nowhere for me to go, nowhere to hide. There was a loud click that drew my eyes to the vampire who stood in the corner of the hallway, a rocket launcher on his shoulder. A puff of flame and smoke erupted from the launcher.

I flattened myself to the ground, and the rocket cleared me by mere inches. The projectile exploded against the wall behind me, and the entire courthouse shuddered and groaned. The humans screamed, filling the air with their panic-stricken cries.

Slithering forward, I opened my mouth, intent on snapping my fangs over the leader, piercing him through. I didn't want to kill him, but he was trying to kill us. I had to stop him if I could. His eyes were on mine, unafraid.

"I can see why Remo keeps you around. You are a useful tool, aren't you?"

I hissed, and venom flicked with the explosion of air, splattering at his feet, where it ate away at the tile. He took several steps back, and I shot forward again.

With my attention on him, I didn't see the rocket launcher go off again. I heard it, though, and rolled, taking the impact on my upper belly.

I braced myself for pain and heat, for the explosion of flesh and blood.

The projectile blasted into me with a shimmering burst of fire and shrapnel, bounced off my scales, and fell to the floor. I rolled on top of it, effectively putting out the flames.

I didn't feel anything more than the pressure of the impact. Dang, my scales really were something else.

"Boss, I'm out of ammo!" the rocket-launching vampire yelled.

The vampires pulled back, running away down the long hall. The leader pointed at Remo. "We aren't done." His eyes slid to mine. "And neither are we, snake girl. I'll skin you alive and make boots out of you before this is finished."

Wonderful, now I was on his list of enemies too. Seemed I was struggling to make friends in my new world, but I was excellent at making enemies.

"Go suck a corpse, Santos." Remo pushed himself slowly to his knees. I waited until I was sure all the vamps were gone. That the hallway was kinda safe. Someone touched my side, drawing my attention.

Tad stared up at me, his hand pressed against me. "You can shift down, sis."

He was right, but I liked being this big. And kinda badass. The prideful thought rolled through me, and I immediately regretted it. Pride was just another sin to add to the list I had going against me.

The loss of adrenaline sucked away the Drakaina form, and the smoke curled around me once more. In seconds I was back on two feet. I wrapped one arm around my chest and the other around my lower bits.

Naked as the day I was born, mind you, but that wasn't as bad as it sounded.

No, it was the crowd of humans behind me that stared with horror-stricken eyes, open mouths, and the occasional whimper that bothered me. Like I hadn't had enough of being judged in my life.

Speaking of . . . Judge Watts stood at the front of the group, shaking his head.

I knew that their stares had nothing to do with me being naked either. What they'd seen was beyond any other supernatural they had ever encountered before. I knew it too; when he'd made me, Merlin had told me I'd be a special snowflake. He wasn't kidding.

I was one of a kind.

Judge Watts took a step, his hands fisted at his side as if he'd like to take a swing at me and was barely restraining himself. "Only because it's the law will I reconvene our session in three days at four p.m. You will send someone in your stead. A lawyer, if you must, but anyone human will do. You will not be welcome in *my* courthouse, and if you step foot inside, I will have you arrested."

One arm wrapped around my chest, I stood there shivering. Tad took a step toward the judge, dropped my papers at his feet, and yanked his robe off over his head. "Give it up, old man."

"That's my robe! Bailiff, order!"

The judge would not give up the robe easily; he fought and grumbled, they tussled, and Tad finally wrenched it off him with a final yank.

"Here." He handed the robe to me, and I pulled it on, the scent of Old Spice, or maybe that was Prejudiced Old Man, heavy in it, making me crinkle my nose.

"Thanks."

"Maybe everyone else wants to stare at you, but the last thing I want to see is my sister parading around naked." He gave a mock shudder and picked up my papers once more. Another time I would have smiled.

As it was, I knew I'd just lost any chance at reclaiming any portion of my life. I sniffed softly, my lips trembled, and I turned away before the crowd could see me cry. I didn't want their pity. I just wanted to be treated fairly. I wanted the same rights everyone else had.

A set of arms wrapped around me, and with the embrace came the soft smell of cinnamon and honey. I buried my face into the crook of Remo's neck.

"I'm sorry, this is my fault," he said.

"No, no, it's not. It would have come out eventually. Roger had a video of me at the stadium," I said.

"Don't cry, we'll find a way to make this work."

My emotions were in a tumult, and my pride had been hurt. "So you can make use of me again? Was that other vampire right? Am I just a tool to you?" I pulled back, sniffed, and wiped a hand over my cheeks while I clutched at the robe.

His dark eyes with that tantalizing hint of violet tugged at me, and the sincerity in his voice eased the sharp dig of uncertainty in my heart. "I doubt anyone could use you, Alena. But maybe we should talk so we can clear the air."

I turned and stopped, staring at Judge Watts. He wore a white wifebeater tank top and a pair of bright-pink boxer shorts. He already hated me; I might as well make it a good and solid hatred.

"Pink panties don't suit you, judge. Then again, maybe they speak to your inner cowardice when it comes to being someone who is supposed to uphold the law and speak for justice. Something you apparently don't know a thing about."

I swept past him with my chin up and my heart breaking inside of me. The crowd parted around me, whispering, some of them even crying out as if my touch would infect them. I couldn't help myself; I stopped in the thickest part of the crowd, right where Roger and Barbie stood. I bent over at the waist and coughed three times into my hands.

Slowly, grimacing, I stood back up, wiped my hands on Roger's shirt, and patted his face. "Oh, sugar snaps, I must be coming down with something."

He choked and scrambled back; now I wasn't the only one with a wide circle around me. The other humans pulled back from Roger as quickly as they got out of my way.

"Alena! How could you do this to me?" he cried out as he pawed at his clothes in an attempt to take the "infected" shirt off.

"Have a good Monday, Roger!" I wiggled my fingers at him. "Maybe you should have your will updated?"

I actually watched the color drain from his face. He swayed on his feet, his eyes rolled back until the whites showed, and he fell to the floor with a heavy thud. No one even tried to catch him.

I shrugged, fought the immediate feeling that I was going to hell for lying (damn my Firstamentalist upbringing), and started forward again, focusing on each step in front of me rather than what I was leaving behind. Problem was, it was a Monday. And it looked like it was out to make sure I knew it was an epic Monday.

One step out of the courthouse and I saw *her*. What was she doing here? I couldn't believe it was mere coincidence; even I wasn't that trusting. More likely it had something to do with Roger.

Fat-nosed Colleen Vanderhoven, the woman who'd been my biggest competitor, she'd even set up her own bakery two streets over from Vanilla and Honey six months after my opening.

Worse than that, she told people my food and goods were contaminated with salmonella, that I stole her recipes, that I'd taken several of her employees from under her, and that I'd even stolen her branding when it had been the other way around. None of it was true, of course, but rumors were a terrible thing to disprove. I'd had to do free taste tests, had the health inspector in weekly checking things, and had to pay my employees more to keep them from running to her with my recipes. All of which had taken its toll and had amounted to even more time spent at the bakery than was truly needed.

She'd offered to buy me out at least once a month since I'd opened. She wanted what I had: a stellar location, a solid customer base, and well-trained employees. I always turned her down, but the last few times she'd gotten aggressive and told me she'd take me to court for slander.

Which was rather rich coming from her.

"Colleen." I snapped her name, whatever upset over the loss of my case against Roger gone in the sheer volume of anger I held when it came to the woman in front of me. "What are you doing here?"

She blinked up at me, her mouth opening. "I have a business meeting here. I'm buying a business. The seller is eager to sell, said he didn't want to wait one second more than he had to." Her way of speaking, duplicating what she was saying over and over, grated on me as much as the thought of her buying Vanilla and Honey.

I knew it. Damn Roger and his greed. No doubt he'd met with her within hours of me first contracting the Aegrus virus weeks before.

"Don't you think for one second you're going to get *my* bakery. Do you understand me? Not for one honey-puffed sssecond," I snapped, struggling over the last *s*.

She blinked washed-out blue eyes up at me that were so sunk into her face, she reminded me of a pig more than anything. She scrunched up her narrow lips, only adding to the image. The fact she'd recently dyed her hair bright pink to match her shop's colors did not help her out.

"Who are you exactly, and why would I want your bakery?"

Of course . . . she wouldn't recognize me. Only those who'd loved me before my change would recognize me through the new look.

"Alena Budrene. And you are negotiating with Dingle Nuts Roger for my bakery, aren't you?" I put a finger against her chest and reminded myself to go easy. I didn't want to kill her.

Well, maybe I did a little bit.

Her eyes lit up. "I heard you got turned into a supernatural. Impressive. Certainly better looking now, though I suppose that won't help you, will it?" She gave me a smug smile. "Since we all know you can own *nothing* on this side of the Wall. Nothing at all. I look forward to negotiations with Dingle Nuts. His stupidity works in my favor." She laughed in my face.

I closed the distance between us until we were nose to nose. I had to give her credit; she didn't back down, though a bead of sweat started at her hairline and slid down her face.

"That is *my* bakery, and I am not giving it up." The words came out hard and clipped, nothing like my normal sultry tones.

She held up an envelope and pulled out a piece of paper I knew all too well. The deed to my bakery, lease agreement and all. At the bottom I could see my signature, and she flapped a note attached to it. "You're right, he is a dingle nuts. He sent this to me in good faith, asking me to meet him here for finalization of the deal. And we both know that whoever holds this holds—"

I snatched it from her and stepped back before she could even register that I'd moved. Thank God for the reflexes of a snake. I cringed. Strike that, I doubted God wanted anything to do with me now that I was a heathen Super Duper.

"And what are you going to do now? You don't have keys." She dangled the keys in front of me, and I took another step back. I wasn't going to take them; no doubt she had spares.

"Ever hear of a locksmith? They can do marvelous things, like changing locks, you pink-haired, fat-nosed amateur wannabe baker."

She gasped. I knew that last was a low blow, but I was ready to fight dirty. She clenched her fist over the keys.

And took a swing at me.

A sudden thought hit me before she did. I didn't exist, not to the human world, so did that mean I couldn't be charged if I hurt her?

The thought was there and gone in a flash, plenty of time for me to consider how I was going to react with my reflexes. I grabbed her fist and clenched down hard on her curled fingers, hard enough her bones ground under my grasp.

"That was not very smart." I stared at her as I bore down.

She screeched, even though I knew I wasn't putting that much pressure on her. Of course, I'd not thought about the keys. The smell of blood rolled up from her hand, and I let go.

She jerked back, clutching her hand to her chest, the keys embedded in her palm. "You are a monster. I will have that bakery; it's *mine*. And there is nothing you can do to stop me."

The snake in me uncoiled a fraction, a silent question coming from it. How badly did I want to stop Colleen?

Short of actually killing her, I knew she was right. She would be able to get the bakery from Roger. All he had to do was apply for duplicate forms from the business offices. Maybe three weeks at the most, and she would have all the paperwork in hand, and they would be able to finish the deal.

I drew myself up. Challenge accepted. I had three weeks to change how the world viewed supernaturals so I could save the thing I loved most in the world.

CHAPTER 3

Once more, Remo pulled me back, his hands tight on my upper arms. "There are more ways than one to make sure you retain your bakery, Alena. Do not follow through."

What did he mean? I glanced up at him, and he gave me a half smile.

"I see the way your eyes narrow, the thoughts rolling through you. There is no way you would ever forgive yourself if you hurt her."

I let him tug me backward, even as Colleen glared at me, still clutching her hand. "I'm going to destroy Vanilla and Honey just to spite you."

My shoulders tensed, and a low hiss slid out of me. Remo turned me around, put an arm around my waist, and hurried us away from the courthouse. "Let it go, Alena."

"She's . . . she's awful!" I spit the word out like it was a cuss.

"I know."

Shaking, I let him guide me down the street. "Where is Tad?"

"Said he had something to do. Suspect he's gone looking for Dahlia. Don't worry, I saw him and he still had all your papers."

I folded the paper I'd taken from Colleen and held it out to Remo. "Do you mind hanging on to this? I seem to be out of pockets at the moment."

He took the paper and tucked it away into a back pocket.

"Are you okay with Tad and Dahlia dating?" I blurted the question out before I thought better of it. Taboos were taboos, and cross-species dating was a no-no. Kinda like baking with garlic and chocolate. Nobody ended up happy with the results, no matter how you mixed the two ingredients.

"For now. They seem to be only testing the waters." He winked at me.

I couldn't help the small smile. Dahlia was my best friend; we'd met when we were both dying from the Aegrus virus. She'd made me laugh when I should have been doing nothing but crying. The fact that Tad was dating her couldn't have made me happier. Even if it meant they were breaking the rules, dating outside their species. Tad was a naga, and Dahlia a vampire. Sure, they both had fangs, but I doubted that would be enough if anyone tried to enforce the no-hanky-panky-between-species clause.

They were good together, and as long as they were happy, I was happy for them.

My thoughts were swiftly brought back to the situation at hand, though. We were still in the shadow of the courthouse when a man approached us. He wore a black suit, with hints of silver flickering through the threads. His hair was a dark blond, slicked back into a ponytail at the base of his neck. It seemed that the lights behind him highlighted his body, giving him a strange otherworldly glow. Like he'd set up the approach, timing it like an actor strutting to center stage for a soliloquy.

Obviously he was a lawyer. Maybe he'd seen the scene in the court-house and thought he could bank on it and get himself a job. Judge

Watts had said I should get a lawyer. Not that I had any money to pay one, but still it might be a good idea to at least listen to him.

He stopped in front of me, forcing us to stop as well. "Are you Alena?"

I clutched my robe around me, and Remo tightened his hold on my waist. "Yes, and you are . . . ?"

He smiled, and the world seemed to dim around him as he held out his hand. I took it, my manners automatic.

"Of course, let me introduce myself."

I tried to pull my hand back, but he hung on tightly enough that if I pulled too hard, I'd end up throwing him through the air. "I can't afford a lawyer, so unless you are willing to go pro bono, I'm not sure I'm your client."

His grin widened and his eyebrows shot up. "I'm not a lawyer."

"Oh." I frowned. "How did you know my name then?"

A cold feeling swirled around my belly as he put his other hand on top of mine, holding me fast. "We were destined to meet, Alena." A slow hum caught me off guard, a resonance I didn't understand.

His smile filled my vision, a little burst of light sparkling in front of my eyes. The snake in me hissed, recognizing him as an enemy before I did. "Oh no."

"Oh no?" Remo whispered. "Do you know him?"

"I'm guessing here, but . . ." I tried again to pull my hand back again, carefully, but the man in front of me held on. "You're Theseus, aren't you?"

He let go then, and I stumbled back a few steps with the backlash. Remo caught me, steadying me.

"I am. I thought I should introduce myself. I'd like to discuss the situation we find ourselves in. You see, I need to kill you to be free of the bonds Hera has placed on me. You obviously want to cause chaos and destruction wherever you go, which in and of itself is not something we can have in the world." He dusted off the arms of his suit.

"What, you aren't just going to try and cut me in half like Achilles?" I kinda hoped he would. We could fight right here, get it over with.

Funny that I just assumed I would win if we battled on the steps of the courthouse. Maybe I was getting prideful. I'm sure that's what my mother would say.

There must have been some hint of my thoughts in my face. Theseus smiled again. "Oh, I don't want to fight you yet. Achilles is a fool, nothing more than a meathead, and really, he underestimated you. It's a flaw of his, one that has hurt him in the past."

"You mean the whole heel issue," I pointed out. Theseus laughed softly, and I wasn't sure just what was happening. This felt too . . . conversational. Too much like he was trying to be my friend. I didn't like it one bit. "Aren't you supposed to kill me and get it over with?"

"Not this time. You've upset Hera. You made her look like a fool. The other gods are laughing at her, something she can't stand to have happen."

Remo stepped up, putting himself a little in front of me. "So you want to make Alena suffer for surviving Achilles?"

Theseus pointed at Remo, a red ruby on his index finger glinting. "Now you begin to understand."

"And you wanted to shake hands with me why?" I didn't know how to handle him. With Achilles, things had been straightforward. He was a bad guy, with thugs, and he'd stolen my brother and threatened to kill him as well as making an attempt on my life.

Theseus was being far too rational for my liking. Far too calculating.

"Ah, because, while I know in the end I will end up killing you, I wanted to see you first. I understand part of Hera's hatred better. You rival her beauty. Shame." He smiled and took a step back. "Be assured, my beautiful snake, you will see me again when you least expect it."

"And then you think you can kill me?" I couldn't help the confidence I felt, and I knew it came through in my voice. "Achilles thought the same thing, and look where he is now. In a home for the mentally insane."

Theseus nodded. "But Achilles was a mere human with extraordinary gifts. I am a demigod, Alena. Immortal. You are not immortal. You can be killed."

His words sank into my heart like lead stones. Immortal. That single word took the stuffing out of me.

He gave me a mocking bow from his waist, flourishing with both hands. "Until we meet again."

A burst of light exploded at his feet, and I reeled back with a cry. Remo caught me a second time, his head tucked against mine. Blinking, my eyes watered like mad, and my vision slowly came back online. Theseus was of course gone.

Remo's face was bright pink on one side, a flash burn. I reached up and touched it. "Are you okay?"

He winked, wincing with the movement of that side of his face. "I could use a little color."

I cleared my throat and looked around us. No one seemed to notice that we'd had a strange visitor who'd just magically exploded out of existence.

Remo snorted softly. "People are blind to what they don't want to see. Easier to pretend supernaturals don't exist in their perfect little world, that they all live on the other side of the Wall."

"Kind of hard with me," I muttered.

He smiled. "True."

People gave us—no, me—some strange stares. No doubt the robe was confusing. Not exactly what I would call high fashion, even in an eclectic city like Seattle.

Finally the adrenaline began to slow in my veins, and fatigue washed through me. That and hunger. Something about fighting and shifting left me ravenous. I could have eaten a whole cow. I blinked and shook my head. Bad image when the Drakaina in me all but nodded at the thought.

"Don't think about Theseus; there is nothing you can do, and worrying won't help." Remo strode at my side, keeping our pace up and really partially helping me walk as I leaned against him.

"Is that how you are dealing with Santos?"

His hold on me tightened ever so slightly. "No, that is not how I'm dealing with Santos."

I wanted to ask how he was going to deal with the other vampire, but I suspected I already knew. "Why is he fighting with you? Is it just territory he wants?"

Remo sighed. "Yes, among other things." He paused, and I could almost feel him thinking, like he was trying to figure out how much to tell me.

"I could just ask Dahlia," I pointed out.

He grunted. "She's a turncoat." There was no heat in his words, though. "Santos and I go way back. We have been at war for years. He wants what I have: power, respect, influence, and territory. But he won't go out and make it for himself."

I thought about what he was saying. "The power . . ."

"The number of vampires who work for me is the main source; they all bring certain abilities and talents, and I put them to work in different areas. I'm particularly good at understanding where to place people to get the best out of them." For a moment I thought of Dahlia and her friendship with me. Surely she wouldn't be my friend only for Remo. He continued.

"I have nearly three hundred vampires in my gang, the largest in North America. Santos has not even half that, and his are spread out, avoiding working for him because he doesn't have the ability to keep them in line. He thinks that if he can kill me, he can take the vampires who are loyal to me. What he doesn't understand is that when a vampire boss is killed, the loyalties of their followers don't automatically shift. They can go wherever they wish. Santos . . . he is a fool. A dangerous one, but a fool nonetheless."

"How long . . . have you been at war with him?" I glanced up as his furrowed brow.

"Since the day I was turned into a vampire. Nearly four hundred years."

"Fricky dicky, that's a long dang time to hold a grudge. Why does he hate you?" For a moment I couldn't understand, and then I thought of Colleen. Maybe I could hold a grudge that long.

A tired smiled crossed his lips. "It's . . . a complicated story, one I'd rather not get into right now."

I mulled over his words, thinking of the many implications of his world that I'd not considered before. "And . . . the influence. You have people who work for you in high places, don't you? Like Officer Jensen, only higher than him."

He nodded and once more redirected. "Yes. But perhaps we can talk of other things besides vampire politics?"

I understood a little. Dahlia had told me that Remo didn't open up; no vampires opened up to the outside word, or to other Super Dupers. But with me, Remo let me in, despite us having the wrong kind of fangs for each other.

"Do you want to get something to eat?" I asked, then immediately cringed at my faux pas.

Remo laughed, spun me around, and stared down into my face. "Are you offering?"

I blushed and looked away. "I didn't . . . I mean, not like that. I wasn't thinking, I guess."

"You should eat," he said, a grin on the side of his lips. "If you are anything like the other shifters I know, food is essential after you flip back and forth."

My stomach rumbled in agreement. "Yeah, I could eat." I froze. All my clothes were gone, and even the stack of papers that proved who I was were with Tad. Worse, though, was the simple fact that I'd left all my money back at home. The little bit of change I'd had in my skirt pocket had been for a coffee.

"Umm, actually, no, I can't. I have to go back to number thirteen." That was Remo's crew's vampire safe house I was staying at on the other side of the Wall. Seemed rather fitting, considering all the bad luck I'd had lately. Yet I couldn't bring myself to leave. Good things had happened there too.

"I'll pay." He cut through to the issue.

My face heated up. "No, it's okay, I can wait till I get back home."

He was shaking his head as I spoke. "There is an Italian restaurant around here that has been in business for twenty years. The humans rave about it." He looked away from me, checked the street signs, and then had us moving again. The thought of lasagna, garlic bread, and Caesar salad had me drooling. I rubbed a hand over my mouth to make sure I didn't in fact have drool on my lips.

We walked in silence, though I saw a flutter of white feathers up ahead of us. I glared at the feathers and the face attached to them. Remo didn't seem to notice Ernie sitting on the streetlight, grinning down at me. I wasn't sure I trusted the chubby cherub. He'd played both sides of the field when it came to Achilles and Hera, and that had almost gotten both me and my brother killed.

At the same time, he'd helped me understand what I was and what I was capable of. So to say our relationship was complicated was a bit of an understatement. I wanted to trust him. I just wasn't sure that was the best idea. For now, I waved at him to get lost. The last thing I wanted was an audience when I was on a date with Remo. Ernie winked and blew me a kiss, then to add to it, he spun around and flashed his bare white bottom at me.

I snorted and averted my eyes. Remo gave me a funny look and raised an eyebrow. I shook my head, not wanting to explain, and not really needing to. Ernie was like that. One minute silly and my friend, the next working for the other team.

But Ernie wasn't going to be ignored.

He flew right in front of us, grinning. "You two on a dress-up date?"

I clenched my teeth. "Ernie, not now."

"Oh, come on. Let me ride along with you. I haven't shot anyone with my trusty arrows in a long time."

"And you're not going to start now," I pointed out. He shrugged, then mock frowned.

"Maybe my arrows could come in handy."

I rolled my eyes. "Would they work on Theseus? Make him fall in love with me so I could boss him around?"

Ernie shook his head. "No, they don't work on the gods and demigods."

"Then I doubt they can help me," I said, and he slumped, his smile sliding off his face.

"You don't need to be mean." He pouted.

"I'm not." I held a hand out to him. "Ernie, I just . . ."

"Never mind," he said as he turned and flew away.

I called after him. "I'm sorry, Ernie!" He flapped a hand back at me that looked suspiciously like he'd flipped me the bird. I sighed. I couldn't seem to do anything right. It was definitely a Monday.

"He'll be fine," Remo said. "He wants to help."

"I know. But . . . trusting him is hard."

Our conversation stalled as we reached the restaurant, and it was only then that another reason not to go to dinner hit me. I was still in a long black robe. With absolutely nothing else on underneath it. A cool breeze ghosted up along my legs as if to point out just how naked I was. I clamped my arms over my middle.

"I think I should just go back to the house. Really," I said.

Remo raised his eyebrows at me, and my heart might have stumbled over itself in an effort to pick up speed. "Why?"

"I'm not dressed. I mean, I am, but hardly." I gripped my waist harder.

He shrugged, but a smile tugged at his lips. "I'll see you home, then. It's the least I can do, since you saved me at the courthouse. Santos almost won the war between us." He tugged at the edges of my robe and pulled me closer to him. "I can take you back across the Wall. Unless you want to stay in the city. With me."

His hands skimmed up my sides and around to my back. Breath hitched in my throat, and I knew I had to say something. "Maybe?" Wait, no, that was not the word. No, thank you. Sorry, I'm busy. I can't, I'm married. Any of those. Not maybe!

Remo grinned, and his fangs flashed at me for a split second. The view did nothing to deter my brain from wanting him to kiss me again. From wanting his hands on my bare skin. Oh dear Lord in heaven, I was in trouble.

"Maybe?" he echoed back to me. This was forbidden, and we both knew it. Tad and Dahlia could get away with the cross-species dating. As Remo had pointed out, they were testing the waters. But Remo was the head boss of the biggest gang of vampires in North America. There was no way it would go unnoticed that he was dating a nonvampire.

My lips parted to answer, and he took it as an invitation, dipping his head to kiss me. His tongue traced my lips, as if tasting my skin, skimming the edges before darting into my mouth. He pressed me into his chest, and I wrapped my arms around his neck. So much for holding back.

In and out his tongue slid, soft and sensuous as it tangled with my own, the sweet flavor of his mouth drawing me in like a drug I craved. A low groan slid out of him as his hands slipped lower to my hips, and then lower to cup my bottom, pulling me tight against him.

A part of my brain flipped on, reminding me that only moments before I'd been thinking about how wrong it was to kiss him because of my situation, and now here I was, locking lips once more. When he loosened his hold on me and moved his mouth to my jaw, nipping the edge, I gulped for air. As if that would somehow power my brain into coming up with an appropriate response. Something along the lines of "You have to stop."

I stared up at the night sky, trying to come up with something, anything, that would slow this down. "You healed up pretty fast."

"Yes, it's a benefit of being a master vampire." He didn't slow, only breathed the words into my skin, which became a vibration that tripped over my whole body. Roger had never roused this kind of passion in me. I didn't think it had anything to do with me being a Super Duper either. However, thoughts of Roger slapped some sense into me more than anything else could have, digging deep into the beliefs I still held on to by a mere thread. No matter how I denied it, the Firstamentalist point of view still clung to me despite my attempted rejection of its beliefs.

I was a married woman, no matter what the judge said. And until I had those dang divorce papers in my hand, I had to behave like a married woman.

"I'm married, even if it's falling apart. I can't do . . . this . . . until it's all done." My words came out in a heated whisper that was anything but off-putting. Even to me.

"You keep saying that"—he nipped at the edge of my collarbone, drawing a low moan from my lips—"but it's not stopping you. I don't think you really believe it. You know it's over. You know they will never give you a proper divorce. You might as well begin to accept it." He licked along the base of my neck, sucking my skin in at spots, then scraping his teeth over the sensitized areas, rubbing his face against me like a large cat marking territory. The stubble on his jaw against my sensitive skin sent the sensations into overdrive, and I fought to keep my mind on track.

Breathing hard, struggling to think straight, I tried a different direction. His words were at odds with the sensations. A part of me didn't like what he implied, but I couldn't pull away from him; the heat between us was too much, too intense, and too . . . lovely.

"Speaking of healing up . . . when did you become a doctor?" I threw the question out like a life preserver, desperate that it would help me. "Was it to impress a girl?"

He pulled back from me as if I'd shoved him, and his face closed down in a split second. My mouth dropped open. All the heat that seconds before had glued us together evaporated like steam in the cold January air.

"It was, wasn't it?" I asked.

Remo didn't answer, just turned and walked away, the impromptu make-out session over as if it had never happened. I was disappointed, and then horrified at being disappointed. What was wrong with me? Were snakes horny beasts? Maybe that was it.

He walked ahead of me until we reached a bus stop. "This one will take you all the way to the Wall." He handed me my single paper back, and I took it, numb.

His cool demeanor should have made me happy. Seeing as I needed space between us. I did. Really. So why was this hurting me so much?

Remo passed me a handful of change, his hand never touching mine. He turned away, leaving me standing there with my mouth hanging open. It was the first time I'd seen some emotion from him other than his cocky smile or smoldering anger.

"Thanks for seeing me home." I couldn't help the parting shot. Mostly because my feelings were hurt. Maybe Santos was right; maybe I was just a tool to Remo, or worse, a weapon to be pulled out when he needed help and kept happy with a few kisses. And when that tool asked questions he didn't like, he was able to walk away.

Maybe worse yet . . . was he using his charm on me, making me believe he cared when he didn't? Could he be using my unruly hormones against me to make me blind to his actual objective of taking down Santos at any cost?

He could do it if he felt nothing for me.

And that stung more than I could have possibly imagined.

CHAPTER 4

The bus ride home was tedious, and my mind wouldn't stop obsessing over the possibilities that lay between Remo and me. I couldn't escape them, and each time I tried, the varied scenarios came flooding back. I finally resorted to reciting recipes under my breath, running through ingredients and instructions for everything from white chocolate–macadamia nut cookies to pasticiotti over and over again.

By the time I reached the Wall, I was beyond hungry, tired, emotionally drained, and footsore. The bus had taken me within two miles of the main entrance to the Wall, but I'd had to walk the rest of the way in bare feet.

I reached the forty-foot-tall Wall and paused, staring at the wide-open gates. A few Super Dupers came and went, but that wasn't what caught my attention. The human protestors sitting to the side of the structure around a tiny burning fire, however, did catch my attention. As I approached, they all jumped up and waved signs at me, as if I wouldn't see them otherwise.

"You don't have to go back in there. Equality for all!" A young woman with dark curls and an earnest, pretty face held her hand out to me, and I stared at it like it was a bomb. She didn't draw back.

"Please, take my hand. We are all one in this world." A lilting Irish accent wrapped her words up in a nice little bundle.

"Supernaturals are sensitive too! They have feelings!" another protestor yelled.

I paused. "Are you actually advocating for Super Duper rights?" They all blinked at me like I'd spoken Chinese, and I cleared my throat. "I mean, supernatural?"

"Yes, here, read this." She thrust a paper into my hand. "You don't have to live behind that Wall; we can all live together in harmony!"

I stared at the paper. It listed all the rights that Super Dupers currently lived without.

Lack of equality. No voice in the government. Inability to own property on the south side of the Wall. Inhumane treatment by the law in general. They were right, but they were also so very wrong.

My lips twitched and I couldn't help it; I burst out laughing. "Listen, I know you believe it, but not all supernaturals are nice. Some of them are downright nasty and will attack you without thought. They will kill you as soon as they look at you."

"You didn't," she pointed out.

I sighed. I didn't know how to explain to her how I felt. I wanted equality; I would get my inheritance and bakery back. But the reality was, not all Super Dupers *should* be integrated into society. I thought about the deviousness of Merlin. The blood-lusting vampires who Remo kept a tight rein on. Even Oberfluffel's werewolf task force. They were all deadly in their own ways and could make mincemeat pies of any human who irritated them. If I was honest, even I could be that deadly. At the stadium, it had been pure luck that I'd not mowed down a fair number of humans in my effort to get to Achilles before he killed Tad.

But whose decision was it to make?

Not mine.

And not the protestors' either. There had to be a better system. I thought about Damara, the satyr and sometimes healer. She'd thought

Zeus was the answer, that he could manage the population of super-naturals and help them integrate into the human world. Maybe he could have, if he'd cared about anyone but himself.

"Super Dupers—I mean, supernaturals—are not safe. You have to believe me that you are in danger here," I said, frustration filling my words. How could I make them see, make them understand?

Almost as if on cue, a twisted werewolf came roaring, literally roaring, out of the Wall's gate, partially shifted. He spied the group of protestors who *cheered* for him as he escaped the Wall.

Their cheers turned to screams as he rushed them, teeth snapping and spit flying. I could have almost sworn he laughed as he chased them around. Like a rat in the kitchen scaring all the old ladies. He passed me once, and there was laughter on his long muzzle. Definitely playing. But it only proved the point of what I was trying to say.

I leapt forward, the robe tangling around my legs. I dropped to the ground, struggled to my feet, and got in front of the group a split second before the werewolf came around for another pass.

"Stop!" I held a hand out, and he skidded to a halt, shook his head, and let out a whine. I put all the strength and power I could into my voice. "Go back, you stay behind the Wall, that's where you belong, you maniac."

He whimpered again, shook his head, and bowed his shoulders, his words slurred, as though he struggled to speak over his mouthful of teeth. "I's just playing."

"No playing with humans; you'll hurt them." I softened my tone, and he lifted a dark eyebrow at me over a bright-gold eye, hope lighting his features.

"You play?"

"No, go home."

He bobbed his head and tried to go around me. "Home, good. Outside."

I pointed at the Wall. "No. The north side of the Wall is your home. Go on now."

Another low whine slid from him as he turned, tucked his tail between his legs, and scuttled back the way he'd come. He glanced over his shoulder once and stuck his overlong bright-pink tongue out at me. It flipped a good four inches out of his mouth. "No fun," he grumbled.

I stood there and made sure he went back behind the Wall. He sat down right at the edge and stared at me. I rolled my eyes. At least he was listening. Sort of.

"You stopped him," the Irish-accented girl said, awe in her voice.

I turned to look at the lady protestor. "Well, I couldn't let him attack you. Even if he thought he was just playing."

Tentatively, she reached out and put her arms around me, giving me a hug. Stunned, I stood there for a second before carefully hugging her back.

"Thank you."

"You're welcome."

I stepped away and headed over to the gate where the werewolf sat panting. He was all black with big golden eyes. But unlike the other werewolves I'd seen, he was neither human nor wolf, but stuck somewhere in between. Like he'd forgotten how to complete his shift.

"Aren't you going home?"

"Waiting for home," he said, which made no sense. How could he be waiting for home to come to him?

"Do you have a name, while you wait for home?"

"Alex." He winked a big golden eye at me, like his name should mean something.

"Well"—I patted him on the head—"don't go beyond the Wall, Alex. It's not safe for you. Understand?"

He bobbed his head once and gave me another wink. "Pretty lady need help?"

"No, I don't." I laughed at him, and he shrugged and lay down at the inside of the Wall, like he really was waiting for something. Maybe his master? Silently I wished him luck in that. As long as he didn't go chasing the humans again—even if he was just playing—all would be well for him. Or as well as it could be in this world of ours.

Another half an hour walk, and I was back at house number thirteen. Inside I could hear laughter and the dual heartbeats of Sandy and Beth. They were Greek monsters too, though a different flavor than me. Stymphalian birds were their designation, and they could shift into the deadly man-eating beasts the same as I could shift into my Drakaina form.

"Hey, girls." I padded through the house and into the kitchen. My eyes stretched wide as I took in the scene, blood everywhere. "Are you okay?"

They looked at each other and laughed, clutching at their bellies as they giggled. While that eased my mind a little, it wasn't until I drew a breath in and tasted the air that I relaxed. The scent was sweet and fruity. Cherries was my guess, not blood.

And then I looked again and slowly shook my head as I picked up one of my pots, the interior covered in dried cherry juice. "Did you pull every pot, pan, and kitchen utensil out of the cupboards?"

Beth laughed up at me and brushed her short blond hair out of her face. "We couldn't find what we were looking for. Don't worry, we'll clean up . . . Mom." She winked, and I rolled my eyes.

"What are you making? Or maybe what are you trying to make?" I couldn't help being pulled into the kitchen, even if it was a complete disaster.

Sandy grinned at me. "We found your 'French Desserts' section in your recipe book. This is clafoutis, cherry flavored."

I smiled and peeked into the mix. I dipped a finger in and tasted it. "You need a bit more sugar; it'll be too tart."

"You got it. Mom."

"Really, you gotta stop that." I laughed at them. "I don't think I'm even older than either of you." In fact, I knew Beth had a year on me, and Sandy was born the same year as I was.

Sandy grinned as she spooned some more sugar into the mixture. "You kinda are, though. You saved us from Merlin, and you've been helping us adjust. You're even teaching us to bake. You look out for us, like a mom would. And . . . we know it irritates you when we tease you."

Beth took the bowl from Sandy and poured its contents into a pan that had cherries scattered about the bottom. "Speaking of teasing"— she raised an eyebrow at me—"what's with the nun habit?"

I pulled a chair out and slid into it. Pushing a few pans out of the way, I rested both hands on the table. "Bad day at the courthouse. I think I lost everything to that . ."

"Asshat?" Beth offered.

"Twat waffle?" Sandy suggested.

"Oh, I like twat waffle." I took a breath and started again. "That twat waffle . . . the judge says he's getting everything."

They gasped and hurried over to me, covered in cherry juice and flour.

They wrapped me in their arms, murmuring their condolences, telling me it was so wrong, and while I knew it . . . that I had them on my side meant the world to me. I leaned into them, tears trickling down my cheeks. "I don't know what I would do without you two."

"We feel the same," Beth whispered, and kissed the top of my head.

"Now you're being a mom." I wiped my face.

She pulled back and shook her head. "Fine, we all take care of each other, that's how it goes."

"On that note"—Sandy let go of me and pointed at my robes— "you should go change. That thing is totally unflattering, and now it's covered in cherry juice."

I had to agree with her; the robe was awful and still smelled of Old Spice. I hurried upstairs and slipped out of it, tossing it into the corner of my room. I put the deed to the bakery on my side dresser, then went to the bathroom and grabbed a wet cloth. I wiped my face and neck, which got the worst of the cologne off me, then tied my hair back into a loose ponytail. I pulled on jeans and a comfy top, then headed back downstairs. Baking the night away would take my mind off the craptastic day, and baking with two of my closest friends was even better.

Back in the kitchen, I pulled out my favorite cookbook. "Here, I'll show you a few things, tricks of the trade, so to speak."

We started on a recipe for filled cookies. With an exterior similar to a sugar cookie, they could be filled with any number of things: strawberry jam, raisins, peanut butter, and pretty much anything else you might think of. I directed them around the kitchen, and they grabbed what we needed as I mixed it all together. The laughter and chatter flowed between us, soothing away some of the day's events. I told them about Remo, and they oohed over the kiss. Awwed when I said I'd touched on a lost love of his, I was sure of it.

"I want to meet someone who melts me," Beth said, stirring her bowl of icing by hand, her eyes distant. "But who will want us now that we're monsters?"

I went to her side and put an arm around her waist. "The right guy. That's who."

She smiled at me, but there was sadness in her eyes, and I knew I couldn't get rid of it for her. I hugged her. "Until then, we bake!"

The flutter of wings spun me around. I more than half expected Ernie, and was prepared to defend my irritation with him, so when I saw it was Hermes, I had to scrub the scowl off my face.

"Easy, Drakaina." Hermes held up his hands. "You look about ready to bite someone in half."

Beth and Sandy waved at him in unison.

I took a breath. "Sorry, thought you were someone else."

He shrugged his thin shoulders, and his feet twitched as though he wanted to be running instead of hovering in midair.

"If you're here, you have a message for me?" I grabbed one of the empty bowls and piled it beside the sink of soapy water.

"Flora wants you to meet her at your bakery." He fluttered up. "Want me to take a message back to her?" The eagerness in his voice was not far off from what I thought a golden retriever would sound like if it could beg to have a ball thrown.

I looked at the two girls, and they waved at me. "Go on, we'll clean up here."

"Thank you." They knew how I liked my kitchen after baking. Spotless. I looked at Hermes. "Sure, tell her I'm on my way."

Spending time with Yaya always made me feel better. Some time with her would go a long way to soothing the last of my hurt. Better yet to do it at Vanilla and Honey, seeing as the bakery wasn't going to be mine soon enough.

With a puff of feathers, Hermes was gone.

"Are you sure you don't want me to stay and clean up?" I looked at Beth and Sandy, and they shook their heads.

"No, we've got it. But you're going to miss out on the clafoutis." Beth smiled, and the dinger on the oven went off. She pulled the pan out and showed it to me. I nodded.

"You two did great. We keep this up, and maybe we can start a bakery here on this side of the Wall."

Sandy sucked in a sharp breath. "Do you mean that?"

I blinked several times as I realized what I'd said. "Yeah, I do. I mean, why not?"

She squealed, and even Beth got excited, her eyes sparkling. "We could totally rock it. Call it the Fantastic Fangs Bakery."

I laughed. "Yeah, that would be . . . nice. I'd like that. Let's talk about it more when I get back."

I waved at them and headed out the front door. The thought of starting a new bakery was more than daunting; I knew the work and hours we'd have to put in. At the same time, I wasn't going to drown myself in the pity party. I steeled my back. No, I wasn't going to pity myself. And I wasn't giving up on Vanilla and Honey, not yet.

I headed for the bus stop that was outside the Wall. It would have been nice if Hermes had found me while I was still downtown.

For a while I'd been using a car that technically didn't belong to me. Sure, it had been Barbie's, but I'd grown to like it. Now it was impounded, and I had no money to speak of, so the bus it was.

I frowned as I walked to the bus stop, my mind racing. What the heck was Yaya doing at Vanilla and Honey at this hour anyway? It was after ten, and . . . more than that, how had she gotten in? I hadn't given her a key to the bakery. "Yaya, what are you up to this time, you crazy old lady?"

I knew the bus schedule by heart, and I also knew I was going to have to wait for at least a half an hour for the next one, then there was the long ride itself. It would be after midnight before I was at the bakery.

The whoop of a police siren made every muscle in me tighten up. A police cruiser inched closer, its lights flickering. I stepped back. What now?

Officer Jensen leaned out his window. "You going somewhere?"

"Why, is that illegal now too?" I raised an eyebrow. I knew that his job was to patrol downtown Seattle. Not to drive around up near the Wall. Which meant he was here for a purpose, and probably that purpose had something to do with Remo. Seeing as Remo was also his boss.

He nodded. "Actually, yes. You aren't supposed to be on this side of the Wall."

I clenched my fingers over the papers in my hands. "And you're going to make me go back?"

"Nope. Remo felt bad for dropping you at the bus. You need a ride anywhere?"

I blinked several times. "Yeah. Can you take me to my bakery?"

"Sure. Hop in." He leaned across and opened the passenger door.

I slid in and buckled my seat belt.

"Considering what you went through today, you look good. I'm sorry about throwing you into things like I did. I . . . knew you could handle it." Jensen smiled at me, then swallowed and looked away. I liked him. He was a friend, handsome with his light-brown skin and deep, dark eyes, not to mention being a man in uniform, but . . . he wasn't Remo.

I kept my eyes on the side window. What to say? What not to say? I didn't want to encourage him, nor did I want to offend him and have him drop me off in the middle of the highway.

"Alena, Remo is no good," he said.

I turned to look at him. His eyes stared straight forward, locked on the road.

"Well, he's helped me a lot so far."

He frowned, his jaw ticking several times before he spoke. "I shouldn't be telling you this, but I can't keep letting you help him. Even with what I did . . . he sent me to get you, using the influence on me to force my hand. He's using you. That much that Santos said is right. Remo doesn't care about you, but he's making sure you think he does. That's his MO. You understand? He doesn't care about *anyone*, and he'll use you until he gets what he wants, and then he'll cast you off like he's done to every other woman in his life. Worse, you'll get hurt or be killed. I . . . don't want that to happen."

I bit my lower lip. His words didn't feel right, and yet I couldn't deny that there was a possibility they were true. "What do you know about the girl he went to medical school for?"

His head whipped sideways so fast the car jigged side to side as he jerked the wheel. "What?"

I swallowed hard, doing my best to work past the feeling that I might be betraying something Remo didn't want to be common knowledge. At the same time, I . . . wanted to know everything I could about him. "He went to medical school, about twenty years ago."

He shook his head. "I doubt it."

I thought about Remo's hands inside of Tad's belly only a week before. How he'd quickly found the puncture that Beth had not been able to discover on her own. Remo had staved off Tad's death long enough that we'd been able to get the healer Damara in to finish the job and save my brother's life.

I didn't argue with Jensen. From the set of his jaw, it was obvious to me he wasn't going to be open to anything that even slightly made Remo look like a good guy. The whole conversation made me wonder . . . was this just another aspect of his knight-in-shining-armor complex? Or did he really think I was in danger? "Why are you still working for him, then? If he's such a bad guy."

His hands tightened on the steering wheel. "I'm tied to him, Alena. Anyone who signs on with him signs their loyalties over. It's how it works with vampires. I never had a reason to care . . . I don't want to see you get hurt, Alena. The best way to do that is to stay close to Remo so I can warn you. The fact that he dropped you off at a bus stop to get all the way home is just another—"

"He sent you to get me," I pointed out.

"After I asked him where you were."

My heart sank a little. I reached up and pulled my hair over one shoulder, threading my fingers through it, then braiding it.

He grimaced. "There's something else I have to tell you."

I leaned back in my seat, trying to quell the twist of nerves in my belly. "What?"

"I don't think Remo wants you to win your case. He . . . he stands to lose a lot of his hold on the Supes if the human court system begins to recognize them. They could then go to protection on the south side of the Wall. Do you understand? He doesn't want you—"

"I got it." I cut him off, not wanting to hear another word about Remo. I needed to digest what he'd told me. And I wanted to ask Remo about it. No matter what Jensen said, I trusted Remo.

"Thanks for looking out for me, Officer Jensen," I said.

"Anytime. You can call me anytime, for anything. And call me Ben. Please." He flashed me a grin, and I smiled back.

"You're a good friend."

He grimaced. "Ah, don't friend zone me."

I laughed, and just like that the tension was broken. We spent the rest of the drive arguing about movies that didn't accurately portray supernaturals. In particular, vampires and the variety of types they came in in movies. Sunlight defying, beautiful, ugly, bloodthirsty, maniacal, and heroic.

"Here we are. Do you want me to wait?" He parked the cruiser at the curb in front of Vanilla and Honey.

"No, I see my grandmother's car. We can carpool." I opened the door, paused, and looked back. "Thanks, Officer Jensen. I mean, Ben."

He tipped his hat and winked at me. "Ma'am."

Laughing, I stepped out and shut the door behind me. He was a nice guy; I liked him, and after the initial awkward tension, he was easy to be around. A thought flashed through my mind. He didn't seem to mind the monsters . . . maybe I should introduce him to Beth? As the thought took root, I nodded to myself.

There was no chemistry between Jensen and I; there never had been. Whatever he felt was only because I'd used my siren abilities on him in a desperate situation. If I gave him a push toward Beth . . . I could totally see it working.

I could picture the group of us hanging out, visiting. With his arm around Beth, Remo's around me, Tad's around Dahlia. I smiled to myself; yeah, I was about to play matchmaker. I couldn't wait to tell Beth.

My thoughts skittered sideways. Jensen was a good guy, and he didn't do a thing for me. So apparently I liked the bad boys now that I was a monster. But was that chemistry fabricated on Remo's part? Could Ben be right about Remo and the way he used women? The problem was that I could see the possibility hidden there, and it bothered me.

I shook my head. "What has happened to the good girl I was?"

Shannon Mayer

The door of my bakery opened, and my yaya peered out. "Good girl? Good girls get run over in life; you need to be a bit of a badass to make it in this world."

"Yaya!" I gasped. "That isn't true. And how did you get into my bakery anyway?"

"Really? I think it is." She shrugged. "Come on, I need help with my recipe. It's not turning out the way I'd hoped." She winked back at me. "As to getting in, I still have a few tricks up my sleeve. I'm old, not dead, you know."

In other words, she wasn't going to tell me a thing.

I took the edge of the door and stepped into the glowing warmth of the bakery. Though I wasn't affected by the cold, I couldn't deny I liked the feeling of heat coursing over my skin.

Kind of like the feeling I got when Remo looked at me.

"Dang it," I muttered under my breath.

Yaya laughed. "Talking to yourself? Oh dear, you must be getting old."

"Ha-ha, very funny." I walked in and went right to the phone. "I need a locksmith before I do anything else . . . I might have taken the deed from Roger without asking." I grabbed the phone book and flipped through the pages as Yaya nodded in agreement, muttering that Roger deserved nothing, until I found a local guy who said he could come at all hours. Good enough. I dialed him up and explained the situation. "Can you come now?"

"Yeah, sure. Going to be double, four hundred," he said with a yawn.

"That's robbery!" I spit out.

Yaya touched my arm. "It's on me. Just get him to come."

"Three fifty," I said, "and some fresh baked goods."

"Done."

I gave him the address, and he arrived in under ten minutes. I showed him the two doors, and he got to work. I went into the kitchen, to see Yaya over a big bowl.

60

"What did you really want to talk to me about, Yaya? You're a better baker than me, and we both know it."

Her fluffy white hair barely came up to my chin as she took each of my hands in hers. "The hearing, did it go well?"

I groaned. "I don't think it could have gone worse."

She grimaced. "Come on, take a look at what I'm doing and tell me about your day."

The smell of spices and caramelizing sugar filled the air as I approached the work table. She showed me the recipe for a caramel-topped, chocolate-filled monkey bread she was trying to make, and I took a look at what she had going on the stovetop.

"Here, just too much heat on the caramel, I think; you're going to burn it." I turned it down and leaned back, took a breath, and told her all about the hearing, the vampires, shifting, and then getting all the way back to the Wall before Hermes caught up with me. I deliberately left out the piece about Remo and me making out, or how I'd turned him off with a single question about his past.

Maybe Jensen was right. Maybe Remo was using me. I mean, if he really liked me, wouldn't he want me to know things about his past? I'd shared everything about myself with Roger when we'd started dating. I didn't think there was a childhood story he'd not suffered through at least once. Now that I thought about it, Roger hadn't bothered to do the same.

The thought of Remo and Roger having any similarities made me ill, and I had to take slow breaths to ease the quick onslaught of nausea.

"Are you okay, Lena?" Yaya touched her hand to my cheeks. "You went a bit green there, avocado in color."

I waved her off. "Just a bad thought."

Her eyes narrowed. "Keeping secrets from your yaya?"

I snorted. "I learned from the best, didn't I?" Yaya had been keeping secrets my whole life, and we—Tad and I—had only just found out. One, Yaya was a priestess of Zeus. Two, she'd had a fling with the god of thunder and lightning that resulted in a curse being laid on our family. Three, well, I didn't know what three might be, but I had no doubt there were more secrets rolling around in that fluffy white head of hair.

She snorted right back at me. "I was protecting all of you the best way I knew how."

"Well, maybe I'm doing the same." I crossed my arms and leaned against the counter. "What am I going to do, Yaya? I have the paperwork for the bakery, so I'll have a few weeks at the most. They won't be able to get duplicates very fast."

"I know this bakery means the world to you, but you won't be the first person who has had to start their life over again after a divorce."

I stared at her. She never talked about Pappou other than to say he was gone and she was glad of him being gone. My mom was their only child, and from what I understood, he'd left shortly after Yaya had announced her pregnancy. Another family secret. I grimaced, knowing that it wasn't important to what we were dealing with at the moment. Even if I wanted to know.

I pinched my lips together. "It isn't the starting over I'm worried about, it's that . . . damn it, it's not fair Roger should get everything. I'd be fine with giving him half. I'd even buy him out so I would have the house and the bakery."

She pulled a pan of monkey bread out, put it on the counter, and drizzled the caramel sauce over it. "Here, try a piece."

I pulled a chunk of squishy dough out, chocolate oozing from the middle, and popped the whole thing into my mouth. "Hot," I said around it. The flavors burst in my mouth, and I groaned as I chewed. Yaya bit into a chunk and nodded.

"Yes, that's better." She nodded to herself. "The first two batches didn't taste quite right."

I licked my fingers and once more went over what the judge had said. "How am I going to find a lawyer who will work without pay, for a Super Duper, no less?"

Yaya squinted one eye and looked at a spot somewhere past my left shoulder. "You need someone who is a good liar, for sure."

"I said lawyer."

"Same thing." She waved her hands at me. "Someone who can spin a good yarn and make you believe him no matter how outrageous. Maybe someone with a little bit of magic on his side."

I leaned forward. "You have someone in mind?"

She nodded. "Someone who could talk his way in and out of a deal with the devil himself."

I reeled back; she couldn't be serious. There was no way she was suggesting who I thought.

"Oh no. I'm not asking him." I shook my head and hunched my shoulders. "He lied to me about everything, Yaya. And he's working for Hera, I'm sure of it. That alone strikes him off the list of possible help." Merlin. Of all people for her to suggest, I was shocked he was even on the list, never mind at the top of it.

"Be that as it may, use his talents, Lena Bean. Merlin is good at what he does; even you can't deny that. And I think you have made him sit up and take notice. You haven't fallen as you were supposed to. I think you should give him a chance to make things right."

I popped another hunk of monkey bread into my mouth and chewed it so I didn't have to say yes or no. Because the truth was, Yaya was correct. There was no one as slick as the warlock who'd turned me from a quiet little church mouse who had never said a bad word in her life and never broken a rule without confessing instantly into a siren that could take on the toughest of heroes and win.

I swallowed my piece of the sweet chocolaty bread. "Fine, I'll go talk to Merlin. But I doubt he'll help."

Yaya laughed and said, "I think he may just surprise you. And one more thing."

I rolled my eyes to the ceiling. "What now?"

"Your parents' thirtieth anniversary is coming up, and you don't want to miss that. I'm going to talk to your mother about having you make the cake."

I snorted. Right, because between dealing with a legal case from hell, Theseus, and being put on a rival vampire's gang poopy list, I was going to want to attend my parents' anniversary. Also known as the father who loved me and the mother who was trying to pretend I didn't exist now that I was a supernatural.

Perhaps I could call in sick on that one.

CHAPTER 5

The protestors waved to Yaya and me as we drove through the main gate of the Wall. "You think the Supe Squad will get back into action soon?" I looked at my grandmother, knowing she had more knowledge about such things than she let on. A lot more, depending on her cache of secrets tucked away like someone's hidden candy stash.

"Perhaps. Their captain is gone, and until the second-in-command truly steps up, we won't know."

It was after one in the morning when she dropped me off. I waved as she pulled away, and she honked several times. As if I wouldn't otherwise know she'd seen me as she left with her clunking baby-blue Granada. Though it wasn't pretty, it did the job. "At least she has a car," I muttered.

Once more back at house number thirteen, I headed up the steps, fatigue nipping at my heels.

I pushed the door open and heard the soft lull of voices speaking in whispers. A smile crept across my lips. Tad and Dahlia were so darn cute together. Almost sickeningly so, actually.

"Coming in, please keep the nudity to a minimum," I called out so I wouldn't catch them in a compromising situation. The last thing

I wanted to see was my brother getting down and dirty with my best friend. Even if I was happy for them.

I kept my eyes averted as I passed the living room, their usual make-out place.

"Alena, I want you to meet someone," Beth called to me.

Surprised, I turned. I saw her first, the short blond hair in a messy do that was both cute and carefree. Her eyes sparkled as she grinned at me. She'd met someone in the few hours I'd been gone? My first thought was *Too bad*. I'd been hoping to gently push her toward Jensen. My next thought was *How had she found someone so fast?*

Then I saw the man whose lap she sat on. His long dark-blond ponytail, his blue eyes, the slick suit with silver threaded through it.

"Theseus."

"No." Beth laughed. "His name is Tim."

I raised both eyebrows even as a cold chill worked its way up my spine. "Tim?"

Her smile widened. "Yes, he saved me, Alena. After we cleaned the kitchen, Sandy and I went for a walk—we were talking about the bakery, you know?"

I nodded, keeping my mouth shut, and she went on. "A car was coming, and I didn't see it. He literally swept me off my feet." She beamed at him, and the only word I could come up with was "lovestruck." This couldn't be real. I had to have fallen and hit my head and I was now hallucinating.

"Beth . . ." I took a step toward her. "You would have demolished the car if it hit you. He didn't save you. Not really."

She frowned at me. "Alena, he saved me. And he doesn't even care that I'm a Stymphalian bird. He's the right guy, like you said."

"I'll bet he doesn't mind," I muttered under my breath. "Look, his name is *not* Tim. This is Theseus, and he's using you to get to me. He doesn't care about you; his job is to *kill* monsters like you and me!"

She sucked in a sharp breath and stood up, her eyes no longer sparkling with good humor. More like sparking with anger. She took a step toward me, and the air around her shimmered. Like she was going to shift into her bird form. What the heck, why wasn't she listening?

I wasn't even sure if we could hurt each other, but I didn't really want to find out either.

"Beth." I held up my hands. "Don't do this. We need to talk about just what is going on here."

The clatter of feet on the stairs almost turned me around. Except I didn't think that what was behind me was going to be a problem.

"Beth, what's going on?" Sandy called from the stairs. Maybe I was wrong. A Stymphalian bird in front and behind was not something that made me feel safe. Not when I was no longer sure if they were my friends. My heart clenched. How could things have changed so much in such a short time?

As if reading my mind, Theseus held up a tiny arrow and swirled it across his knuckles. An arrow just like the ones Ernie had to make people fall in love with one another.

"Oh, you little bastard," I whispered.

Beth ignored Sandy's question. "Tim is not Theseus. Theseus would want to kill me, not save me. Sandy was there; she saw him save me." Each word was bitten out, and each one pitched higher than the next.

Sandy took another step, the stair creaking. "He did pull her out of the path of the car." Her words were careful, like even she wasn't sure what was going on. I dared a glance back at her, and she shrugged, her eyes worried.

I took a step back, seeing the pickle Theseus had put me in. Behind Beth he smiled at me, the smug satisfaction evident in every line of his face, the tiny arrow tucked away somewhere. His arms were thrown over the back of the chair, and his legs were stretched out as though he were preparing to watch a prizefight.

In that moment I knew there was no way I'd be able to convince her he was anyone but Tim. The best thing I could do was back off and try to find a different route.

I held up my hands to her. "Fine. I retract my statement. He's not Theseus."

She slowed her advance, and the shimmering around her eased off. "I think we should go, Tim."

"Of course, beautiful girl." He stood, stepped forward, and slid an arm around her waist, though his eyes never left my face. "We can go to my place."

She beamed up at him. "I'd like that. Sandy, you're coming too, right? You're with me? You know he's not Theseus. Alena is wrong."

"A threesome, really?" I couldn't help the words. Beth glared at me and I glared back. We were friends, we'd survive this, I had to believe it. Even if it felt like something was broken that couldn't be fixed. A crème brûlée spilled on the floor, ready to be tossed in the trash.

"No," she snapped. "I just don't want her around you."

Anger coursed through me, and a low hiss rumbled through my chest. Theseus tightened his hold on Beth's waist and slowly guided her to the door while I stood there shaking with the growing fury.

"Alena, lovely to meet you." Theseus winked and they were out the door. Sandy crept down the rest of the stairs and paused at the door. "I'm sorry, Alena. I have to go with her. I don't want him to hurt her."

"I get it, just . . . be careful. He *is* Theseus, and he's here to kill us all."

Her eyes were sad and she looked away. "I don't know. I . . . I just don't know."

She closed the door behind her with a soft click, and I counted to ten in an attempt to get control of myself.

"Son of a bitch!" *That* word slipped from me in a burst of emotion. I stomped through the house, looking for something to hit, something to . . . I don't know, destroy, maybe.

"Your scales are showing."

I spun and glared up at Ernie, my voice coming out in a fair imitation of Yaya's you're-in-shit-now-you'd-better-run-if-you-want-to-survive tone.

"You! You gave him one of your arrows! I thought you were my friend, you little fat-bottomed jerk!" I took a step toward him, and he floated to the ceiling, his eyes widening.

"What? No, I didn't . . . Oh my gods." He put a hand to his face. "I thought there was one missing. I . . . he took one, I didn't give it to him, you have to believe me."

His eyes begged, and I tried to see through my anger and betrayal. Tried and failed.

"How could he have taken it from you? You just leave them sitting out there on the street to be grabbed?" I snapped.

"No, it . . . they're made for me. I leave them behind at the forge, though, because I don't want them to be taken." He held his hands out to me. "Please believe me, I didn't give it to him."

"Maybe you should hide them better." I slumped against the wall and stared up at him. "Your timing is rather suspicious, even without the arrow business. Theseus was here, and he's got Beth in his thrall because of your arrow."

He nodded and slowly dropped from the ceiling. "You believe me?"

"While I probably shouldn't"—I watched him draw closer—"I do. I don't think you'd actively try to get us killed. So if it isn't because of Theseus, why are you here?"

Hurt flashed over his face, and I closed my eyes. "I'm sorry. It's been a poop-filled day," I apologized.

The flutter of his wings stopped. I opened my eyes to see him sitting on the back of the recliner. "I've been trying to find a moment to talk to you all day. I didn't want to interrupt you and your yaya, even though that monkey bread smelled amazing. And I was pretty sure you didn't want me interrupting your . . . talk"—he waggled his eyebrows—"with Remo."

I glared at him even as my face heated. "So instead you decided right after Theseus walks out with two of my friends is a good idea?"

He sagged in the air. "How many times do I have to tell you I'm sorry? I'm torn in two directions. If I completely tell Hera I won't help her, I will get no inside information for you, something that you need."

I put my hands on my hips and glared up at him. "And do you have any such info?"

"Well, no, not yet—"

I snorted and turned my back on him, struggling to breathe through the anger. *Theseus . . . damn him to hell and back.* I might not say the words out loud, but I could say them in my head and not feel too bad.

"Alena, tell me what happened. Please?" Ernie dared to float in front of me, lowering himself to the edge of the sink.

I let out a sigh, and with it the worst of the anger faded.

"He has Beth believing his name is Tim, and that he cares about her. She was ready to fight me just because I tried to tell her he was Theseus and not Tim." I rubbed a hand over my face. I slumped into a kitchen chair. "Why isn't he just attacking me? I hate to say this, but at least I could do something with that."

Ernie pulled one wing around him and played with the feathers. "Look, Theseus isn't like Achilles. He was king of Athens, and the goddess he's tied himself to is Athena. Goddess of wisdom . . . so he's not going to play a purely physical game with you. He'll twist your world inside out and then some. He handles things almost opposite to how Achilles does. I mean, look at Achilles. He didn't even update his clothing or weapons; he came at you with all the old-school stuff, including the Bull Boys. Theseus is smarter than Achilles. A lot smarter, and the fact that he's lining your friends up against you . . . I hate to say it, but it doesn't surprise me."

His words made sense. "Yeah, that's what I'm worried about. Can you tell me anything about him, other than what you already have?" I looked at Ernie, watching him for one of his tells. His left foot bobbed several times before he stilled it. I looked away with a soft snort. "Never mind."

"No, I want to help, Alena, I do. Let me think a minute what I can tell you." He flew to the table and sat on the edge next to me. "Okay, it's obvious he's learning what the world has to offer him in terms of taking you down. He would have watched that video your idiot husband took of you fighting Achilles in the stadium. I mean, it's all over the Internet. He'll have learned from it. That is his style. He's feeling things out right now and trying to make your life harder by taking away your allies. And he has some abilities with charm. I bet that's why Sandy went with him. Yes, he took my arrow and used it on Beth, but not on Sandy. But she still went with them, right?"

I frowned as I nodded.

He went on. "It only works on those who are susceptible."

I waved both hands in the air as if batting away steam. "Yeah, but he's still going to have to fight me at some point, right?"

"He may not. What if . . ." He stumbled to a stop and clamped his mouth shut. "I can't tell you anything else."

My jaw clenched and I fought against the tears. Forget it, I needed a good cry. I lowered my head, hid my face, and let the tears fall. Mostly angry tears, but I'd lost two friends in the space of as many minutes, and the pain of that hovered in me as well. Ernie fluttered down and patted my back. I took a swing at him.

"Go away, Ernie. Just go away."

"Alena, I am trying. I don't want to lose your friendship. But I don't want to get killed either. Can you understand the position I'm in?" His voice was about as dejected as I'd ever heard it. I lifted my head and wiped my eyes. His brow was wrinkled, and he wrung his hands over and over. I didn't want to lose another friend. I sniffed once and held an arm out to him. He flew into me and grabbed me around the neck.

I hugged him, patted him lightly on the back. "I don't understand, Ernie, but at the same time, I've seen Hera; I wouldn't want to go up against her for anything in the world."

He hiccuped a sob, surprising me. I pushed him back gently. "Why are you crying?"

The words spilled out in a tear-soaked rush. "You're too damn nice, Alena. You shouldn't forgive me, even though I want you to. You should probably never talk to me again, because there will probably be a time when I have to work for her or get my wings removed."

I blew a raspberry with my lips. "I'm not that nice. Remember Achilles?"

Ernie shook his head. "You were protecting your brother and Remo. Theseus"—he grimaced and then leaned in closer to me, his voice dropping to a whisper—"he won't make that same mistake. He knows you won't fight for yourself. He won't attack your people until after you're dead."

I sat back and opened my mouth, ready to ask a question when a knock on the front door grabbed my attention.

I looked at Ernie. "Are you expecting company?"

He shook his head. "No. Zeus has gone underground; he's the only one who might show up from my end of things. I left him a message, but his answering machine said he was going out of town. No one has seen him since that night at the club."

Zeus. Another issue I had a feeling I'd have to face at some point. I stood and walked to the door, taking a deep breath as I drew close. The sweet scent of vampire musk, licorice, and blood whispered across the air.

"Remo," I breathed his name and jerked the door open even as I realized I'd made a mistake. Remo didn't smell like other vampires. He smelled of cinnamon and honey. Not blood and licorice.

Santos grinned at me, flashing his fangs fully, something I knew from Dahlia was a sign of aggression. Like a baboon flashing its teeth right before it attacked. I slammed the door shut and threw the dead bolt.

"Alena, behind you!" Ernie shouted the warning and I spun, dropping into a crouch with instincts I didn't know I had. A weapon of some sort blurred as it shot over my head.

"Well, well, so she has a feathered friend too? Roast chicken along with the snake tonight, boys!" The vampire right in front of me grinned up at Ernie. Which took his attention completely off me. They seemed to be coming in from all sides: the kitchen, the front door, and there was even a pair sliding down the banister.

"You leave him alone!" I shot forward with both feet and kicked him in the shins. He screeched and slammed to the floor on his belly, a gust of air shooting out of him.

The door behind me burst inward, and I scrambled away from the flying splinters. Really, it was more the vampire I was trying to get away from.

"Oh, you aren't going anywhere, little snake girl," Santos crooned. "I've got something special for you." He laughed, and I did not laugh with him.

I rolled onto my back and scooted away. Which sent me right into another set of legs. I looked up, way up, at a mountain of a vampire, one that easily topped seven feet. He had shaggy, long red hair and a full bright-orange beard.

"Viking?" I couldn't seem to help the one-word question.

He roared down at me, fangs exposed and spit flying. He spread his legs as he lifted a huge ax over his head, no doubt to chop me in half. I scooted between his legs and shot a fist upward as I passed his family jewels. The crunch under my fist brought an instant groan from all the vampires in the room.

"Alena, get the hell out of here, they've got a snake catcher!" Ernie screeched.

A snake catcher? What in all that was holy was that?

There was no time to discuss just what a snake catcher was, but I found out anyway.

I made it into the kitchen and pushed to my feet when a thin metal wire flipped over my foot and wrapped in tight to my jeans, cinching shut like a noose around my ankle.

A sizzle crackled through the air, and I stared at Santos on the other end of the noose. The long wire was attached to a five-foot-long steel rod. Like a dog catcher's favorite tool. It had to be what Ernie meant. I tugged hard with my leg, and the pole was ripped out of Santos's hands.

"Idiot, you think you can outmuscle me?" I snapped at him. Though I was terrified, I wasn't going to let him know it. I wanted them to believe me dangerous, even if I struggled with the concept.

"I can smell your fear, Alena. And I like how it tastes," he purred.

Poop on it, so much for my bravado.

I backed up farther as I wiggled my foot in a vain effort to get the noose off, but it was stuck tight to my jeans as if it had magnetic properties of some sort. I kept my eyes up, reached the kitchen sink, and groped behind me. I came up with a frying pan in one hand and a large cookie sheet in the other.

The vampires circled in tighter, laughing. "Look out, boys, she's going to brain us with her kitchen wares!"

"Five against one, that's not very fair," I said.

"Oh, it isn't five against one." Santos grinned. "I have a crew outside too, just in case you manage to slip"—he made a snake-wiggling motion with one hand—"through our fingers."

Another sizzle crackled in the air, and the smell of burning material tickled my nose. Heat suddenly erupted on my leg where the noose had hooked in tight.

I screamed as I went down, writhing with an intense burning pain, not unlike an oil burn I'd had when I'd made my first attempt at deep-frying apple fritters. Only this was a thousand times worse. I couldn't think past it, couldn't make myself care that I was surrounded by enemies.

"See, I told you that potion would work," Santos crowed, but I barely registered his words; I had to get the noose off. I scrabbled at my leg, but every time I touched the noose, my fingers burned, scalding.

"Grab the handle," Santos instructed, "and I'll get on top of her."

This was going down faster than a stack of pans off the top shelf. I had to do something now, or I was going to end up in more trouble than I'd been in so far in my new world.

And that was saying a fair bit.

CHAPTER 6

With my teeth gritted tight, I reached for the noose as one of the vampires reached for the long handle. I grabbed the metal wire, crying out with the pain in my hands that mimicked the unreal pain in my leg, and loosened it just enough to slide my foot out.

I jerked away from the noose as though it were a snake. Scratch that, as though it were a snake catcher. I pushed myself to my feet and climbed onto the kitchen counter.

"What, you can fly too?" Santos laughed up at me, his dark eyes filled with anything but humor. "My, my, Remo is going to be upset when he sees the damage on you."

Breathing hard, I struggled to think straight. The pain encompassed every aspect of my mind and thoughts. I wanted away from the vampires; I needed somewhere dark and quiet and cool to heal my wounds. Somewhere to hide.

I turned my back and dove for the tiny window over the sink. The shattering glass didn't hurt me except where it landed on my hands and leg that had already been damaged, leaving me open to yet more injury.

Shouting erupted all around as I hit the ground with an unlady-like splat. I pushed up and took off, running as fast as I could, doing my best to ignore the intense pain as it spread up my leg. I'd had burns before and worked through them; I could do it now too. The snake in me urged me on, self-preservation kicking into overdrive.

A flutter of wings drew my attention to the left, and I followed Ernie, blindly, unable to see through the wash of tears.

"Get into the water!" Ernie seemingly appeared at my side, and I stumbled to a stop. "Get into the water, you've got to wash it off!"

The sound of flowing, gurgling water drew me to it. A haze of pain coated my vision, so I followed the sounds until I was standing knee deep in a fast-flowing current. I sank down, burying my hands into the ice-cold water. A shuddering breath escaped me.

Ernie was in front of me; I could feel the wind off his wings as he trod air. But I kept my eyes closed, swallowing down the nausea that rose even while the pain eased a little.

"Alena, talk to me." He touched the side of my face, and I slowly opened my eyes. The world shimmered and slowly solidified.

"I feel like I'm staring through a bowl of gelatin." I shifted my leg and groaned as the pain spiked again. I let it float back down to the rocks on the riverbed and forced myself to remain still, the flowing current pulling whatever had been on the snake catcher's loop away from me.

I blinked up at Ernie, a sudden thought making my adrenaline surge once more. "Did I lose them? Do I have to run again?"

He flew straight up into the air and stared back the way we'd come. "I think they gave up. You were moving too fast, even injured, for them."

I lay back in the water. "Tell me if they come."

He stayed where he was, but he kept glancing at me. "How bad are you hurt?"

"I don't know, it's like I dipped myself in oil and set it on fire."

He grimaced and looked out around us again, doing a slow circle. Where was Remo when I needed him? Dang it all, this was kinda his fault; he could at least have the decency to show up when . . .

I lifted one hand out of the water. My fingertips were seared right through both my human skin and the snakeskin underneath, showing muscle and even a hint of bone. I shuddered, and not from the icy water. My snakeskin could take a rocket launcher. Santos had said the potion would work. Was that what had done it, or was it a special kind of metal on the snake catcher? Whatever it was Santos had used cut through me like fat-nosed Colleen going through a cheesecake. "Ernie."

"Yeah?"

"What kind of material was that he had? It was like my kryptonite, wasn't it? Silver, maybe? Could I be reactive to a metal like some other Super Dupers?"

He dropped like a stone, his feet dipping into the water, his whole body shaking. "They found you. You have to run again."

I lurched to my feet and stumbled out of the water. "Where?"

Ernie did a quick spin in the air. "The Supe Squad could take them, even unorganized as they are. If you can make it."

I slogged out of the water, limping hard. The burn had faded, washed off in the river. But the open wound was anything but pleasant. At least it didn't make me lose my mind like the . . . whatever it was that had cut me open.

"You lead, I'll follow," I said. "I can't think past moving."

"Hurry, this way."

I could only hope that he didn't lead me straight to Theseus. Or worse, Hera. I forced myself to work through the pain. When I'd burned myself baking, I'd still had to bake, I couldn't stop. This was the same. Work toward the goal through the hurt, through the sharp stabs. Hard breaths slipped out of me through clenched teeth, and I tried not to think about the warm blood sliding down my leg.

"The blood, that's how they're finding me."

Ernie groaned. "As long as they don't stop and lap any up, you'll be okay."

"Deep-fried dog turds, that . . . would be bad," I whispered and forced myself to a higher rate of speed. I'd not even thought about the vampires getting a boost of power if they stopped and took some of my blood. They wouldn't, though, would they? They wouldn't know that my blood gave a vamp the increased speed and power that didn't normally come to them even if they had lived thousands of years.

A streetlight flickered into view, and suddenly I knew where we were. Three houses down on the right was Merlin's place. The windows were dark, though, and the door was boarded up. Not that I thought he'd help anyway, no matter what Yaya said.

"Ernie, I can find the station from here. Go get Remo. Please."

Ernie flew backward in front of me. "Are you sure?"

"Please, find Hermes and get Remo. I can't fight them like this." I wasn't sure I could fight them at all.

I ran down the street—okay, limped quickly down the street. From the corner of my eyes I saw movement between the houses, the flitting of shadowy forms.

They were surrounding me. With a whimper I forced myself to move faster, ignoring the stab of pain with each step, ignoring the hard ground beneath my bare feet.

Two vampires shot out from either side of me, and a new burst of energy fired through my veins. I dodged them, but only barely, as they reached for me. One of them had that damn snake catcher.

Shouting erupted all around, and their cries drove me forward. Something slammed into my knees, and I was sent flying through the air. I hit the ground hard, a large body on top of me. I stared up into the red beard.

"Viking."

"Ball-crushing bitch," he snarled.

I shouldn't have laughed, I knew it. But I did anyway. I burst out laughing, unable to contain the hysteria, the fear driving it more than anything. Funny enough, Viking did not laugh with me.

He grabbed me around the neck and hefted me up, strangling me with one hand. I clawed at his arms and, slowly, consciousness faded.

As my awareness slipped, the Drakaina in me woke.

And she was not happy. It was like watching a movie from inside my head. I shot a hand forward, driving it into the back of Viking's elbow and breaking his arm so badly the bone shot out the crook of his elbow. He screamed and dropped me, but I didn't back off.

I grabbed him and yanked him forward, as if I were going to kiss him. Only I didn't kiss him. I drove my fangs into his face, scoring his skin with the venomous tips.

Screeching, he slapped his good hand over his cheek and reeled back. I spun and caught the next vampire by his hair and twisted, yanking his neck at an impossible, bone-shattering angle.

As the blood pumped through me, I fought with my inner nature. I was not this girl; I was not this violent snake monster.

Santos approached, the snake catcher in his hand once more. "Well, well, so you do know how to fight."

The words that slipped from my lips were not my own; they couldn't be, because I wasn't like that. "I will destroy you, vampire." The husky slither of my voice seemed to curl around him. "Drop the weapon."

He dropped it as though it were a hot frying pan.

His eyes widened and fear coursed over them, followed swiftly by a hatred so intense it all but crackled in the air between us. I swallowed hard, and the snake in me receded.

"Go back to your home," I commanded. "And take all your vampires with you."

The power in my voice shocked me as much as it seemed to shock him.

He snapped his fingers, and he and his vampires, even the wounded ones, slunk away into the darkness.

I stumbled back and put a hand to my head. "Oh my good grief."

The street around us was silent as a grave, and I didn't like that comparison. I took a step, and then another, until I was running once more. I didn't stop until I hit the doors of the SDMP station and burst into the main lobby. I dropped to my knees, sobbing with relief.

"Ms. Budrene. What in the devil's name are you doing here?" The hard voice had never sounded so lovely to me. I looked up into Smithy's icy blue eyes.

"Santos and his crew. They attacked me."

His eyes widened as they swept over my body, taking in my injuries. "Where?"

"Near Merlin's house."

He swung around and barked at the men behind him. "Boys, get on it. Drive them out of town."

With a chorus of snarls and howls, the Supernatural Division of Mounted Police, werewolves to a man, rushed out the doors. Smithy did not go with them. He dropped to a crouch. "Thought you were some sort of badass Greek creature? That's the rumor."

A wobbly smile curled my lips. "You and me both. They had something that cut through me—badly."

He nodded, his eyes on my leg and then flicking to my hands. "Shit. You aren't kidding." He let out a tired sigh. No doubt he was regretting coming into work today. "Come on, I'll get you cleaned up and you can tell me exactly why Santos is after you."

He didn't hold his hand out to me, didn't offer for me to lean on him. Smithy wasn't that kind of man, and I was glad for it. The last thing I needed was attention from another man that I didn't know what to do with because my siren abilities kicked into overdrive. Like Jensen.

And maybe even like Remo. A sigh slipped out of me as I limped after the larger-than-life police officer. The silence was heavy in the station without the ebb and flow of his men.

"So what happened?" he prompted.

"I . . . well, I protected Remo at the courthouse earlier today."

Smithy glanced at me. "Remo needed protecting? Since when?"

I frowned, bristling at the underhanded insult. "Since today, when he was attacked by Santos's entire crew with a rocket launcher in the middle of the human courthouse because our system is down with Oberfluffel missing in action." The words snapped out of me, but Smithy didn't appear bothered.

"And you happened to be there?"

A groan slid from my lips as I touched my fingers together, pain snapping through me. "Divorce proceedings."

"Well, that's like trying to paddle up shit creek with your bare hands." He snorted and shook his head. Like I was an idiot for trying to change things, just like everyone else thought—that an actual divorce was a ridiculous dream of mine.

I wanted to smack him, and would have if my hands weren't still throbbing and dripping blood with every step I took.

"Where exactly is Oberfluffel anyway?" I asked.

He cleared his throat. "*Oberfall* has gone on . . . a sabbatical."

I snorted softly. A sabbatical for a werewolf? "Please, even I know better than that in my short time as a Super Duper. Does that mean you're in charge, then?"

Smithy gave me a trademark icy glare. "Not that it matters to you, but yes, I am, at least until he returns. And sabbaticals do happen, especially for werewolves when they are struggling—" He stopped in front of a door that said "Medic." He pushed it open and I followed him in, sitting myself down on the only stool.

Smithy did not finish his sentence, and I didn't push him. What did it matter to me that Oberfluffel was struggling? Not one penny's worth of sour candies.

He fumbled through a cupboard and pulled out a tiny first-aid kit. Like the size of a child's lunch box. I raised an eyebrow. "Seriously?"

Smithy shrugged. "We don't generally need help healing. Werewolves are tough like that."

I tried to open the kit and failed, wincing with every touch of the blistered and burned-through tips against the cold metal. My fingers were useless.

"Do you mind?" I held it out to him, keeping it between my palms. He rolled his eyes, but he did take the tiny medical kit and open it up. Moving swiftly, he pulled my burned leg up to his face, which pulled me to the edge of my seat.

I balanced precariously on the edge. If he let me go, I'd crash to the ground. "Hey!"

"The wound is deep; I can see bone in places."

I swallowed hard and tried not to think about it. "Can you just put some ointment on it and wrap it?"

His eyebrows shot up. "Really, you think that's going to help you out here? A bit of ointment and a bandage?"

I flushed. "I don't know, remember I'm new at this? I was thinking the ointment was magic."

"Nope, just Polysporin." He held the gold-and-green tube up for me. Well, that was disappointing. Like getting a dried-out brittle cookie you thought was fresh and warm from the oven.

"I agree, I think you need more help than a wolf can give you."

Smithy and I jerked at the same time, spinning toward the vampire in the doorway. Smithy tightened his hold on my calf. "Remo. You need to keep your territory clean of the cockroaches, or I'm going to assume you are one of them."

Remo's face was all hard lines and tightly controlled anger. "My people are on it. You can call your dogs off."

Smithy did not let go of my leg, but instead pulled me even higher so I was balanced on the edge of the seat. Barely.

"Excuse me, I'm not a weapon to be thrown at him." I couldn't even grip the edge of the chair with my chewed-up fingers.

They ignored me, and the tension in the room kicked up several notches.

Remo stepped closer and pried Smithy's hands off my leg. "Call your *dogs* off, Captain. *I* will deal with Santos."

Smithy didn't shift a single inch. For that alone I had to give him credit. "You haven't been dealing with him at all, or he wouldn't dare encroach this far into our territory." They were eye to eye, toe to toe. And while I wanted to believe Remo would win, I didn't want to be in another fight, particularly in my current state.

And I recalled all too well that my injuries were a direct result of helping the vampire in front of me.

"Hey. You two knock it off. I'm injured. It's partially your fault, Remo, and yours too, Smithy. If you'd work together, you could keep Santos out." The words burst out of me before I thought better of them, but even as I said them I knew they were true.

Two sets of eyes swiveled to me, both icy now. I lifted my chin. I would not back down.

Ernie burst into the room, panting. "I went you one better! I found Damara, the satyr who healed your brother . . . Whoa, there is some major testosterone going on here." He waved a hand in front of his face. Behind him popped up Damara, her horns entering the room first. I sighed in relief.

"Damara, thank you for coming. Ernie, you're a doll for finding her," I said.

He beamed and she slipped in past the two men. She subtly bumped both of them as she passed with the curling horns on top of her head. "Both of you out, I don't work with an audience."

Smithy grunted and stepped out first. Remo stayed until she bleated at him. "I said get out!"

"This is my fault." His shoulders tightened. "It won't happen again." He spun and slammed the door behind him.

Damara bent over me. "Men, touchy creatures no matter what species."

I stared at the closed door, wondering just what Remo thought he'd do to make Santos leave me alone.

"Well, you should know, since you have two men." I winced. I meant, I knew that Tim and Gavin were her two satyr boyfriends, and while it was common for their species to be into the extra partner scene, I probably shouldn't be pointing it out. "Sorry."

She laughed. "No, it's true. But I have them well put in their places. They know that they only get to be a part of my life until something better comes along. So they both fight to keep our trio alive and well."

That was an interesting take on a relationship. Until something better comes along . . . I suppose that's what Roger did. I hunched my shoulders, sucking into myself.

Remo's eyes and his words floated in front of me. *"It won't happen again."* I tasted the words, like trying to identify a new flavor in the cookie batter. Could they mean something other than what they seemed? My mind raced ahead while Damara probed at my ankle and dug into the bag at her side.

"Remo's going to try and stay away from me, isn't he? To keep me safe by no longer being around me," I said softly.

She glanced up at me. "It's the way of an alpha, regardless of species. He'll try to protect you any way he can."

I grimaced, then sucked in a gasp as she pressed something to the open wound. The pain flared up around me, and the world went black.

CHAPTER 7

I snuggled deeper into my bed, breathing in the vanilla scent I'd specifi-
cally put in the wash to coat my sheets. I rolled and stretched, sunshine
spilling over my face, lighting up the back of my eyelids to a lovely glow.
I lifted a hand to scratch my cheek and froze as my fingertips touched
my skin. Fingertips that were whole, without chunks of them missing.

The events of the night before washed over me, sending chills
through me as if I'd sat back down in the flow of the icy river. A quick
inspection of my hand showed the skin completely healed, the wounds
gone, and the pain too. I pulled my legs out of the sheet and breathed
out a sigh of relief. My ankle was once more intact, though there was a
scar around it where the loop had bit into me.

"You were lucky."

I jerked around to see Damara sitting beside my bed. She yawned
and pointed at my leg. "Much longer without my help, and I think you
would have lost it."

"Lost it? You mean my foot?"

Her eyebrows rose. "I mean your entire leg. Whatever they used was
spreading up through your entire limb, not just your foot."

I pushed to a sitting position, cold chills rolling through me, even though I sat in a patch of sunlight. I pulled the sheets up. "Do you know what it was?"

She shook her head. "I've never seen anything like it, at least not in the Supe world. Tell me what happened."

"They had a snake catcher, a rod with a long noose at the end. The noose cut into me and burned like hot oil. Even after I got the noose off, it burned. Ernie led me to a river, and that washed it away."

"So not oil based, then." She tapped a finger on one of her horns, her eyes thoughtful. "Plant based, probably. But I don't know of any plant that can cause an injury like this. And nothing specific to cause an injury to a Drakaina. You are one tough cookie, you know. The fact that you healed so fast is testament to that."

"Thanks?"

She laughed. "Look, I'll see what I can find in the old texts. I'll pass it on to Ernie if I get anything. But for now, try to avoid that shit at all costs."

"No kidding." I swung my legs off the bed. "Damara, I owe you."

"No, you don't. Whether you realize it or not, you're making Zeus pay attention again, even if he is in hiding right now. That alone is worth helping you." She smiled. "Keep at him, Alena. If he won't listen to those who are on his side, maybe he'll listen to a monster who could swallow him whole if she chose to."

I grimaced. "I have a feeling he'd take that an entirely different way."

She laughed, stood, then walked to the door. "True, but that gutter mind has always been a part of him. You healed fast, expect to be hungry. And craving whatever your body needs to restore your reserves; don't ignore it, no matter how strange it might seem."

I didn't like the sounds of that. My belly grumbled, and I clutched it with both hands.

Damara left me alone in the room, and I quickly dressed. I heard her go out the front door, her heartbeat fading as she walked away.

As I went downstairs, the house was eerily quiet. No Sandy, no Beth. My eyes watered at the thought of the two girls who were my friends fighting on Theseus's side. I didn't want to fight them, not because I was afraid, but because I didn't want to hurt them. The Drakaina in me, I could almost feel her nod. They were tough, but I was tougher, which meant if we faced one another, they would get hurt. I didn't want that.

I listened for Tad's heartbeat, but he wasn't here either. Dahlia would be in the basement sleeping for another couple of hours.

I stepped into the kitchen, and a sigh slid out of me. While it wasn't a total disaster, glass from the window littered the floor, and the clean dishes from the rack were spread everywhere. Getting a broom, I swept the floor. The scent of licorice floated through the air, the same smell I'd picked up on the night before. It had to be Santos. Just like Remo, his opponent had a signature scent, one I would not be forgetting anytime soon. Licorice was one of those flavors that cloyed in the mouth when used too liberally. I had a funny feeling that Santos's presence would be the same.

I followed up the sweep by mopping the floor, as if I could erase everything that had happened the night before. Next came the dishes, and from there I slid into baking mode, pulling a recipe book off the shelf and laying it on the table.

My belly rumbled as I stood in front of the fridge. "All right. Eating first."

I opened the door and stared at my options. There was a pack of raw chicken drumsticks I'd pulled out of the freezer to be cooked for dinner the night before, a couple jars of pickles, milk . . . my hands were reaching for the chicken before I was even cognizant of the need for meat. I grabbed the three-pound package and put it on the counter. I grabbed the jug of milk next and set it next to the chicken. Protein in two forms. I stripped the plastic off the chicken and took the cap off the milk.

"I could deep-fry them, throw them in a batter," I said as I pulled the first drumstick out and held it up to my mouth. The smell of raw meat normally turned my stomach. This time? Not so much. My saliva glands went wild, and I bit down on the chicken, snapping the bone in half. I didn't chew.

I swallowed it whole. And the next, and the next, until the package was empty. I grabbed the milk jug, almost a full two gallons, and put it to my mouth. The cold, fresh milk slid down my throat. I slammed the empty jug down and stared.

"Holy crap," I whispered, then looked around. I wasn't sure if I felt bad about saying "crap," or the unreal meal I'd just had.

The snake in me felt like it curled up, content with the food I'd literally swallowed whole. I cleared the empty jug and chicken packaging off the counter and into the garbage, then wiped the surface down.

I hadn't even tasted the chicken. Maybe I would get salmonella.

I grimaced. Even I knew that wasn't likely.

"God, I am a monster," I said to the kitchen, as though the space would respond. I paced the small room, my mind racing almost as fast as my heart. There was only one way to make myself feel better. Time to bake.

I knew Tad liked chocolate chip cookies, so I made those first, the recipe memorized. I added extra chocolate and threw in some puréed pumpkin for good measure. He wouldn't even taste the pumpkin, but it gave the cookies a fluffy, light consistency, and it was a sneaky way of getting him to eat his vegetables. Just one of my baking secrets.

I smiled to myself, panic and fear easing as I moved through the kitchen, my mind floating in that state of bliss only baking brought me. After the cookies, I made meringues in strawberry and lemon, scraped together a peanut butter–caramel cheesecake, and then whipped up a batch of baklava. No problem. The time passed, hours falling away in the rhythm of whipping cream, measuring ingredients, recalling recipes, and checking the oven.

Somewhere in the midst of it all, the sound of the front door clicking open shot through the peace. I froze in the middle of pouring the honey syrup over the pan of baklava, fear slicing through the happy place I'd been in. I grabbed a rolling pin and a large pot from the stove. I gripped them tight, ready to fight. "Who's there?"

"Just me, sis, and you are baking, and I love you to pieces!" Tad shouted, running into the kitchen, sliding to a stop. His green eyes lit on the chocolate chip cookies, and he snatched one with each hand. "You are the best."

"Tad, where have you been?" I tried to soften my tone, but with everything that had happened, I'd been worried about him. What if Santos had gone after him too? Or worse, Theseus?

He stopped midchew to talk around the mouthful of cookie. "Don't take this the wrong way, but I've got my own place; I've had it since I was turned, you know. I'm not rooming here with my sister."

"Dahlia's here," I pointed out.

He nodded. "Yeah, we've been dating like two weeks. I'd rather not move in with her that fast."

"Point taken." I wiped my hands on a tea towel. "Your night was okay?'

He grinned at me. "Probably not as good as your night. Remo take you out on the town?"

I started to laugh, and once I started I couldn't stop. Tears streamed from my eyes, I struggled to get enough air, and I knew my brother was staring hard at me.

"Sis?"

"Oh, Tad. You have no idea what a cluster of gopher poo I dealt with last night."

"That's a new one," he muttered. "Why was it bad? You and the boss have a fight?"

The boss. Like Remo was my boss and Tad's too.

"He is *not* my boss. And he's not yours either." I pointed a wooden spoon at him.

Tad grabbed another couple of cookies with one hand and a few meringues with the other. "Sure, but he's the mob boss around here, which kinda makes him everyone's boss when you think about it."

"Tad"—I rolled my eyes to stare at the ceiling—"he may be the mob boss, but he doesn't know everything."

"What happened last night?"

"I'll wait for Dahlia. Then I only have to tell it once." I turned back to the baklava and finished pouring the honey over it. I cut into the delicacy and popped a slice into my mouth before placing the pan on the table. At least I could taste my food again. The flaky pastry seemed to melt in my mouth, and I chewed slowly, enjoying the flavors.

Tad looked at the number of goodies on the table, spread out like a buffet. "Sugar craving?"

I sat down and chased the baklava with a cookie. "Maybe. Better than my other options." I dug into the cheesecake next, and Tad sat beside me, helping himself to a slice.

"Hey, I've been thinking about Dad," he said between bites. "You know, it would make sense that he only has a little bit of Super Duper blood. Maybe he doesn't even realize that he's tainted. That would explain his denial."

I scooped my spoon through the cheesecake and eyed the bite up. "Maybe. But I don't think so. He'd just laugh it off. Or do the blood test like we offered. I think he knows exactly what he is."

Tad reached over and put his hand on mine in an uncharacteristic move. "We'll figure it out."

I smiled and put my hand over his. "Yeah, I just worry . . . that when we find out, we won't want to know. You know?"

He bit his cookie in half and shrugged. "But neither of us will ease up until we know."

The word game went on a few more minutes, each of us using "know" as much as we could. A silly game from our childhood that had driven our parents batty.

The sun dipped lower and lower. Ten minutes and Dahlia would be up. Ten minutes . . . I leaned my head on Tad's shoulder. "Did you ever flat out ask Dad?"

That was our little family secret. Both Tad and I had gotten the deadly Aegrus virus, forcing us to choose between dying or being turned into Super Dupers. We'd both chosen to live, despite the way super-naturals were treated in our world, and despite our ultraconservative Firstamentalist upbringing.

The kicker was that the only people who could contract the Aegrus virus were those who weren't fully human—not something the general populace even knew. I mean, I'd found out only after I'd been turned into a Super Duper. We knew our mom was pure human, which meant our dad was anything but normal.

"He's denying it." Tad shook his head. "Says we were just lucky we could be turned instead of dying and we should leave it at that." He shook his head, waving a cookie back and forth. "And he said it with a straight face. I thought maybe I'd get a wink or something, but nothing."

"In other words, we should be taking him to Vegas to play poker." I snorted and took another bite of cheesecake, the last of the rumbles in my belly finally easing. "He's hidden himself well for a long time. I mean, even Mom doesn't know." Which was so, so weird to me. How could you not know your spouse was a Super Duper? The thought was ridiculous, at least to me. Then again, I had no room to judge; I'd not known Roger was cheating on me.

"Maybe it runs in our family, turning a blind eye." Tad didn't seem to see anything wrong with pointing out my faults. That's a brother for you—to the heart of the matter regardless of how tender of a spot it is.

I struggled to swallow the last piece of cheesecake, thinking about Roger and what he was putting me through. A shimmer of indignant anger rose in me. I would not let him *put* me through anything. I would get that dang divorce if it was the last thing I did.

"You okay? Your eyes totally just flashed . . . snaky." Tad stared at me, eyes wide and brows raised.

"Yeah, had a moment of insight. I'm not walking in Mom's footsteps anymore; I'm not turning a blind eye to things done to me." I smiled, though I was far from happy. Determined? You bet your sweet hind end. "Roger isn't getting away with all my money, the house, or my bakery. I don't care what I have to do, I'm getting a divorce. And I'm getting Vanilla and Honey back."

He grinned, but I saw the doubt in his eyes. "You know I'll stand by you, no matter the outcome."

I didn't smile back. "But you don't believe in me."

He shrugged and his grin faded. "Reality is what it is. You can't change it, and I know that. Eventually you'll realize it too. I just hope it doesn't hurt you too bad."

I pushed to my feet. "Just watch me, then."

Tad saluted me with a cookie. "Whatever you say, General Lena Bean."

The sound of footsteps on the basement stairs turned us both around to see a sleepy green-eyed Dahlia step into the hallway.

Her bright-red curls were wild as always, but not like she'd just woken up. More like she'd just come from the salon with an artful coif that was perfectly messy.

She yawned, flashing her fangs, and ran a hand through her hair, but that did nothing but make it even more wild. "Your baking smells amazing, even if I can't eat it."

"Did I hear something about baked goods?" Ernie shot in through the open window, his focus zeroing in on the table laden with treats. I shook my head. "Go ahead." A part of me wondered where he'd been, if he'd been off telling my secrets to Hera or Theseus. I pinched my mouth shut and did my best to push those thoughts away. They wouldn't help me any at this point.

"You are a glutton." I forced a laugh and turned my back while Tad and Dahlia greeted one another, busying myself with the dishes at the sink.

I clunked the pots and pans together hard enough I could almost block out the sound of their kisses. Ernie flew to the edge of the sink and dangled his feet in the sudsy water while he chewed on a handful of cookies. "These are really good."

"Thanks."

"Don't like hearing them make out?" He grinned, and I grimaced.

"Something like that."

He looked to the side and curled up his nose. "They don't seem to care that we're here."

I laughed softly. "Yeah, that's part of the problem."

Dahlia spoke, and I assumed that meant they were done saying hello. "What's up, my snake friend? You're all wound up like you're about to strike something. I can smell it all over you." I didn't like her metaphor; it was too close to the mark.

"Santos attacked me last night." I turned back to them in time to see Dahlia's jaw drop and her eyes look like they would fall out of her head.

"How do you even know Santos?" she blurted out. "He's—"

"Remo's rival, I know. Santos attacked Remo at the courthouse while Tad and I were there. I helped Remo, so Santos put a target on me and made good on it not long after."

Dahlia shook her head, her eyes wide as saucers. "That's crazy. But you're saying this like Remo wasn't with you. He was with you, wasn't he?"

I shook my head. "I upset him and he let me go home on my own."

"Oh, he is going to be pissed. At least you're okay. I mean, you obviously survived them. Did you run away?" She smiled and leaned back in her chair. Tad put an arm over her shoulders, nodding.

Did I run away? I blinked several times as I struggled with the reality that Dahlia didn't think I had it in me to take care of myself either.

Tad nodded. "Well, it's not like she's going to fight them on her own. How did you get away?"

I folded my arms over my chest, hugging myself tight as if I could squeeze their disbelief away. "Santos has something that . . . well, I think it could have killed me. He hurt me bad enough with it last night he almost had me." I refused to admit that I had indeed run away in order to survive.

Their reactions were polar opposites. Tad sat there and stared at me, while Dahlia jumped up and ran to me, grabbing me in a hug. "Are you okay?"

"Yeah, Damara fixed me up, but she said . . . I almost lost my leg."

Dahlia hugged me tighter, and I hugged her back. I was lucky to have her as a friend. Tad continued to stare at me until I snapped my fingers at him. "Hello, I almost died. Do you not care?"

He shook himself. "Sorry, I just . . . I have a hard time believing you were hurt that bad, and then you're here now, all healed up."

"You don't believe me?" I spluttered, shock and hurt bundling up in me once more. Yet I had no proof. What was going on here?

Ernie swept in between us. "I was there, Tad. I saw the whole thing. She really was hurt that bad. If it hadn't been for Damara, she would be missing a limb for sure."

At least Ernie was standing up for me. But my own brother . . . he didn't believe me. Didn't believe in me. Dahlia didn't either, though, and that hurt only a small amount less.

Dahlia frowned at Tad and then looked back at me. "What do you want to do?" she asked, stepping back so she could look me in the face.

"I have an idea, but I don't know how good it is." The thought had been growing in the hours I baked, slowly forming into a perfect recipe, if I could pull it off. "Santos put something on the weapons, like an acid, and *that* is what hurt me. It burned right through my snakeskin, eating its way to the bone in no time."

Tad blanched. "I should have been with you."

I waved him off. "They would have hurt you too, and there was no way you would have known. If anyone should have been with me, it should have been Remo." I shook my head and bit my bottom lip, but the words were already out.

Dahlia nodded, then frowned. "I can't imagine him walking away from you, though. You've got him all tied up in knots. It's killing him that he isn't supposed to be with you. The whole cross-species thing, you know."

I did know. I rubbed a hand over my eyes, unsure that I wanted to share Remo's past, as little as I knew about it. I had a feeling he wouldn't want anyone else to know. "I can't tell you what happened. They are his secrets, not mine."

Her jaw dropped. "He told you . . . about his past? Good God, he does have it bad for you."

Ernie snickered around a mouthful of meringue, spitting bits of it out as he spoke. "Like a major hard-on. You should have seen him on her after the courthouse."

"Ernie!" I screeched. "You are such a Peeping Tom!"

Dahlia kept her focus. "Did he tell you about his past?"

"No, he didn't," I spluttered, as if denying a crime. "I kinda guessed. Look, that's not the issue at hand. I need to find out what that stuff is Santos has, and if I can stop him from using it, then all the better. Because he's going to come after me again. If it will burn through me, it could burn through Tad too."

Dahlia's eyes went thoughtful. "And you are thinking of what exactly?"

I took a breath and straightened my back. "Of switching allegiance to Santos."

CHAPTER 8

"You're out of your mind! He'll never go for it!" Dahlia's denials burst out of her as she paced the kitchen from end to end.

"I think he will," I said softly. "He kissed me at the courthouse; he wants to hurt Remo, not just me. If he thinks he's stealing me away from Remo . . . he'll believe me. I know he will. He obviously wants to hurt Remo, and what better way than to take someone he sees as Remo's secret weapon?"

"Do you know where he is?" Tad asked.

I looked at Dahlia. "I don't have to. Dahlia does, don't you?"

She groaned and shook her head. "This is a bad, bad idea. Santos isn't like Remo. No matter how tough Remo is, he is fair. Santos is an asshole of the largest kind with a god complex."

"You mean he's an elephant bum hole?" I raised an eyebrow, my lips twitching.

She pointed a finger at me. "Don't try to lighten this moment. This is deadly serious."

A sigh slid out of me. "I know, but the reality is I need to find out what he's got on me. And how he got it. Does it not seem crazy coincidental that Santos, after his first run-in with me, mere hours later has something that can hurt me? Something even Achilles couldn't manage on his own? This doesn't make sense."

She stopped pacing. "Do you think Theseus has finally shown up?"

I groaned and tipped my head back. "I know he has, actually. He's convinced Beth he's a good guy named Tim. And she and Sandy are still with him." A fact that made me all kinds of fear filled. Like an overstuffed cream puff filled with curdled cream, my nerves and fear spilling in every direction.

Ernie spluttered. "What? I didn't know he's calling himself Tim. What a tool."

"Huh?" The strangled sound barely escaped Dahlia's lips before she spit out, "Tim? What's he trying to do, blend in with the normals? Are the girls okay, though?"

I nodded. "I think so. I think . . . I think he's not going to hurt them yet. Beth was ready to fight me over him."

"Oh my God, I miss out on so much being out during the day!" She threw her hands in the air. "Okay, come on, let's go."

"No, just tell me where Santos is. I'll go on my own. I don't want you to get hurt," I said.

She pointed a finger at me. "Listen, we are friends, so you aren't going alone. I could never live with myself if something happened to you when I know I should have been with you. And . . . honestly, you can't do this on your own. You aren't a fighter, we all know it."

And there was the truth, more than anything else. She didn't think I could do it without her help.

"And you aren't going without me." Tad stood and brushed his clothes free of cookie crumbs.

Dahlia and I shook our heads in unison. "No."

Ernie snickered. "Don't argue with two badass chicks, my friend. They'll do you in when you aren't looking."

Tad looked from Dahlia to me, and back again several times. "I'm coming with you. One of you is my sister, the other is my girlfriend. I'm not going to be that guy who is ever okay with either of you just walking into danger without me either trying to stop you or going with you."

"Sweet, but stupid. It's why I like you," Dahlia muttered.

He grinned as though it was a compliment of the highest kind.

"There are more problems than Santos, and honestly, what does he want with you, Tad? You're a naga, not a vampire."

"You're not a vampire either, sis." He pointed a finger at me.

I pointed a finger at myself.

"But he wants me because of my connection to Remo, because of what he sees me capable of, regardless of what you two think I can do." I gave them each a hard look. "He doesn't want you, which will make you as expendable as an empty cupcake wrapper." I waved both hands in the air at him as a thought hit me. "But you could help find Theseus. I don't know where he took Beth and Sandy. Maybe you can see if they are okay? I bet he'd let you get close to him. We need to watch him and see if he's amassing an army or something."

Tad frowned. "The last Greek hero I dealt with didn't go so well for me."

He had a solid line of reasoning there. "Don't engage him. Or maybe . . ." I had another thought, one I really didn't like. "What if he's trying to get my own friends to fight me for him? That's what Ernie thought might be happening. Then he'd welcome you."

Dahlia's eyes shot to mine. "You mean actually get Beth and Sandy to fight you? They would never do that."

I shivered. "Monster against monster." I didn't know if the two girls' metallic feathers could cut through me, but if I were a betting sort, I'd say yes. "After what I saw last night, I'd believe it. Beth was . . . enthralled with him. And even Sandy was uncertain. I'd just been with them hours before, and they were totally different."

Ernie groaned. "It's the arrow with Beth. If they are used the wrong way, it isn't just love they can induce but obsession. I didn't see her, but I'd bet that's what he did. So don't discount her if it comes to a fight.

And Theseus has enough of his own charms to bend Sandy if she's already not sure."

Tad nodded slowly. "Okay, so you want me in that enemy camp? I can be your spy guy?"

I swallowed hard, hating that I had to ask him to put himself in danger. "Yes, go and tell Theseus you want to be in his camp."

"And my reason?" He arched a dark eyebrow.

Dahlia laughed. "Oh, that's easy." She swung an arm over my shoulder and kissed my cheek. "I chose her over you."

Tad rolled his eyes. "You think he'd buy that?"

"If you tell him I used my siren abilities on Dahlia, I think he might." I slowly warmed to the idea. "Be careful, please. Ernie"—I turned to the cherub—"will you go with Tad? Give him backup?"

Ernie's face was grim, hardly looking like the cherub of love and sex. "Theseus will take him on, I'm almost sure of it." Which made me think my general idea of what was happening with Theseus was spot on.

I didn't think I liked being right in this case. I didn't want my friends turning against me, even on a good day. I had few enough of them as it was to end up losing more.

Within minutes of the decisions being made, the four of us were off and running in our respective directions.

Buckled into the passenger seat of Dahlia's little punch buggy car, I glanced across at her when she started the engine up. She had a little glimmer of tears at the edge of her eyes.

"You really love him, don't you?"

"Damn it, yes," she muttered. "I don't want him to die. He came so close with Achilles. You really think he'll be safe going to Theseus?"

I clung to Ernie's words about the hero we were dealing with. "Theseus has a different game plan than Achilles. I don't think he'll hurt anyone until he's dealt with me." I covered my face with both hands. At least I was hoping. "What if I'm wrong?" I whispered.

"We're a team, Alena." Her voice firmed even as mine softened. "And Tad can help you by doing this. Let him. He'll be careful; we've all learned from what happened with Achilles. You were right to send him to help, and Ernie will watch out for him too." She pulled onto the road that took us north. I did my best to push away thoughts of Tad, Beth, and Sandy being hurt, though it wasn't easy.

Hours later, we crossed through the Wall and continued to head north, leaving the border behind, along with any real civilization.

I looked out around us at the desolate road, the lack of people not lost on me. We were out of the main city and working our way steadily north. "Where does Santos, I don't know, is 'live' the right term? Hole up? Hide out?"

"He's got a place on Grouse Mountain. The hike up is a total bitch; they used to call it the Grind. There's a checkpoint at the bottom, and if we get through that, we'll have a trek ahead of us."

"He walks up and down every time he makes an attack on Remo?" I lifted both eyebrows.

"Ah, no, he has a gondola that takes him up and down, but it's heavily guarded."

"You know a lot about his place." I glanced at her and she nodded again.

"He snatched me right from Merlin's, and Remo fought to get me back. I mean, it took me about five minutes in Santos's group to realize I wanted nothing to do with it."

"Wait, Remo rescued you?"

"Yes, sort of."

"Why? I mean, I'm glad he did, but . ."

She sighed. "He'd come to Santos's place to try and negotiate some sort of deal right after I was turned. Santos agreed to the meeting and the contract between them. They shook hands and everything. But as soon as Remo turned his back, Santos attacked him. There was a fight, and I already knew that Santos was a nutjob, so I knew which side to be on. He'd told me I would be part of his harem, but I never saw any other women, vamps or otherwise. I was scared that he was going to kill me. So I fought at Remo's side, against Santos. Remo took a blow that would have killed me, but he protected me at his own expense. I carried him out. He's like the brother I never had."

Suddenly her utter devotion to him made perfect sense. He'd saved her from Santos, who by my own experience was not someone I would want in my life, never mind as my boss.

I looked in the rearview mirror and caught a flash of something, and the faintest of vibrations that was not Dahlia's engine. I spun in my seat and stared back down the road. Another flash of metal catching the starlight. "I think we're being followed."

She glanced back, squinting. "I don't see anything."

Out of the darkness roared two big trucks, the rumble of their engines giving them away, even if they didn't turn their lights on.

High beams flicked on as I thought about it. Dahlia yelped. "I can't see! It's too bright for my eyes!"

I reached over and grabbed the wheel. "Hit the gas; I'll steer."

The car shot forward and I screeched, struggling to keep us on the road. Steering from the passenger side was not as easy as I'd thought it would be. The tiny car wobbled back and forth as though we were on some sort of carnival ride, accompanied by the screeching of two women as they careened out of control at speed.

"More gas?"

"I don't know!" I yelled back at her.

"Well, make a decision!" she yelped, and I dared a glance at the two trucks bearing down on us in the rearview mirror. Or at least I tried to. Their lights were so bright I couldn't see them or the drivers.

"Keep the speed steady. I think." I tightened my hold on the wheel and slid across the divider line so I could steer better. Not that it helped. The two trucks pulled up on either side of us, pinning the little car between them. They pressed us like a waffle maker squishes batter. The screech of metal was almost as loud as the high-pitched screaming that erupted from both of us.

"This is not going as planned!" I yelled. "Kitty puke on cookie sheets!"

The road beneath us changed, going from smooth pavement to huge bumping potholes. Each dip and valley sent our heads bouncing into the ceiling of the car. "Slow down!"

"Brake?"

"No, just less speed."

Too late. Dahlia hit the brake, and the tiny car squealed as it slowed and the two trucks that had flanked us ripped past. The screech and tear of metal as they slid away from us made me shiver, my skin crawling with the vibration of bending metal as much as with the shrieking sounds. My eyes rolled, and I fought to stay in the moment.

"Out, get out quick!" I pushed her toward the door.

"It's stuck!"

"You're a vampire! Kick it open!" I yelled back.

"Right." She booted the door and sent it flying off its hinges. She tumbled out, and I was right after her. "Come on, this way." Dahlia bolted off down the rocky pothole-strewn road. I hurried after her, running hard.

The two trucks were ahead of us, backup lights on. We ran past them. I caught a glimpse of a long red beard in the driver's seat of one truck. Damn it, what had Santos done, gathered up every Viking vampire he could find? This was not going to play well in my favor.

"How far?" I yelled.

"The checkpoint is at the start of the Grind," she said as I caught up. Like we were out for an evening jog and not running from two oversized trucks driven by vampires who probably would kill us as soon as look at us.

"That doesn't actually tell me how far," I pointed out.

"Far."

I pressed my lips together and tried not to think about how stupid I was to imagine this would go my way. I mean, after the catastrophe that was my life, why did I think this would be any different? I was a useless, pride-filled heathen. Dahlia and Tad were right not to believe I could do this on my own.

The words were not mine, but my mother's, and they struck a fire inside me that burned away the words of my past. I was not useless, and I would not be forced into a corner ever again. I reached out and grabbed Dahlia's arm, slowing her.

"They won't have the stuff with them to hurt me; we need to face them."

"You don't know that for sure." Her eyes were wide, dilated in the deep darkness.

I tugged her to a stop. "Pretty sure."

"Alena, we can make it."

"No, I want them to take us there. *We* are strong enough to do this, Dahlia. We aren't weak-willed, shrinking flowers that need to be rescued. Despite your name." I smiled and she shook her head.

"You're crazy."

"Maybe. And you're my best friend."

She laughed. "Crazy's best friend? Not a title I was aiming for."

Two sets of overamped headlights raced toward us.

"They're going to try and run us over," Dahlia said.

"Then jump out of the way," I said. "They would have some sort of walkie-talkie system, right?"

"Yes, why? What are you thinking?"

There was no more time for conversation. The trucks slowed as they approached us, but they didn't turn their lights down. Dahlia blinked and her eyes watered. "Assholes, those lights mimic UV light."

"Get behind me. I'll tell you if we have to fight." She did as I asked, putting her hands on my shoulders and dropping her head so her forehead touched my back.

The trucks were both turned off, the engines grumbling to a halt, but the lights remained on.

"You know," I called out, "you'll drain your batteries if you leave the lights on like that."

Viking number two was the first one to step out. I smiled at him. "You look like someone I met the other night. He was mean to me. It didn't end well for him."

"You killed my cousin, you brassy bitch. You think you can take us on our own turf?" He strode toward me, and I drew in a slow breath, hating what I was about to do. To be fair, the snake in me approved wholeheartedly.

I pushed power into my words, filling them with seduction of the highest caliber. "You don't *want* to hurt us. You *want* to take us to Santos."

He stumbled midstride and shook his head. "I . . . no, that can't be right."

"Remo's an ass; he's almost gotten us killed," Dahlia called out from behind me, her hands still gripping my shoulders tight. "We don't want to work with him anymore. It's obvious Santos is stronger."

"You see?" I added, "You can take us to Santos. I mean . . ." I took several steps closer to him until I could touch him. I fought not to recoil, but I knew that my touch on him would heighten my ability to influence him. I ran a fingertip down the center of his chest. "A big strong vampire like you wouldn't be taken down by a couple of girls, right?"

He grinned, flashing his fangs. "Of course not." He agreed so fast I stood there, not sure what to say. That seemed too easy.

And suddenly I understood my ability to manipulate that much better. I couldn't force him to believe something he didn't already think was true. He *truly* believed he was stronger than two women, I could see it in his eyes almost as if it were spelled out in thick blue frosting. I leaned into him, as if I were unable to stand on my own two legs.

"And we're so tired. Could we use the gondola? Our tiny feet and weak muscles could never handle that big hike."

He swept an arm around me and scooped me into the air. "Well, that's obvious. Come on, both of you."

I turned my head so he couldn't see me and grimaced at an open-mouthed and staring Dahlia. That had worked better than I'd thought. I batted my eyes up at Viking Boy, and he leered—yes, actually leered—back. I fought not to shudder as he lifted me into the oversized truck, his hands sliding dangerously close to my ass.

"I wouldn't do that. Santos wants her untouched," Dahlia said. Viking Boy jerked his hands off me as though I'd electrocuted him. Score another point for the girls' team.

Dahlia climbed in and the truck started up. Only once we were going did I realize the other vampire hadn't gotten out of the second vehicle.

Dahlia looked out at the other truck too. It didn't move an inch as we cruised over the dirt road and farther toward the base of the mountain.

I blinked several times, heavily, at Dahlia. As in, *What do you think?* She shrugged and shook her head and mouthed, *Guard.*

Of course they wouldn't leave their entrance road unprotected.

Viking didn't speak to us as he drove, though his hand kept wandering over my upper thigh. I kept brushing him off while saying, "No touching," heavily weighting the words with my siren power. Or whatever it was called. The fact that he kept trying told me I was probably right about my guess in terms of the person I was trying to influence already believing my words. The whole Jedi mind trick only worked when they already wanted something along the same lines of what I suggested. Which is why the seduction worked so well on most men, since most men saw me only as a piece of ass.

My theory also explained why turning off the seduction was such a crapshoot.

His hand gripped my thigh, and I shoved it off. "I said enough."

"You want it, baby. Santos doesn't have to know." He took his foot off the gas, and the truck rolled to a stop.

I leaned sideways, pressing against Dahlia. "Any suggestions?"

"I think he's going to have to learn the hard way, just like his cousin," she said.

That's what I was afraid of. I really didn't want to hurt anyone. But I didn't feel like being groped by the big vampire either.

CHAPTER 9

I lifted my legs up, keeping them closed at the knees as I slowly drew them to my chest. Viking Boy's eyes widened, and I realized something.

He was dumb as a stick if he thought I was going to spread my legs for him right there in the truck with Dahlia right beside me. What an idiot.

I kicked out as hard as I could with both feet, driving them into his chest. The feeling of things breaking, of my foot going right through his rib cage and hitting his heart, was unreal—unexpected. He flew backward, out the open window and into the darkness without a sound. I slid over into the driver's side and started the engine back up. My hands shook on the ignition, forcing me to try several times to get the engine turned over.

"You think he won't come after us?" Dahlia grabbed the back of the seat and stared out where we left him.

I shook my head and struggled to breathe past the horror. "No, he won't be coming after us."

"How do you know that?"

I grimaced. "One of my feet went through his chest." The warm blood trickling down inside my shoe was enough evidence. That is, if I'd ignored the feeling of his chest spitting open.

I pursed my lips and focused on the road in front of me even while my mind ranted at me. Sounding rather like my mother.

Murdering monster, you are evil and going to hell. It doesn't matter that he was touching you; it wouldn't matter if he even raped you. This is punishment for all your sins, you know that. When will you learn to just lie down and take what is your life? Stop fighting.

"I will not." I bit the words out as I clenched the steering wheel, the shaking in me subsiding.

"Won't what?"

I sucked in a quick breath and held it to stave off the tears that threatened. "Nothing. Let's get this over with."

I put the truck in park and cut the engine. I didn't want to hurt anyone, I really didn't. But I wasn't going to let anyone take advantage of me anymore. I'd done it my whole life, let people walk all over me. Because it was the right thing to do. No more. I wasn't going to do it anymore. Starting with Santos.

I squared my shoulders and hurried to where a low gondola waited. Up the platform we went and climbed into the small box. Dahlia grabbed the controls and hit the button on the speaker box. The soft static of an intercom floated through the airwaves.

"Password," said a disembodied voice.

"Shit balls, I didn't think they'd bother." Dahlia scrunched up her face. "Now what?"

"Just hit the button again."

She did and the voice came back.

"Password."

"Looks like we're hiking," she said.

"No, I want Santos to wonder how we got up here, how we used his gondola." I thought back to my last negotiations with the bankers for money to add new equipment to the bakery. About how I'd had to use what leverage I'd had. I'd bluffed, told the bankers I'd withdraw all my accounts and go to their competitor, who'd already offered me what I wanted. Of course, it wasn't true, but the bank manager hadn't known that.

I hit the intercom button and leaned forward. "Then you can tell Santos his personal guests left because you couldn't be bothered to bring them up."

I let go of the button and put my hands on the railing. Willing the gondola car to start moving.

The voice didn't come back, and Dahlia shook her head. "It was worth a try, but I think we'd better . . . hey, we're moving!"

I smiled as the gondola shivered and rose in the air. Mind you, maybe they had a way to cut the lines when we were high in the air, hovering over some bottomless pit. I put a hand to my head. "I've got to learn to stop thinking sometimes."

"What's the plan from here on in? Good cop, bad cop?"

I shook my head. "No, we both hate Remo. He tried to force himself on me, and beat you up for protecting me."

She shook her head and made a circling motion around her face. "Won't work. I'm not beat up at all."

I grimaced. She had a point. I put my hands to my head, thinking. There had to be a way to convince him . . . slowly a smile spread as the idea grew. Dahlia stared at me. "I don't like that look, Alena. It's devious. And you aren't devious."

I laughed and shook my head. "Not devious, honest. I gave you some blood, and you healed super fast."

Her eyes widened. "Do you really want to play that card? I mean, if he knows your blood can do that—"

"He'll be even more willing to keep me alive if he thinks I have something to offer him more than my ability as a weapon." I nodded, already happy with how it would pan out.

"And if he uses that damn snake oil shit on you, what then?"

The thought of being burned that badly again had occurred to me, I'd just been ignoring those particular thoughts. In the bakery business, I learned my lessons quick. Apparently not so much out here in the Super Duper world. "If he tries, we'll have to deal with it then."

"That's what I thought; you don't really have a plan." She shook her head, sighing under her breath. "I'm going to lead, you stay behind me. We don't know if that oil will burn me, and if it does, you can heal me up. I can't heal you." She gestured for me to stay behind her as she spoke.

I spluttered a protest, feeling like the pan of spun sugar she was afraid would melt in the rain. "This whole thing was my idea; I'll lead."

She grabbed my arms and her eyes hardened. "You aren't as tough as you think you are, Alena. Strong, yes. But you don't have the killer instinct to survive. Even with the Viking back there, you felt bad. I could see it. And no matter what happened with Achilles, you were lucky to face him with all of us helping."

Her words could not have shocked me more. "You really don't think I can do this either, do you?"

Her eyes were soft and filled with pity. "No, I don't. I love you to bits, but I don't think you have it in you to make the hard decisions, and in this world, that will eventually get you killed. And maybe all those people around you killed too." She let me go and smoothed her wild curls back, though they just sprang up again. "Follow me, Alena. Let me do the heavy lifting."

Hot, angry tears burned the edges of my eyes. No one thought I could do this on my own. It was no different than my family when I'd wanted to open the bakery. They'd tried to stop me, tried to tell me I wasn't capable. Except for Yaya, that is. She had always believed in me.

The gondola lurched and hopped along the cables. Dahlia grabbed the railing to balance herself. I stood in the center of the tiny box, swaying slightly but riding it out.

"Don't be angry." Dahlia looked over her shoulder at me. "Please."

"Don't tell me what I'm capable of," I snapped. "Just don't."

She shrugged and stepped back from the railing. "Fine. You want to lead? Then lead. Try not to get us *both* killed."

Her words were covered with a layer of heat that I'd never gotten from her before.

We locked eyes, and I didn't back down. I was not weak. I wasn't, and I'd prove it.

I took a step forward as the tiny boxcar slowed and bumped against something. I moved so I was right in front of the sliding door. It opened, and I walked through with my head held high.

In front of me was a huge wooden mansion, three stories tall, and it sprawled over the top of the mountain and into the trees so I couldn't see where it ended. Windows glittered like dark eyes staring out at us, winking in the torchlight like leering old perverts, beckoning us closer. I shivered, not liking the imagery or where it took my thoughts one bit.

I steeled my back. No matter how little Dahlia believed in me, no matter how little Tad believed in me, I knew I could do this. I had to, if not to prove them wrong, then to prove to myself that I wasn't the anchor holding my friends down. That I could protect myself and them when the crunch time came.

The open path ahead of me was lit with torches on either side, and I strode between them. I snapped my fingers back at her. "Keep up, Dahlia."

She sucked in a sharp breath and then hurried to do as I'd suggested. I didn't want to make a scene of things. But she was wrong; I could do this.

Even if I was terrified that I *would* screw it up and get us both killed.

A roll of fog curled up around my ankles as I walked, and for a second I thought I was shifting.

"Theatrics, he loves a show," Dahlia breathed out.

I didn't react, just kept moving. The thick cover rolled up in front of me, and I kept moving into it, as if I didn't care that—I slammed into a body, nose to nose.

Yelping, I bounced back from the fog and hit Dahlia, and the two of us tumbled back onto the ground, limbs tangling. So much for a strong first impression.

Her eyes narrowed, and she pinched her mouth shut as I struggled to get upright as fast as possible. "Great intro," she mumbled.

I looked up to see Santos emerge from the fog, rubbing his nose. A giggle full of nerves bubbled up in my chest. "You know, you should tell people you're trying to make a big show of things. I thought it was a test of courage, not your entrance music, so to speak."

Dahlia let out a soft groan. "Don't irritate him further."

Santos lifted an eyebrow, and again I got that sense I knew him from somewhere, like I'd met him before all of this. I pushed to my feet and held a hand out to Dahlia. She didn't take it, and I turned away from her.

"Tell me," Santos drawled, his words humming along my skin, "did you come to surrender?"

"Not exactly." I tucked my hands behind my back, then brought them around the front and finally folded my arms. "I . . . Remo is not who I thought he was. He tried to force himself on me."

"And I give a shit, why, exactly?" He smiled. "How do you know I wouldn't do the same?"

Oh dear, this was going downhill faster than if someone had indeed cut the gondola cables. I opened my mouth, but nothing came out. What could I say to that?

"Because we know things about him and his operation." Dahlia stepped up. "Perhaps we could trade information for protection."

He leaned back, a big booming laugh rolling from his mouth. His fangs flashed in the flickering torchlight, reminding me that I shouldn't underestimate him.

"My blood." I paused and glanced at Dahlia, who shook her head. "It—"

"Tastes good? All blood tastes good. Did you think you were something special? Something I've never seen before? I've been around as long as Remo, and I've seen it all. You're just a souped-up version of a naga." He made a dismissive wave with his hand, and I frowned.

All around us, vampires shot from the darkness, weapons in hand.

Dahlia pressed against me. "If you're going to lead, now is the time to do it."

She was right. I gathered what courage I had left to me and swallowed hard.

"Listen here, hamster balls, I *am* special." I took several steps until we were so close I could see the violet-blue flecks in the darkness of his eyes. I lowered my voice and pushed power into the words, knowing they were true, and knowing he knew it too. "I am special."

His eyelids fluttered, and he lifted a hand that slowed the advance of his troops. "You . . . are special."

I lowered my voice to a bare whisper, banking our lives on what I said next. "And you want to talk with me and Dahlia in private."

He raised his other hand and waved it around. "Leave them to me; I want to talk to them in private."

So apparently he had already wanted this? Or was I getting stronger? Sweating, I fluttered my eyelashes up at him. "Tell them not to disturb us."

"You will not disturb us!" He bellowed right in my face. He did not smell like Remo at all. The scent of licorice hovered in the air between us. The same smell I'd picked up on the oil that had burned me. I had to fight not to step back. Santos stepped to my side and curled an arm around my waist, tugging me tight to his side.

"Come along."

I glanced at Dahlia. She shrugged, her eyes wide. What choice did we have if we didn't want to fight our way out? And we'd come for a reason; I needed to find out just what Santos had on me.

How had he been able to find something that could hurt me so badly, so fast? I mean, it was like he'd been just waiting for me to show up so he could use it. Which made no sense. I'd been a Super Duper for such a short time.

"I asked you what it was exactly that Remo did to you, to turn you against him?" Santos tightened his grip on my waist, and I realized I'd zoned out on him.

"Oh, well." I cleared my throat and made myself look around. We approached a two-story wood cabin that was, from what I could see, easily a ten-thousand-square-foot house. "He tried to push himself on me. Dahlia stopped him, and he hurt her. I realized then we'd chosen the wrong side."

The words were stilted, and without a lot of emotion or detail, but Santos nodded. "He's a complete control freak. Always has been. Here, let's go to my office." He opened the main door to the monster log house, and we stepped inside. The warmth of two large fireplaces, one at either side of the entrance hall, curled around me.

Though I wasn't bothered by the cold, the warmth called to me. I rubbed my hands over my arms. "This is lovely."

Dahlia snorted.

"Yes, rather lovely, the previous owner had, oh, shall we call it excellent taste." He winked as if I were too stupid to get the pun. "He and his family were exceptionally delicious," Santos said and then frowned at me. The fog that had slid over his eyes faded, and I smiled up at him as my belly clenched with fear.

I pushed my siren ability into my words. "You were going to take us to your office?"

His smile widened once more, a wicked smile that might have curled my toes if I hadn't met Remo first. Good grief, what was wrong with me? Was this part of being a siren, wanting the bad boys? I sure hoped not.

"Yes, this way." He headed to the main staircase that spread up into the second floor. Santos led the way and we followed. He glanced back several times, a slight frown on his lips. He was pushing off my suggestions faster than the Viking had.

Down a hallway to a set of double doors, and we were inside his office. Nope, wrong again.

He shut the doors behind us and locked the door with a chuckle. "Multiuse room. Please make yourselves comfortable."

The master bedroom was so big even the king-size bed looked tiny. Across from us was a pair of French doors that led onto a wide balcony, where I could hear the bubbling of a hot tub. A thick rug covered the wooden floor near the bed, and the smell of stale sex whispered over my nose. Oh dear, this was worse than burning a million-dollar square. And yes, that was an actual recipe.

I couldn't make my feet go farther into the room. Dahlia stayed behind me. "Now what, oh mighty leader?" she whispered.

Santos turned as he unbuttoned his shirt.

"Oh dear."

His grin widened.

This was getting out of hand. I put everything I had into the words I spoke, fear driving me. "Santos, sit down."

He dropped to the floor so fast it looked like his legs had been knocked out from under him. Dahlia slid to the floor beside me, her eyes clenched shut tight.

I whipped around. "Dahlia?"

"Ask him," she managed to say, though her lips looked like she struggled to form the words. I drew a big breath and hurried to where Santos sat on the floor, his eyes fogged with confusion.

I crouched in front of him, my hand seeming to lift of its own volition as I cupped his face. He leaned into my hand with a sigh.

"Santos, where did you get that oil from? The oil that burned me?"

He purred into my hand before answering, the vibration of the sound trickling along my skin in a not unpleasant way. "Was brought to me, a week ago. A man in a suit told me if I used it on you, he would reward me. He will help me take out Remo." He leaned harder against me and licked the palm of my hand. I forced myself to sit there and let him.

"A man in a suit?" I didn't like where this was headed. If Theseus got his hands on the snake oil . . .

"Yes."

I struggled to keep my voice even. "What did he look like?"

"Handsome, bright-blond hair like the sun, blue eyes like the ocean." He sighed and nipped at my hand.

I put my hands on both sides of his face, squeezing him. "Did he have a name?"

"Theseus."

While I wasn't surprised, I didn't like that he'd been planning things a week before he'd even met me. Then again, it lined up with what Ernie had said. Theseus was playing a game, like chess, but only he could see the board and the pieces.

"Can you tell me what he said exactly?" I knew I was pushing my luck. Touching him, I could feel his mind begin to revolt against the control I was exerting. I went to my knees and brought his face close to mine, so close he could see nothing but me. The struggle in him slid away.

"He said to hang on to the oil, to use it if I stumbled on a great large snake, and to keep it safe for him. He wants to humiliate you, to make you suffer."

He leaned in and brushed his lips over mine. I pulled back.

"I need to know how much of the oil you have and where you keep it."

"Not a lot, only a flask. We diluted what we used on you to not waste it. Theseus told us to do that. I didn't think it would still hurt you, to be honest." Like he had a choice in his current honesty.

I jerked at the thought of the oil, the pain that had sent my mind into complete shutdown, being *diluted*. "Where is it?" I repeated, my words hard.

"In the cellar, behind the vodka."

I started to let him go, and Dahlia put a hand on me. "Tell him to go to sleep."

She had a point. It would buy us time. "Go . . ." A thought hit me, and I glanced at Dahlia once before I changed my mind.

"Why do you hate Remo?"

Dahlia sucked in a gasp. "Oh, that's gossipy. I forgive you for everything earlier."

My lips twitched.

Santos breathed out a tired sigh and leaned in so his forehead was on my shoulder, and I kept my hands on the back of his neck, touching his bare skin. "He was always my boss. In charge of me since we were children. I couldn't stand it any longer. And I killed his favorite girlfriend, which probably didn't help."

Since they were children? I pushed him off my shoulder and stared at his face. Mentally I took away the long hair and added the piercings Remo had. "Fricky dicky, you're his brother, aren't you?"

Dahlia gasped and Santos grunted. "Not that I like to tell people, but yes. Remo's my older brother."

CHAPTER 10

"Go to sleep for one hour," I commanded and let him go. He slumped to the floor, his head hitting the wood hard enough to make the thump echo in the room. I backed away from him, my mind racing.

"Holy shit on a Ritz Cracker! They're brothers! That explains so, so much. Talk about sibling rivalry to the max." Dahlia gasped and I grabbed her arm.

"Come on, we've got to hurry. I don't know if that's actually going to hold him."

"What do you mean? He was totally under."

I unlocked the bedroom door and pushed her out ahead of me. "That's the thing. He fought me all along. I don't think we'll have an hour."

"How long?"

"Minutes," I breathed.

"Shit."

I nodded. "My thought exactly. Do you know where the basement is?"

She bolted ahead of me. "Through the kitchen."

We ran down the stairs, and I tried not to think about all the things that could go wrong. The flask not being where Santos said, the other vampires coming in to check on their boss, Santos waking up. Any one of those things would spell disaster for us.

The gargantuan house was quiet as we leapt from the first landing of the staircase, dual thumps as we hit the floor in the main hall. Dahlia turned to the right, and I kept at her heels. We bolted through the kitchen . . . okay, she bolted and I slowed. The kitchen was my dream kitchen, and I couldn't help but stop and stare. I ran my hand over the marble countertop with flecks of silver veining through it and found myself stopping at the high-end utensils. I grabbed two wooden spoons, longer than normal and used for large vats. I tucked them through my jeans' belt loops. Not exactly weapons, but maybe in a pinch they would give me something. I ran my hand over the customized stove, and the—

"Alena, not now!"

"Right." I snapped my eyes away from the pretties and followed Dahlia through a door I'd not noticed. The stairwell was narrow and nothing like the rest of the house. Old, dusty, musty.

"Cold storage isn't really the same as a basement," I said.

"Whatever. This is the only basement I know about."

At the bottom of the stairs there was a click as Dahlia pulled a string and light flooded the tiny space. At least, tiny compared to the rest of the house.

"Look for the vodka," she said.

I nodded and started checking the different labels. Very quickly I realized it was more of a wine cellar than a pantry. "Why would they keep so much booze? You can't drink it."

"But our victims can. If a vampire wants to get a real buzz on, they drink down a drunk."

"Oh." I breathed the word out and kept looking. "Here, I think this is vodka?"

Dahlia hurried to my side. "Yeah, Russian brand." We pulled the bottles off and threw them behind us. They crashed into the far wall. Behind the last bottle, the glittering of a large flask beckoned. "You'd better grab it." I took the bottle of vodka and clutched it to me.

Dahlia grabbed the flask and spun the lid.

I squeaked and took several steps back. She breathed it in. "Smells like licorice."

"Yeah, that's it, then."

Time to go. I spun and froze. Two shadowed figures slid down the stairs. Apparently our luck had run out.

I stared at the vodka in my hands and made sure my voice was loud enough they would hear me. "Dahlia, Santos said to get to get the good Russian vodka, right?"

She stepped up beside me. "Yeah, we better hurry. We don't want to disappoint him."

The two figures fled back up the stairs, leaving before they even asked what we were doing. Their fear of Santos worked in our favor.

I led the way, vodka in hand. Just in case we were stopped. We emerged from the stairs into the kitchen where the two vampires waited. I didn't recognize either of them. Both were men, both big with over-grown messy brown tangled hair and eyes the color of mud. Twins.

I licked my lips and held the vodka up. "Bottoms up."

Their eyes were dead—no pun intended—as though there was nothing going on behind them. Dahlia squeezed my arm. "Whatever you do, don't look back."

"What?"

"Go, up to Santos's room."

"What?" The second time was far more strangled. Why in the world would we go back to Santos's room?

We stepped into the living room, and I knew why. If I'd been paying attention to all the signals my extra-special senses had been giving me, I would have smelled the vampires; I would have been aware. But my fear had gotten in the way.

"Sugar biscuits." I breathed the words, and Dahlia grabbed my arm, all but dragging me up the stairs. The vampires didn't move, only watched us go. We were down the hallway and back in Santos's room in a matter of seconds, though with the weight of the eyes on us, it felt much longer.

Dahlia slammed the door. "Shit, this couldn't get much worse."

A groan behind us spun me around. Santos sat up, a hand to his head.

"Dahlia, we're in trouble."

She glanced at Santos. "Just put him under again."

He lurched back, his eyes glancing off mine and then away. "Guards!"

I leapt for him, swinging the bottle of vodka. It crashed into his head and he went down again, blood pouring from the side of his face. "Sorry!"

"Don't apologize to him!" Dahlia yelled as she ran past me. I didn't think, just ran after her. She crashed through the double doors that looked down the mountain. Even when I jumped out and off the balcony I wasn't really thinking, because if I had been, I would have remembered we were on the second story. I screeched as I fell, instincts tucking me into a ball. I hit the ground hard, but it didn't hurt as much as I thought it should. Flat on my back, I stared up at Dahlia. She still had the flask.

"We've got to teach you to land on your feet." She grabbed my hand and hauled me up. "Time to run."

Behind us came the sound of yelling and gunfire. Not good. But at least this time they didn't have the oil. Score one for our team. I ran for the gondola, but Dahlia grabbed me. "Are you crazy? They'll cut the cables the instant they figure it out."

She had a point.

So we ran down the mountain, using the path that had been cut into it for years of hiking pleasure. The switchbacks wove down in a tight zigzag, which meant we weren't getting as far as it felt.

A vampire landed in front of us, underlining the point I'd been about to make. I shoved him hard with both hands, sending him over a side cliff.

"That won't stop him," Dahlia said.

I looked back the way we'd come, and it seemed that the sky above was filled with what looked like flying vampires as they leapt their way down the mountain. And here we were, staying on the designated path like a couple of nincompoops. "Jump!"

Dahlia leapt first, and I followed. The first jump took me down three levels of switchbacks, and I landed on my knees. I glanced back in time to see the vamps already back in the air with their next jump.

"Go, go!" I yelled at her. The worst thing to happen wouldn't be dying, as far as I was concerned. It would be having that oil land back into their hands and used on me in some form of torture. I wasn't sure I could handle knowing it was out there and ready to be used against me again.

Fear for my life and skin drove me. Fear for Dahlia slowed me. I could take the vampires. But I knew Dahlia couldn't, not this many.

Dahlia jumped, and this time I waited for the vampires. She screeched at me. "Alena, no!"

I didn't look at her. "Get it home! Get it to Remo!"

I stood and squared my shoulders. Time to put on my big-girl panties if I wanted Dahlia and me to both get out of here alive, and that dang oil free of Santos.

I pulled out the two wooden spoons I'd snagged from the kitchen. The first vamp landed in front of me, shirtless, blood all over his chest, as terrifying as anything I'd seen in the Super Duper world. His buddy landed behind me with a thump. I turned so I could keep eyes on both of them. It was the twins we'd seen in the kitchen. The one to the left of me took one look at the wooden spoon and laughed, going so far as to throw his head back.

His twin on the other side of me mimicked him. I had a split second to do something before they would be on me.

I braced my legs wide, clutched the fat scooping end of my weapon, and thrust the wooden spoon forward like a spear, aiming straight for the heart of the twin on the right, between two of his ribs that flexed with his laughter. Not really expecting it to do much more than snap off in my hand, I did it anyway.

What else could I do? The weapon at hand was simple; I had no other choice.

The wooden spoon slid between his ribs, and his whole body jerked. The laughter stilled and he stared at me. "Killed with a wooden spoon?" Like he couldn't believe it, even though it had happened. Blood bubbled out over his lips as he slumped, his fingers brushing along the edge of the spoon.

"I'm sorry," I said and pulled the spoon out with a slurping plop, like a too-thick batter that wouldn't let go. I spun and, with a backhand, drove the second spoon handle through his brother's chest as he stood there staring, shock keeping him in place. "Not possible," the big vampire spluttered.

"Tell that to my spoon." Instinct took over, and I hammered the handle through his chest as if I'd been staking vampires my whole life instead of mixing batter.

Twin number two crumpled to my feet, and I looked up. Two more vampires faced me from the path immediately over my head, their eyes wide.

"She killed Bub and Bob. With spoons."

The other vamp shook his head. "I'm not throwing my life away, not for Santos."

I steeled my shoulders. "Don't think I won't spoon you too!" Okay, so maybe that wasn't the toughest thing I'd ever said. But it made the point.

They ran back up the way they'd come, scrambling so fast they sent rocks flying in their wake.

I listened to them bicker as I stood there.

"Tell Santos they got away. That they killed the twins and got away."

"Yeah, good plan."

I stood there, two spoons dripping with blood and a light tremor running over my body. Adrenaline and grief mixed together.

I forced myself to pay attention and jump down the mountain after Dahlia. Maybe we were home free, but it didn't feel like it. Not one bit.

In fact, it felt like things were tightening around me, like the snake catcher as it closed over my leg, an image I couldn't banish no matter how hard I tried.

CHAPTER 11

We took the Viking's truck and drove as though demons chased us all the way back into town, though there was no one behind us. I drove and Dahlia sat with the silver flask clamped between her hands, her hands on the lid. My two wooden spoons lay somewhere on the side of the mountain, evidence that I was more of a killer than I'd ever thought possible.

Dahlia kept glancing at me. She'd open her mouth as if to speak, but nothing came out. Finally, when we closed in on house number thirteen, she managed to spit out a question.

"What happened back there? Why did they stop chasing us? They don't give up easily."

I pulled over, thought better of it, and pulled back onto the road. "I don't think we should park this in front of where we're staying."

"They know where you live, Alena," she pointed out. "And what the hell happened? Talk to me. There is no way they would have just given up."

I slowed the truck and backed up, the engine rumbling as I hit the throttle. We reversed so fast I ended up partly on the sidewalk, the truck half in and half out of the road. I slammed it into park and slid out of the driver's side. "I don't want to talk about it."

Dahlia met me at the front of the truck. "Why? Did you shift? No, you couldn't have; you still have your clothes. What the hell happened? You're whiter than—"

"A bowl of flour?" I offered with a weak smile.

She rolled her eyes. "How bad could it be? I mean, it's not like you killed any of them."

I stepped back and tucked my hands into my pockets. "Yeah, it could be that bad." I took a step and then another, moving quickly toward the house. "Come on. It's getting close to morning."

Dahlia fell into step behind me. I knew she wouldn't be upset that I'd killed them. Surprised, yes, but not upset. She didn't understand what it meant to me to break that rule.

Being raised to believe that killing was a mortal sin, that my soul, whatever was left of it, would be cast into utter darkness when I died . . . that prospect was not exactly comforting. Besides that, killing people was just . . . wrong. Even if I hadn't been raised as a Firstamentalist, I would have believed it was wrong. Killing people was wrong.

As if reading my mind, Dahlia touched my arm. "They would have killed you, and then me. I don't know much about church stuff, but I'm sure there is something about defending your own. Isn't there? Like looking after your family?"

I hunched my shoulders as I stepped into the house. I listened for heartbeats and picked up two upstairs. Sandy's by the flutter of the first, and . . . Beth's. A sigh of relief flowed out of me. She had to have seen what Theseus was up to. That was a weight off me. I didn't realize just how worried I'd been about them until I heard their hearts and knew they were home and safe.

"Alena?"

I turned to Dahlia and motioned for her to follow me. "Let's see if we can tell what this stuff is."

"No, you answer my question. Isn't there something about defending your family?"

Why was she pushing this so hard?

I pressed the heels of my hands into my eyes, thinking about all the studying I'd done, all the reading and meditating about the teachings of the Firsts. "There is one section about it, yes. That if there is no other route, you should defend your family. But not yourself; if you are attacked, it says you should turn the other cheek." I opened my eyes. "I was defending myself, Dahlia. They were attacking *me*, not you."

Her green eyes softened. "Alena, you are like a sister to me. And so I'm only going to say this once." She put her hands on my shoulders and shook me gently. "Pull your head out of your ass."

My eyes bugged out, and she went on as if I'd agreed with her. "Those vamps were after me too. They would have killed me. They are trying to kill Remo, and even if you aren't in love with him, I know you care about him. This is war, not just between you and whatever heroes come, but between you and the vamps now too. And maybe in some ways they are going to be even more dangerous. Because there isn't just one. They are an army of supernaturals with no morals. No desire to make nice. That's why they are with Santos."

I blinked several times. "I'm never going to be okay with . . . killing."

"I would worry if you were." She touched a hand to my cheek and smiled. "You are too compassionate by far, but you are also one badass monster when you want to be. You are a hot mess of contradictions, my friend. Like a bacon-and-chocolate dessert." She winked to soften her words.

I couldn't help the smile that slowly curved my lips or the laugh that followed. "Yeah, that I would agree with."

I was a hot mess, all right. We headed to the kitchen, and she held the flask out over the sink and unscrewed the cap. The scent of licorice flowed into the room, so strong it burned the inside of my nose. I backed up until I was at the far side of the room. "It smells like fennel," I said.

"Isn't that an herb or something?"

"Yeah, I use it sometimes in my baking." I coughed into my arm. "Cap it up, I can hardly breathe."

She screwed the lid on and leaned as if to open the window, then stopped and pulled back. "Right, forgot you already permanently opened it."

I rolled my eyes. "I don't understand how fennel could burn me so badly."

She shrugged. "Maybe it's just the base for something else? Like a carrier?"

I tugged at my bottom lip with my teeth, thinking. "I'd ask Ernie, but . . . I don't want to take him from Tad right now."

"What about that skinny flier? Hermes?" she asked.

My eyes widened. "Good idea. HERMES!" I hollered his name and she flinched. The two sets of heartbeats upstairs fluttered and beat faster as Beth and Sandy woke up.

That was good; I wanted to talk to them anyway, see how things had gone with Theseus. To make things right with them both, to tell them that I was just trying to protect them.

They thumped down the stairs in tandem and entered the kitchen side by side.

Sandy's dark hair was all mussed up and she cracked a big yawn. "What time is it?"

Beth frowned up at the clock, irritation clear on her face. "Too damn early. What is all the yelling about?" That was not her usual tone or style. What if the arrow and Theseus's claim on her were still there?

"I need Hermes's help," I said. "I've got something here, and I'm not sure what it is exactly."

Beth raised one blond eyebrow. "Well, that's not a shock. There doesn't seem to be much you *do* know about."

Sandy sucked in a sharp breath, and Dahlia let out a growl. I shook my head and decided to go the safe route. "Beth, I know you were upset with me, but I was trying to protect you—"

"Tim broke it off with me. Said you were the reason why, that he can't stop thinking about you," she snapped.

"I didn't and wouldn't—"

"He said your beauty took his breath away." Her eyes filled with tears. "He said you looked at him, and he knew you were the one for him. You texted him. I saw the text."

My jaw dropped. What the hell was he up to? "I never looked at him like that, Beth, and I've been far too busy to text anyone. He's lying to you! You have to believe me that I'm not interested in Theseus—Tim—like that."

"HE ISN'T THESEUS!" Her scream coincided with Hermes winging through the window. If one could skid to a stop in the air, he did. I glanced at him; his eyes were wide and his mouth hung open.

"Did you call for me?" he managed.

Beth screamed, the sound crawling over my body like tiny daggers, and for just a second I thought she was going to shift. Sandy put a hand on her. "Beth, calm down. This isn't Alena's fault. Tim is just one of those assholes who uses one girl to get to another."

"It *is* her fault!" she cried as she spun and ran from the room. I stood there, staring at the place she'd been, my heart breaking at the thought of losing my friend. Of losing Beth to a man who would kill her as soon as kiss her.

Sandy shook her head, glanced at me, and shrugged. "I'll try to talk to her."

"Thanks," I said softly. "I didn't text him; he's playing a game."

"I know." She frowned, turned, and left the room. I blew a big breath out that fluttered my lips.

"Holy snickerdoodles."

Hermes cleared his throat. "You have a message you want me to take?"

Crap. Of course, that was his job, not educating me on snake oils. "Um. Yes. But first could you take a look at something?"

His eyebrows shot up. "I don't know much. I'm just a messenger."

"But you must have learned lots when you take messages. I only need to know if this is fennel." I pointed at the flask Dahlia held up. He spun around, his wings barely moving.

"It's a flask," he stated. I rolled my eyes.

"Dahlia, crack it open for him."

She spun the lid and held it up for him. He peered in and nodded. "Yup, that's fennel. Pure and distilled, by the looks of it."

I frowned. "Any idea why it might burn me?"

"Oh, that's easy." He paused. "But why aren't you asking Ernie?"

"Oh, that's easy," I mimicked him. "I don't trust him not to go running to Hera."

Hermes blinked several times as if digesting my words. "Yeah, it's tough being caught between the gods, we all do what we have to in order to survive. You shouldn't be so hard on him."

I nodded. "I'm trying, and so is he. Now, can you tell me why this is so awful for me?"

"Prometheus's Fire," he said as if that explained it all. I made a motion with my hands for him to continue. He shrugged and floated to stand on the table. "Look, Prometheus hid his fire from the gods, and when he hid it, he put it in there."

"In the flask?" I wasn't following.

"No, he put it inside a fennel stalk. So if you know what you're doing, you can distill fennel down to fine oil that will burn like a son of a Hera. Last person who made it was Hephaestus. Did it up in a crucible in his forge. It's one of those things that is incredibly effective against monsters. It won't hurt only you, but those two Stymphalian girls too."

"What about other supernaturals?"

"Nope, just good old-fashioned Greek monsters," he said.

Hephaestus. I wracked my brain, coming up with a blank. "Please, what does Hephaestus do again?"

Hermes groaned. "This is why I don't like answering questions. Can I just take your message, please?"

He had a point. The rest I could find out on my own; I was just being lazy. "Sure. Go to Remo, tell him . . ." What the fricky dicky was I going to tell him?

Dahlia helped out. "Go tell Tad to come back. We need to talk to him."

Tad, damn, I'd not even thought of my brother. My first instinct had been for someone to get Remo to come see me. For the comfort of his presence, as well as his insight into the situation. Hermes was gone in a shot faster even than usual. No doubt he was worried we were going to pepper him with questions if he stayed a minute longer.

I paced the kitchen, my thoughts rolling. This was a moment where I could use Ernie's help, and the best way to get the cherub to show up without asking him was to bake something.

I waffled back and forth until finally giving in. I scrubbed my hands and arms clean of the last splatters of vampire blood before I turned the oven on. Next I pulled out a bowl, set it on the counter, and ransacked the kitchen for the ingredients I wanted for a batch of muffins. Flour, sugar, oil, chopped walnuts, pumpkin seeds, and chunks of chocolate, along with the usual suspects to keep the treat from falling. A pinch of salt to set it all off.

"You know, I'm surprised you weren't five hundred pounds when you were human." Dahlia leaned in and poked a finger at the batter. I slapped her hand away.

"I didn't eat everything in sight. I just taste tested, that's the trick." I spooned the batter into muffin tins, then made a quick sugar crumble that I put on top of each one. I slid the pan into the hot oven and set the timer.

Within minutes the smell of the muffins filled the air and dispelled the last of the licorice scent.

A flutter of wings turned me around. Ernie beamed down at me. "I thought I smelled muffins. How long?"

I sat down in one of the kitchen chairs and leaned back. "A few minutes. Long enough for you to tell me about Hephaestus."

Ernie plopped himself on the table, his chubby cheeks puckering. "What has Happy got to do with anything?"

"Happy?" I blinked at him.

Ernie shrugged. "Hephaestus is a mouthful, and I've been saying it for a long time. Besides, calling him Happy irritates him. Which is amusing once you get him all worked up. He's kind of a grumpy bastard." Ernie winked, and I shook my head, unable to smile back after everything that the night had held for me.

"Tell me about him," I said. "I really want to know."

Ernie shrugged again as though he really didn't care. I didn't buy his act for a second. "Okay, but he has no part in what Hera is up to."

"Tell me anyway."

"Well, he rules the forge, making weapons and dealing with fire. I mean, he rarely comes out of his blacksmith shop, to be honest. He doesn't deal in the politics like others do. Really." He sniffed the air. "The muffins are almost ready."

I ran my tongue along the roof of my mouth, against one fang. I felt like I was missing something, like that one ingredient that would turn a flopped recipe into a bestseller.

"Nothing else about him?"

Ernie shook his head. "He's married to Aphrodite, but that's been a rocky marriage from the beginning. I don't think they've had sex for a hundred years or more."

"Goddess of love?"

"And sex. She's really my main supervisor."

Now that was interesting. Ernie slowly took his eyes from the oven and lifted them to mine. "What?"

"Aphrodite is your supervisor. You're working for Hera."

If I recalled, Hera was a jealous bitch. Like seeing the ingredients of a recipe come together, I slowly grasped the truth. "If that's true, then those two Greek goddesses could be working together. Does Hephaestus make your arrows?"

Ernie nodded, a light going off in his head. "And Aphrodite imbues them with power . . . oh my gods. Theseus and the arrow. I knew I didn't misplace any of mine!"

I glanced at Dahlia, who nodded her agreement.

"What do you want to bet Aphrodite convinced her hubby to help? Maybe for a quick roll in the hay?" Dahlia asked as she lifted an eyebrow at me. I nodded.

Ernie flew so he was between Dahlia and I. "Wait, this is more than the arrow, isn't it? What are you two referring to?"

Dahlia pulled the flask from behind her. "Oil of fennel. Prometheus's Fire. Snake oil, burns through Drakaina skin and can kill monsters. Ring a bell, *Ernie*?"

His shoulder's drooped and he fluttered to the floor, something I'd never seen him do. "Damn, I was hoping she was just spouting off."

"Who?" I demanded.

"Aphrodite. I think . . . I think you've pissed her off too."

Oh, well, wasn't that just a bucket and a half of rotten peaches.

CHAPTER 12

"What could I have possibly done to upset Aphrodite?" The question burst out of me at the same time the oven timer dinged. I moved on autopilot and pulled the muffins out, dumping them upside down on the cooling rack with a thump. Ernie grimaced and held a hand out like I'd kicked a puppy. I grabbed a muffin and tossed it to him.

He grinned and gave me a wink. Tossing the muffin back and forth between his hands to cool it, he answered me. "The thing is, she's kinda jealous. Achilles, despite his rather wounded ego, has been talking you up. 'Beautiful Monster' is what he's been calling you. I walked in on her ranting about making sure people knew who the real beauties were in the world, not some Drakaina that just showed up out of nowhere."

"Beautiful Monster. Sounds like one of those cheesy new romance novels," Dahlia muttered. I shushed her.

"But . . . Achilles hates me," I said.

"Yeah, but you totally flipped his switch. Achilles loves a strong woman." Ernie grinned as he took a bite of muffin. "You're breaking hearts everywhere you go, Beautiful Monster."

I groaned and shook my head. "Beth thinks I turned Theseus away from her, that he's in love with me too."

Ernie stopped chewing. "What?" Bits of muffin flew out of his mouth, landing on my lap. I flicked them off.

"Long story. Look, can you just tell your boss I'm really not doing this? That I just want to be left alone?"

He chewed thoughtfully on his muffin for a moment. "She won't believe me."

I blew out a puff of air. "Some help you are."

He flew up so we were eye to eye. "Listen, it's not my fault. Didn't you ask Merlin to make you special?"

I glared at him and snatched the remainder of the muffin away. "Don't you try and make this my fault that your boss is obviously nuttier than a batch of Christmas cakes."

He made a grab for the muffin, and I held it back. "I don't know how much to trust you, Ernie. How do I know you aren't going to run to Aphrodite and tell her . . . I don't know what you'd tell her, but something to make her angrier. How do I know you won't run to Theseus, or Hera?"

His mouth hardened into a fine line. "You'll just have to trust me that I'm doing everything I can."

I handed him the muffin and stepped back. "I've done that before, Ernie. Trusted men who were supposed to be there for me. Roger. Remo. Tad. You. Even Zeus said I could trust him."

The front door clicked open, and Tad's heartbeat preceded him. "Do I hear my name?" He stepped into the room, his eyes lighting on the muffins. "Thought I smelled these from outside."

I looked back at Ernie. "You have to earn my trust now, Ernie. I'm not just giving it to you like a free cookie."

He put the last of his muffin down on the table. "Then I guess I'd better go. Since I'm not trusted, that is."

Without a backward glance, he flew out the open window, disappearing into the night. I swallowed the desire to call him back and tell him all was forgiven. I couldn't afford to be the nice girl anymore, and it killed a part of me to embrace that truth.

I looked at Tad and refocused. "Did you find Theseus?"

"Shit, sis. You going to just act like Ernie isn't a friend? You pretty much booted him out." He frowned at me, a muffin in each hand.

I glared at him. "I didn't boot him out, I gave him a choice. And if you want to keep your muffins, I think you'd better reconsider those words. Ernie is dodging questions and working for more people than he has fingers. Explain to me how I can trust him."

Tad popped the whole muffin in his mouth and grinned around it. "Mfffn gdd."

"Yeah, buttering me up won't save you now," I grumbled, but I still smiled.

He swallowed the muffin down and licked his lips. "Theseus is holed up in Seattle, not far from Mom and Dad's place, actually."

A nervous zing of energy snapped through me. "Seriously?"

"Yeah, you know that big house on the corner? The one that's been for sale for like a year because it was way overpriced?"

I nodded. "He bought it?"

"I don't know if he bought it, but he's living there. It's gated and everything, I tried to get in, but he's not doing interviews until tomorrow."

"Interviews, you can't be serious now."

He nodded. "He says he understands my desire to get away from you, but he's got other people looking to be on the 'right side.'"

Although it was good to know where Theseus was, I wasn't sure how it was going to help me. Tad leaned back in the chair. "You ready for dinner at Mom and Dad's tonight?"

I groaned. "Damn. I forgot about that." The fact that I'd even been invited had been a shock until I realized that it had been Dad making sure I was part of the family event.

"We have to decide what to do with this." Dahlia held up the flask. "Can we just pour it out, down the sink?"

I frowned. "I don't know."

The front door clicked open, and the three of us froze. While I picked up a heartbeat, I didn't immediately recognize it.

Yaya called out, "Darling granddaughter, are you baking?"

Relief swept through me. "When am I not, Yaya?"

She greeted Tad first with a pat on his cheek. A thought rolled through me like a wave of undulating coils. "Yaya, what are you doing up at this hour?" Hard to believe it was only the middle of the night, with all that had happened so far.

"I'm old, Lena Bean, and that means I do what I want. And I don't sleep worth shit anymore." She rubbed at her right hip. "What I wouldn't give to be young again and free of this."

She pointed at the flask. "What's that?"

"Fennel oil. We were just going to pour it out."

"Oh, gods, don't do that! It has to be properly disposed of." Yaya flapped her hands at Dahlia as she unscrewed the cap.

"How? Why?" I blurted out. "I rinsed it off me in the river, can't I just pour it out there?"

Yaya lifted both eyebrows and closed her eyes. "No. It's not really an oil, though they call it that. It's imbued with power from the forge of Hephaestus. Which means it is a weapon designed for destruction. If you just pour it out . . . there's no telling what it will do."

Well, that was just awesome. "So what do I do with it?"

"Hide it." She pointed at Dahlia. "Let your friend keep it safe while she sleeps."

That was actually a good idea. "You okay with that, Dahlia?"

Dahlia swept past me with a nod, clutching the flask tight. She kissed Tad solidly on the mouth. "Keep an eye on her, I have to sleep. See you three at dinner tonight." She held the silver flask up and I nodded.

"Thanks," I said. "Wait, you're going to be at dinner?"

They ignored my question.

Tad swatted her on the butt as she sashayed away. "I always keep an eye on her."

The sounds of her footsteps faded as the sun rose behind me. "She was cutting it close," I said.

"She loves you and wants to keep you safe," Tad said as he took another muffin. "We all do."

Yaya nodded. "He's right, we're all here for you."

The statements were meant to be heartwarming, I'm sure. But all I could hear was that I wasn't capable of taking care of myself. I frowned. "I'm going to go shower and sleep for a couple of hours."

I walked away before Tad or Yaya could answer. I wasn't really tired, though if I were still human, I knew I'd be falling asleep on my feet. There was something about danger that supercharged my ability to stay alert and functioning. That was probably a good thing, since some of the people closest to me were nighthawks. I'd noticed I could run on only a few hours of sleep each day or night and keep going.

Go me.

Up the stairs and into the bathroom, I did my best to ignore the pacing of Beth's feet in her room. Sandy was quiet, either sitting or lying down by the rate of her heart. I flicked the shower on as hot as the water would go and stepped in with a gasp. I stayed in for a good ten minutes, letting the water run over my face, muffling the sounds outside of the bathroom.

Letting me believe for a few minutes that I was still normal. I snorted and sucked in a lungful of hot water, which sent me into a coughing fit.

I flicked the water off, grabbed a towel, and headed for my room. Beth and Sandy were no longer upstairs. I flopped into bed, set my alarm for three hours, all that was left of the night, and fell fast asleep.

The buzzing of the alarm went off what felt like seconds later. I jerked upright and checked the clock. Three hours shouldn't have been enough, but I was alert. With a yawn and a stretch, I slid out of bed and dressed in a flowing short skirt and a beautiful lacy mauve top that skimmed the edge of my belly, giving glimpses of my skin here and there. I braided my hair down one side of my head and left the rest loose to hang past my shoulders.

And not once did I let my mind wander to all the problems.

Yeah, right.

I couldn't stop wondering if, when night fell, Santos would be back.

If Beth would attack me or go back to Theseus. If we could mend our friendship.

When Aphrodite would make a full move, if she hadn't already.

If Remo missed me at all.

I closed my eyes on that last one and knew it was the question I wanted the answer to more than any other.

I hurried downstairs. Tad was passed out on the couch, snoring loudly. Yaya was nowhere to be found, but a note said she was looking forward to dinner. I snorted to myself. No doubt she knew the poop show it was going to end up being. How could it not, with a Firstamentalist mother and her two Super Duper kids sitting down together?

Beth and Sandy were gone too, and I let out a sigh. I hoped they were just out shopping, being normal. And not being sucked back into Theseus's grasp.

Slowly, my thoughts came together, and a possible solution formed like watching dough rise. Maybe there was a way. "Tad, I need to go to the bakery and whip something up for dinner tonight."

He groaned, and I grabbed one of his feet and gave it a shake. "You brought your car, didn't you?"

Another groan. I rolled my eyes. "Look, I get it. I've only had three hours too, but there is nothing I can—" I stared at his sleeping face.

Only, he wasn't sleeping, not really. Blood seeped from a thin line along his forehead. "Did someone attack you?"

His eyes fluttered open. "Beth."

"Beth?" That was crazy. "Why? What did you say?"

He drew a slow breath. "I tried to stop her from taking the flask."

My heart sank to my toes like a lead weight dropping through a piecrust. "No . . . Is Dahlia okay?"

"Yeah. Dahlia is fine. Slept through the whole thing, I think." He struggled to sit up, so I helped him.

"Tad, this is bad."

"She's working for Theseus, then? For real?" He squinted at me and then covered his eyes. "Damn, two of you is too much."

"Lie back down. Stay here and rest. I'm going to take your car and go to the bakery." A place of sanctuary, a place I could hide for a little while from the truth that was causing me to shake. Theseus had the oil. And I had no idea how to stop him. He was moving his chess pieces carefully, and I couldn't seem to outmaneuver him.

"Why not bake here?" Tad grumped.

I shook my head. How did I say that the bakery might not be mine much longer and I wanted as much time there as I could get? "Special equipment, ingredients and such. You and Dahlia come for dinner in her car, okay?"

He grunted. "Be careful, sis, he's out for you."

"I will. You too. Bro."

He laughed, his chest shaking. "Don't ever say that again."

"I make no promises." I scooped his car keys from the hook beside the door and stepped outside into the surprisingly bright winter sun. And right into Smithy's chest.

I blinked up at him. "Captain. Can I help you?"

Ice-blue eyes stared down at me. "My men have been pulled off duty. Captain Oberfall is back."

I bobbed my head. "Okay, thanks for letting me know. And thanks for the help the other day."

He didn't move. "I heard a rumor you took out the twins."

I frowned, not understanding at first. Then I blanched as I realized he meant the twin vampires that had been in Santos's gang. "Um. Maybe?"

"With wooden spoons? Your smell is all over the handles." He held two bloodied wooden spoons up, and I pressed my back into the door.

"Are you going to arrest me?" I whispered.

"Nope. Any woman who can kill a vampire with a pair of wooden spoons . . ." He shook his head. "I wanted to thank you. Personally."

It was then I realized he wasn't in his uniform but instead wore a pair of tight jeans, a black T-shirt, and a thin camouflage jacket.

He held out his hand that didn't have the spoons. "I was wrong about you. I'd like you to consider joining the Supe Squad and working with me."

My jaw dropped as he took my hand. "Oh no, I don't think that's a good idea. The spoons were an accident."

Smithy shook his head. "No, it wasn't. Killing a vampire is never an accident. It's hard work. They don't die easy."

"They underestimated me," I blurted out. "It means they don't take me seriously. No one does."

Smithy's lips twitched. "Yeah, I got that. Look. I was wrong about you. And I want to try and make it right. For my part in things."

His words had more weight to them than just what they seemed. I could feel it in the air. I stared into the blue eyes, and a flicker of something I didn't expect flowed between us. The image around Smithy wavered, the werewolf I knew sliding away to leave someone very different in his place. Same blocky muscular build, and the eyes were still the same flinty blue, and even his hair was the same. But he had scars across his neck and up the sides of his face. The scars, though, weren't what made him look so different. The fact that he wasn't really a werewolf was what caught my eyes. He reminded me of Zeus, the way he just stood there, looking at me.

He held out his hand. "Hephaestus."

"Happy?" I blurted out before I could catch myself. He grimaced.

"Damn Eros. No, do not call me that." He frowned. "You can still call me Smithy if you want."

"Smithy, as in blacksmith?" The pieces clicked together for me, and I whipped a hand out and slapped him hard enough to snap his head sideways. "You made that oil of fennel."

Smithy, Hephaestus, whatever he wanted to call himself, slowly turned back to me. His eyes were all but glacial. "My *wife* asked me to. Let me tell you something, Drakaina. You don't turn down your wife, especially not when she is a goddess of love and sex. Get my drift?"

"You did it so you could . . . boink her?"

His jaw dropped and a laugh boomed out of him; he roared with it until his eyes ran and he actually went to one knee. "Oh, gods. Alena. You are nothing of what we expected."

What *we* expected. Chills and horror collided as they raced through my synapses. "What do you mean?"

Smithy stood and crooked a finger at me. "Come on, let's have a chat."

I stood unmoving. "Why would you help me? Your wife is working with Hera to have me killed. And you've been hiding in plain sight all this time, pretending to be a werewolf. Why?"

The words hovered in the air between us, and he gave me a slow nod. "How can I put this? The pantheon is complicated at the best of times. Yes, I gave my wife what she wanted, and she gave me what I wanted." He smiled, the grin all wolf and lechery. "That being said, now that I know what she and Hera have been up to, I don't necessarily agree with it. While I can't go against my wife, exactly, I can give you some ideas. And yes, I hid in plain sight. Gods get bored too, you know. It's the bane of a long-lived life."

I wasn't buying it. "I ask you again, why? You gain nothing but an angry wife if you help me."

He squinted one eye at me. "You know why I took the job as second-in-command at the SDMP? I'm bored, Alena. The world is boring. And then you showed up, and things started happening." He smiled, and I realized for the first time he was a rather handsome man. I didn't even mind the scars.

Our eyes connected again, heat simmering between us in a way I didn't expect. I flushed and looked away, not liking the flash of whatever it was that zipped between us. I had enough on my plate with my crap-tastic soon-to-be ex-husband, a taboo cross-species growing relationship with Remo, and Theseus making a bid on my life to be dabbling in this kind of tension with a Greek god.

"So I make things interesting? That doesn't seem to be much reason to put your marriage and life on the line."

Smithy snorted. "Please, like all marriages within the pantheon, it's for show. Why do you think I jumped at the chance to get back in her bed? Unlike her, I don't stray."

My eyes involuntarily shot to his, and he slowly nodded. "I respect your stance on trying to get a divorce, even though it won't happen. You're as trapped as me, Drakaina."

I lifted my chin. "I have a hearing again tomorrow. I'm not giving up."

That smile crossed his face, and I found myself staring. Well, this was not a development I'd expected.

"I wouldn't expect you to. The real heroes don't."

"I'm not a hero."

He shook his head. "A hero's journey is rarely one where they see themselves as such. Do me a favor. Trust Eros. He's on your side, as I am. As Zeus is, even if he's doing nothing but partying it up at his house out on Olympic Drive in the Highlands area."

I lifted both eyebrows and his mouth twitched up.

Smithy rubbed his jaw. "Not exactly subtle, I know. He'll probably hide if you show up, but it might be worth a visit." Smithy winked. "In case you need to talk to him."

I opened my mouth to thank him, and he closed the distance between us. I held my breath as he dipped his mouth and let it hover over my lips. "If I weren't married, Alena, you would be in trouble for a whole different reason."

That was all he said. He stepped back and turned away from me. I blurted out the question I couldn't help but ask.

"Did you know what I was from the beginning? When you first caught me?"

"No," he called over his shoulder. "No, I didn't. Nor did I realize you'd rolled me at the gate until after. And even then I didn't understand. It's been too long since we've seen a real monster, Alena. And maybe it's been too long since we've seen a real hero. You are changing the rules, even if you don't know it."

He slid into the SDMP pickup truck at the curb and pulled away without saying anything else. My heart bumped against my rib cage, and I made myself walk down the steps to Tad's beater of a car. I was out on the human's side of the Wall in a matter of minutes, and while there were officers watching, they waved me through.

Another few minutes and I was on the highway headed south to my bakery.

"What in the name of all that is made of sugar and spice just happened there?" I couldn't wrap my brain around Smithy, Hephaestus, whatever his name was. He wasn't a werewolf, he was hiding in plain sight. Just like Zeus working for the local Blue Box Store. I lifted a hand to my lips. He hadn't kissed me, but he'd wanted to.

And I think I might have wanted him to as well. Not that I would have. It was bad enough that Remo and I had kissed . . . a curl of guilt spooled out of me when I thought of Remo. Like I'd been unfaithful to him. When in reality it was Roger I was married to. I put a hand to my head as I drove. "Seriously, you are messed up," I whispered to myself. I did my best to focus on what Smithy had said. He would help me. And he told me to trust Ernie.

"Ernie, if you can hear me, I'm sorry. I'm going to the bakery, and I'll whip you up something as an apology."

A puff of feathers all but exploded in the seat beside me, and the fat, smiling cherub stared up at me. "It's about time. What changed your mind, girlfriend?"

I laughed. "Hephaestus vouched for you."

"He did?" He gaped at me.

I nodded. "I don't know why I believe him, but I do."

"He's a total stick in the mud. No fun. I haven't seen him in years, how did he look?" Ernie settled into the passenger seat.

"What do you mean you haven't seen him in years?"

"Like, I don't know, a few hundred years? He went off the radar after Aphrodite's last conquest. She broke his heart one too many times." Ernie shook his head. "Made him a real asshole, hard and jaded."

I could see that. Not that it mattered to me. "He almost kissed me."

"WHAT?" Ernie roared, his voice filling up the small space. "Are you yanking my wings? Tell me you're yanking my wings!"

"No." I kept my eyes on the road. "He leaned in and was close enough to kiss me, and he said, 'If I wasn't married, Alena, you would be in trouble for a whole different reason.' And then he left."

"Wow," he breathed out. "Now I know why Aphrodite hates you. It isn't that you are beautiful, because there are lots of beauties out there." He moved so that he sat on the dash and faced me like an oversized bobble-head doll. "You caught the eye of her husband, something that has never happened. He isn't like the others; he takes his vows seriously."

I scowled. "I didn't catch his eye. He . . . he just said I made things interesting again."

Ernie groaned and covered his face with his hands. "Even worse. If a god finds you interesting, that's bad. Bad."

"Look, what does it matter? She doesn't even like him, you said that yourself." I tapped a finger on the dash beside him. "And I'm still married to Roger."

"Look, it's a territory thing with these Greek ladies. They want what they want, and they don't share worth shit. The thing is, Hephaestus hasn't gotten laid for a long time, at least not since he made the fennel oil, I guess."

"Maybe that's why he's so miserable," I said.

Ernie barked a laugh. "No doubt. But Aphrodite uses it to keep him under her thumb. She really can be a bitch."

"Again, none of this really matters right now. I can only deal with one thing at a time, Ernie. First thing I've got to do is get through this family dinner with a mother who thinks I'm a monster and a brother who is bringing his vampire girlfriend to meet her. Tomorrow I have court. And if I can get through that without issue, then I'm going to have a long nap."

"What about Theseus?"

"He's not doing anything. So neither am I." I took the next exit and wove underneath the highway. I knew I was lying to myself. Theseus was manipulating my friends around me, slowly cornering me. But I didn't know how to stop him.

"That's not a good plan. You need to be ready for anything with him."

"That's impossible," I said.

"Yeah," he muttered, "that's what I'm afraid of."

CHAPTER 13

Vanilla and Honey came into view, and in front of it a sign that hadn't been there before. A "For Sale" sign with a "Sold" sticker slapped across it in bold lettering.

I yanked the steering wheel to the side and parked at the curb hard enough to crash the hubs into the cement. Ernie grimaced. "Easy on the old car, Alena."

I jerked the keys from the ignition and stepped out as a semitruck roared past, fluttering my skirt around my legs. The rumble of the big rig vibrated up through the ground and into my body through the soles of my shoes. I embraced the energy and used it to propel me forward with long strides.

From around the side of the bakery Roger appeared . . . with Colleen Vanderhoven right behind him.

Roger half turned and smiled at her. "As soon as we can get the duplicate paperwork, we'll finish the sale, Colleen."

"You'd better, because you and I both know your Barbie doll spent the down payment I made already. I want those recipes your wife keeps in her vault." She poked him in the chest with one finger I knew would be filthy from the one time I'd tried to shake her hand. Her greasy neon-pink hair was pulled back in a low ponytail that would hang in any batter she tried to whip up.

Suddenly, the break-in I'd busted up the week before made sense. The robbers hadn't been looking for money.

They'd been looking for my recipes. A low, rumbling hiss escaped my mouth as I strode toward them. They stood in front of the bakery, oblivious to my approach.

"I can't get the locksmith in until I have proof this is my bakery," Roger said. "You know that. The paperwork should be here in the next week or so."

"Vanilla and Honey issss *my* bakery, Roger." I snapped the words at him as I struggled to keep my fangs in place. They kept lowering as the anger in me rose, and I kept pushing them back up with my tongue. The effort made speaking interesting.

Roger spun to face me and at the same time scrambled backward. "Stay there, Alena. I don't want to get sick."

Colleen snorted. "She's not sick, you fool. I can see it. Can't you? Not even a sniffle on her stupid face." Her brown eyes narrowed as they landed on me. "Poor little rich girl, all the money in the world handed to you, and you end up not being able to use it because you're a supernatural. How awful. The bakery is going to be *mine*." She snapped her fingers at my face. I clenched my teeth to keep from biting her.

"I suggest you leave, lady." Ernie floated at my shoulder as he glared at Colleen. "She's about two seconds from shifting into a seriously badass snake. She could swallow you whole, without a problem. Well, maybe two gulps—you're a bigger girl, aren't you?"

Colleen's wicked gaze slid from me to Ernie. "You're a mouthy one, aren't you, for being *miniature?*"

He put his hands on his hips. "Look who's talking, fat nose."

I stepped close enough that our chests touched, and I stared down at her, using every inch of my height to its full effect.

"Colleen, I will burn the bakery to the ground before I let you have it," I said. "And I'll tell the insurance adjusters I did it so you get nothing, Roger."

He gasped. Colleen pushed away from me, spluttered, then finally spun and walked away. For the first time I'd rendered her speechless. Roger not so much.

"You wouldn't dare burn it down!"

"I would!" I yelled. "I would. Better that it be in ashes and dust than in her hands. No money for you . . . you . . . *asshole*!"

I stormed away from him, put the keys in the lock, and let myself into the cool interior of the bakery. I leaned against the door. Roger banged on it, thundering with his fists.

"You're crazy, you're not getting anything tomorrow. Nothing. You're the monster, I'm the human, remember? And I have a lawyer who is going to destroy you." In classic Roger fashion, he shoved a card into the mail slot. It fell to my feet, a single name blinking up at me.

Merlin.

I dropped my head to my chest, all hope fleeing in a matter of seconds.

Roger walked away, and I listened to his heartbeat flutter and slow the farther away he got.

"You held it together, Alena. That was good." Ernie flew in front of me at eye level. "You kept your snake under control."

I bent and scooped up Merlin's card. "He hired a warlock to defend him in a human court. How would he even know who Merlin is?"

Ernie shook his head. "He wouldn't. Unless he was approached. Which would only happen if he had the Aegrus virus."

I groaned. "I made him think I was sick yesterday. I coughed all over him. They would have stuck him in quarantine . . . What do you want to bet Merlin paid him a visit?"

"Well, that seriously stinks like nymph shit."

I grunted and pushed off the door, turning only to lock it behind me. In case Roger came back. "Ernie, he's right. I'm going to get nothing tomorrow. Especially if Merlin is helping him. Even Yaya wanted me to hire him. I mean, think about it. If he can convince me, a Firstamentalist born and raised, that being turned into a Super Duper is okay, what judge stands a chance with his slick words? For all I know, he really is a lawyer." I bent the card in half.

Ernie's wings drooped. "He is a lawyer, but I don't think he's practiced in a long time."

"Roger outed me. Maybe I could do the same to Merlin?" I unbent the card and stared at it. "Then he couldn't represent Roger."

"The humans won't even realize he's a supernatural," Ernie said. "Even if they gave him a blood test, warlocks are the one brand of Supe that don't show up. They're just magical humans. They can slide through without being noticed."

Well, that explained things, but it didn't help me.

I stood there, despair flowing through me. "I don't have a shot then, Ernie. Between the judge and Merlin, Roger has won. I might as well not even show up."

"Don't give up. Please," he said.

"Why does it matter to you? Nothing changes in your world if I win or lose."

I walked through the front of the store, around the counter, and into the kitchen. I flicked on the lights and grabbed a few bowls before he answered.

"You're fighting not just for yourself but for all of us. This could change the way Super Dupers, as you say, are seen. We could all have rights if you can get them to really acknowledge you."

I glanced at him as I grabbed a bag of flour. "But, Ernie, you're not really a Super Duper like me. You're a part of the Greek pantheon. Isn't that different?"

"Maybe at one point, but not anymore. We've all been lumped into the same category."

I started mixing the cupcakes I'd planned on for desert. Butter pecan with candied pecans and cream cheese icing to top them off.

Ingredients went into the mixer, and I made myself think about the hearing the next day and what my yaya had said. "Maybe Merlin isn't really going to help Roger. Maybe he's going to help me by sinking Roger's case?"

Ernie's eyebrows rose to his hairline. "Would you even want that kind of help from him? You'd end up owing Merlin something."

"Owing him something is better than giving Roger anything. What I really need is someone who's familiar with the law, who can help me through the loopholes." I cracked three eggs and dumped them into the batter.

Ernie was quiet long enough that I looked up. He had a strange look on his face as his cheeks flushed red and the lines between his brow furrowed.

"Are you constipated?"

He spluttered, "I am not. I'm thinking."

I smiled. "Not what it looks like from here, like you're all backed up."

"Potty humor, really?"

I shrugged, still fighting a grin. "I have a brother and a father. I know what constipation on a man looks like."

"Look, are you going to be serious here? I have an idea," he said.

I stared at the cupcakes as I ran my tongue over the roof of my mouth. "I think I have one too. You first."

Ernie sat on the counter. "You have someone who knows the law inside and out, and he likes you."

I shook my head. "Remo? The session is in the afternoon. Not as late as my first one. He won't be awake yet." I spooned the batter into cupcake molds, making sure to get the perfect amount.

"I mean Hephaestus. You said he is Smithy, right? So he knows the law, and he's smart. And mean when he wants to be. You need someone downright mean on your side, someone who can stand up to Merlin."

I slid the pan of cupcakes into the oven and started on the next one. "But I wouldn't need him if Merlin didn't show up, right?"

Ernie flew around so we were eye to eye. "What are you thinking?"

I batted my eyelashes at him. "What if I took Merlin a peace offering that happened to have a little venom in it? Just enough to make him sick? Too sick for court. I mean, it could be an accident, right? Will my venom work that way?"

Ernie's jaw opened and closed several times. "Damn, that is . . ."

"Brilliant?" I offered.

"I was going to say wicked badass, but brilliant will do. And yes, we can make your venom work that way." He chuckled. "You won't need much at all. Put a drop into a cup, and then we can dilute it down with some kind of liquor."

My theory was good, but making it happen was a little more difficult. I tried to pry one of my overlong fangs forward, but it stayed clamped to the roof of my mouth. I blew out a raspberry of frustration.

"Sure, they drop when I don't want them to, but when I do want them around, they're cemented to me," I grumbled.

Ernie pursed his lips a moment before speaking. "What makes them drop?"

"Anger. Frustration." Remo, something about Remo softened them up. Just his name floating through my mind loosened the hold my fangs seemed to have. I reached up and pulled one forward. A single drop of venom plopped into the glass cup I had under my mouth.

I let my fang go, and it snapped back into place.

"What did you think of? You weren't angry." Ernie had a smirk on his face. Like he already knew the answer. Maybe he did; he was the Greek version of Cupid.

"None of your beeswax."

"Remo, huh? Or maybe Smithy now too?"

I whipped around, a wooden spoon in my hand. "Neither. I'm a married woman. I don't think about things like that about other men, like that, you know that."

The jumble of words was a mess of a defense.

"Hey, don't be pointing weapons at me!" Ernie lifted both hands high above his head while he laughed.

"Stop it."

"You're deadly no matter what you've got in your hands." He smiled. "I wonder how you'd do with an actual weapon instead of kitchen utensils if you got in a fight."

I stared down at the drop of venom in the bottom of the glass. "If I dilute this with ouzo, you think that would work?" I reached above the sink and flipped the cupboard open. A variety of liqueurs and alcohol stared back at me. Ernie fluttered close.

"I thought you didn't drink."

"I don't drink. They're used in baking."

"And the ouzo, why that one?"

I grabbed the bottle labeled as such and uncorked the Greek liquor. The faint licorice scent rolled up to my nose, and I immediately pulled back. "Seems fitting with everything that's happened lately."

I filled the glass with the drop of venom to the top with the ouzo. I gave it a quick stir with a spoon and then stopped. "With my venom this diluted, will it do anything at all?"

Ernie grimaced. "It won't kill him, I know that much. As powerful as your venom is, you still would need a straight shot into his body with your fangs to pump enough in to kill him."

I tapped the glass with the spoon. "But will this make him sick enough to not go into the courthouse?"

"Should. But I'm not taste testing for you."

Pulling out cream cheese and icing sugar, I began to make the frosting. Butter, a splash of vanilla. And a quarter teaspoon of the ouzo mixture, just enough for a faint smell of licorice and fennel to fill the air.

Ernie stared down into the mixer as it whipped the concoction up. The timer dinged, I took the cupcakes out, and Ernie grabbed one and flew to the other side of the room. "I want one before you cover it with your nasty spit."

I snorted. "I'm making a second batch of icing. I have to take these for dinner to my parents."

"Groovy." He rubbed his hands together with glee. "I missed out on your muffins, so I have lost time to make up with your other baked goods."

As the cupcakes cooled, I set the first batch of frosting aside and started on the second. Then I threw some pecans, sugar, and butter into a pan, caramelizing them. I poured the nuts onto a piece of parchment paper to cool.

Both frostings and the topping made, I picked up the best-formed cupcake. I put the venom frosting into a piping bag and piped it onto the cupcake for Merlin. I put on a good two inches of the thick white frosting, making a perfect swirl like a soft-serve ice-cream cone.

I tossed the toasted and caramelized pecans into the food processer and then took the sprinkles and dusted the top of the cupcake. I held it up for Ernie's inspection. "Good enough to eat?"

"If I didn't know what was in that frosting, I'd steal it from you right now. It smells good too." He licked his lips.

A thought rumbled around in the back of my head. I had more than one person I'd like to give a venomous cupcake to. Like Zeus . . . I grabbed a second cupcake and frosted it up with the ouzo-and-venom icing. Maybe I could make him wish he'd been more helpful. Dang, I really was turning into a monster. I kept on piping the frosting, a grim smile on my lips.

"Who's that for?" Ernie bobbed around in front of me, his lips dipping into a tiny frown. I grinned up at him.

"You wait and see."

A knock on the back door slowly drew me around. I listened and no heartbeat floated back to me. I swallowed hard and checked the clock. It was late enough that it would be dark already. I grabbed a rolling pin in one hand.

"Dahlia?"

"No." Remo's voice slid under the door, and my heart rate kicked up more than a few notches.

"What do you want?"

"I came to apologize. May I come in?"

I looked to Ernie, who just shrugged and said, "I'd give him another chance. But I'm also a sucker for a bad boy; they make me tingle in all my lady parts." He winked.

I rolled my eyes. "Some help you are. Can you go to the front or something? I don't want an audience for—"

"For making out with your vamp boy toy. I got it, I'm all about the love, you know." He flew out of the kitchen, laughing the whole way.

I put the rolling pin down and went to the door, wiping my hands on my apron before I grabbed the knob. I paused, though, and tried to gather myself.

"I can hear your heartbeat pounding as well as if I had my ear to your lovely breast, Alena. You might as well open the door," Remo said.

Cocky jerk. My mouth twitched, and then I remembered everything I'd been through in the last twenty-four hours. That he'd said he'd help me, but when I'd asked him to come via Hermes, he'd not shown up. And I'd had to deal with Santos on my own.

I jerked the door open. "What do you want?"

His dark eyes, so like his brother's, now that I knew the truth, widened. "I said I came to apologize. Hermes brought me your message, but I wasn't ready to see you yet."

I gripped the door hard in preparation to slam it. "And now you are? Fine. Apology accepted. I'm *busy*. Please go away."

He strode forward and planted his lips on mine.

I couldn't help myself, I wrapped my arms around him. We stumbled backward into the counter, the clatter of pots and pans tumbling behind us, as he lifted me up to sit on the edge so I was taller than him. The taste of his mouth, the feel of his body, every part of him called to me, to my senses. He said something in Italian, a soft murmur of apology against my lips. "I should not have left you alone. I don't know how else to keep you safe."

"I can take care of myself," I whispered back, even while I struggled to break free of the spell his kisses wove around me. My hands were all over his shoulders and the back of his head, holding him tight.

It took all my strength to pull away, and even so, my hands lingered on his shoulders, as his lingered on my back and waist. I slid off the counter, though my legs were a bit wobbly.

"Still married," I said.

His smile was tired, and he stepped back, giving me room. "Did Santos hurt you?"

I ran a hand through my hair and quickly told him about the fennel. How it had been meant for Theseus to use against me, how Dahlia and I had retrieved it, and how it was missing yet again.

"Beth has truly turned on you?"

"It's like she's still under a spell," I said. "No matter what I say, I can't seem to convince her that he is not Tim, but Theseus. And poor Sandy is just going along with her out of loyalty, I'm sure. I'm afraid he's going to hurt them and there is nothing I can do."

Ernie flew back in. "Couldn't help overhearing that bit. Beth actually is mesmerized by Theseus. Not quite the same as a spell, but close. That's the kind of arrow he had, the obsession one I told you about. He's using her own desires against her to keep her under his thumb. He's good at that."

"How long will the arrow last?" I asked.

Ernie shrugged. "Until she doesn't want it to. Kinda like your influence as a siren. It only works on those who already are in line with what you want."

"Wonderful." I tipped my head back to stare at the ceiling. Remo made a soft noise that brought my eyes back to him. His dark eyes with the violet edge were completely dilated. "What?"

"You threw your head back. It's all but an invitation to a vampire." His voice was carefully neutral and he looked away.

"Oh, sorry."

"Awkward much," Ernie muttered. "Look, let's get these cupcakes and go. You wanted to see Merlin before you go to your parents, right?"

I shook my head. "I'll take it to him after." I grabbed the bowl of frosting, doing my best to block out the smell of cinnamon and honey that was Remo. I spooned the thick frosting into a fresh, clean piping bag and got to work finishing the cupcakes, still tasting his mouth on mine. Still trying to get my hormones and thoughts back under control.

Remo stood to one side, watching me. "Did you really use wooden spoons on the twins?"

I jerked in the middle of piping and blinked up at him. "Yes."

He didn't smile, didn't laugh. "Good. Don't hesitate when it comes to Santos and his crew, Alena. Never hesitate. He will hurt you."

"Even though he's your brother?" The words slipped out of me, and I forced myself to hold his gaze.

His jaw twitched. "Most especially for that reason."

I swallowed hard and went back to the cupcakes. In a matter of minutes I'd finished and dusted them with the caramelized pecans.

"Can I have one now?" Ernie begged.

"No." I slapped his hand away. "These are for after dinner." I glanced at Remo. "Dahlia will be there . . . would you like to come with me?"

"For dinner?"

"At my parents', to be clear."

His eyebrows shot up. "You want me to meet your parents?"

A thought hit me. "Actually, I'd like you to smell them." I didn't think his eyebrows could rise higher. I was wrong.

"Excuse me?"

"Come on, I'll explain on the way."

CHAPTER 14

"You don't know what kind of supernatural your dad is?" Remo asked again as he took the off-ramp nearest my parents' house. I'd let him drive so I could make sure my cupcakes didn't get bumped around; okay, to make sure Ernie didn't eat any. "How is that possible? You have a sense of smell at least as keen as a vampire's."

I shrugged. "He just smells like my dad to me."

"Does it matter, I mean, really? He is what he is, and that is what made you susceptible to the virus. None of that can be changed," Remo pointed out.

I didn't know how to explain that it did matter, at least to me. That there was something our parents weren't telling us, and I had a feeling that once we knew what kind of Super Duper Dad was, we'd understand why things were the way they were. That we'd be able to make sense of our family.

We pulled into my parents' driveway, and my stomach clenched. I clung to the edges of the container that held nearly two dozen cupcakes. I glanced into the back, where Ernie sat, two cupcakes in a container beside him. "Ernie, are you coming in?"

"Nope." He yawned. "I'm going to stay right here and guard the magic cupcakes. You have fun facing down your Firstamentalist mom with your vampire boyfriend, while you are still technically married. I'd rather stay out of the family feud." He winked and my mouth dropped.

"Ernie!"

Remo stepped out of the car and held a hand out to me. "He's just teasing you."

"No, he's right." I let Remo help me out, telling myself it was because of my short skirt. Really I just wanted to hold his hand for a moment. "This could get ugly fast. My mom . . . she's not very open minded."

Remo smiled. "I'm known for my charm."

"It's not your charm I'm worried about; it's your fangs."

He winked at me as he took the cupcake platter from the seat. "Ladies first, and I promise not to bite anyone."

I took a breath and strode toward the front door as if I were headed into battle. I hadn't been home since shortly after I'd been turned, and *that* had been a scene and a half. Achilles had attacked me, and we'd blasted Mom's favorite coffee table into tiny pieces, but that wasn't the worst of things. No, the worst was confirming my mom wouldn't acknowledge me, even though I stood right in front of her.

I rapped my knuckles on the door and took a half step back. Who knocked on her parents' door? This was ridiculous. I took the knob and twisted it to the left. "Dad?" I called out as I stepped in. I glanced back at Remo and nodded. Maybe he didn't need an invite, but better to be on the safe side.

I forced my feet to move, walking over the threshold of the door with more than a little trepidation. I could hear two hearts beating in the direction of the kitchen, one at the back of the house, and . . . five in the direction of the family room. Eight people. There shouldn't be that many. Even if Dahlia had a heartbeat to pick up on, there wouldn't be eight. I drew in a breath at the same time Remo did.

He put his mouth next to my ear. "They aren't all human."

I put the cupcakes down on a side table next to the door. "What if Theseus has my family?"

"Then we will stop him." Remo stepped in front of me and pointed toward the kitchen. "Fewer people."

I nodded, and we moved quietly toward the sounds of two heartbeats and . . . an electric mixer burst into the silence along with a voice that made my head drop.

"Beatrice, what is wrong with you?"

I put a hand on Remo's arm and shook my head. "It's family. Aunt Janice is married to my dad's brother." Half brother, to be correct, but I wasn't going to get that detailed. I counted heartbeats again and slumped. "Which means the other heartbeats are her husband and two kids."

"They aren't all human," he repeated with a nod.

I licked my lips. "You sure you aren't just picking up on Tad?" Even as I said my brother's name, I knew exactly what Remo meant. There was a strange smell floating out of the kitchen.

I frowned, and my tongue shot out and flicked once in front of my face, tasting the air. Blushing, I turned my face away from Remo, even as the smell registered in my brain.

"Goblin?"

Remo nodded. "And they are usually as mean as their name."

"Am I . . . ?"

Remo touched my hand. "No, you aren't like them. It would still linger in you even now. I smell nothing of the sort in you, and remember, I have tasted your blood. There is no goblin in you."

I didn't realize how tense I was until he spoke, dispelling my sudden fear that I was even more of a monster than I already believed.

Suddenly my childhood summers with my cousins made more sense. Samantha and Everett were the same age as Tad and I which meant we'd had to suffer through school with our cousins, as well as through family functions. They'd always been bigger and taken great pleasure in torturing us when the adults weren't looking.

There was a high-pitched screech from the kitchen, and I ran down the hallway without a thought, skidding to a stop at the white tile. Aunt Janice stood next to the sink as the sprayer from the hose shot her in the face. She spluttered and held her hands up as the water doused her good. Mom got the water turned off. "Those boys, they're at their tricks again."

Aunt Janice spat out a mouthful of water and grabbed a tea towel to wipe her face. "My Everett would never do such a thing. You'd think Tad would grow up by now."

Mom's jaw tightened, and then she saw me. "What are you doing here?"

Not hello, not even bothering to call me by name. "It's a family dinner, isn't it? And Dad invited me."

Aunt Janice turned and squinted at me. "You look different than the last time I saw you, Alena. Did you dye your hair?"

"Yes." I wasn't going to explain I'd been turned unless I had to.

I backed up, bumping into Remo. He put his hands on my arms, steadying me. "Are you going to introduce me?"

Oh dear. I nodded, manners taking over. "Of course. Aunt Janice, this is my"—I swallowed and forced the word out—"boyfriend, Remo." Oh my God, I felt like I was in high school again. That is, if I'd ever brought a boyfriend home from school. Which I most certainly had not. The only saving grace was that Aunt Janice was not a Firstamentalist.

Aunt Janice stared at Remo, and her throat bobbed as she squeaked out, "Hello."

He took her hand and gave it a quick shake before turning to my mother. He smiled at her, and I knew there was no way she could miss the tips of his fangs.

Mom raised a single eyebrow at him and then glanced at me. "Really? When you aren't even divorced yet? I raised you better, Alena."

Sucker punch to the gut. I should have expected her to say something like that, yet it still hurt.

Remo laughed and held a hand out to her anyway. "Well, you can't blame her, can you? The court system says she's dead, so technically she's widowed. Which makes her free and clear to do"—he glanced back and winked at me—"what she likes."

I flushed, heat racing all the way up my face to my hairline. Much hotter, and I'd be able to finish cooking dinner on my cheeks.

Mom crossed her arms and raised herself up as if she could somehow look down her nose at Remo, who stood at least a foot taller than she did. Probably more. Yet she still didn't seem intimidated by him.

"If she is a widow, then she should at least give herself time to mourn. I think that would be far more acceptable than prancing around in inappropriate clothes and dating men with piercings in their face like they are some sort of gang member."

Oh, God. That was the thing that bothered her the most about Remo? Maybe she hadn't seen his fangs after all.

I touched Remo on the hand. "Let's go find Tad and Dahlia."

"Alena, there isn't enough food for extra guests," Mom called after me. "You and Tad were not asked to bring a guest each."

Remo laughed, but there was a tired edge to it. "Do not worry, both Dahlia and I ate before we came. We were unsure of the hospitality."

Mom gasped, and my jaw dropped as I struggled not to splutter. Aunt Janice smirked and her shoulders shook. I managed to point a finger at her. "Not a word."

"Or what?" She put her hands on her ponderous hips.

"I'm not the only one with secretsss," I said, my tongue hovering a little too long over the last *s*.

Aunt Janice paled. "You wouldn't."

I snapped my fingers at her, turned, and walked away. I glanced at Remo as we walked down the hall. "I am so sorry."

"No need. You've met my brother. If you recall, he tried to kill you not once but twice. At least your mom isn't swinging a knife at my head."

I laughed before I thought better of it and then looked at Remo. He smiled, his eyes soft. "See? Your family isn't that bad after all."

That's what he thought. I wasn't so sure.

We were in the main living area, and anxiety cut through me as sharp as any kitchen knife. Something was wrong; I felt it in my belly like I'd eaten too many sweets.

"I think we should go," I said softly.

Remo tipped his head. "Are you sure?" Not "Why," not "We just got here," but was I sure.

I nodded. "Yeah, this was a bad idea."

I had no idea just how bad it was until the door swung open as we approached it. Like a weird twist in an even weirder, cold medicine–induced dream.

Roger stepped inside, Barbie right behind him. His eyes were on something in his hands, so he didn't see me right away. "Beatrice, I brought the papers for you and Clark to sign . . ." He trailed off as he raised his eyes and saw Remo and me. Roger was all but shoved into the house from behind, Barbie barreling in behind him.

"Oh, you were right, this is nice. You should have asked for more money for the house if they're living out this way." Barbie all but cooed the words as she stared around my parents' home.

Remo's hands were on my shoulders, and I didn't understand why at first. I leaned toward Roger as my breath hissed out of me.

"You . . . what are you doing here?" I snarled.

Roger held up a stack of papers as his face turned as white as a crème brûlée prior to being lit on fire. I kinda wanted to light him on fire and finish the job.

Everything happened at once. Dad, Tad, and Dahlia stepped into the room from the far side of the house. Yaya and Uncle Robert burst in from the back porch, Samantha and Everett trailing them. Remo and I stood in the center of the room, him holding me back from physically going after Roger. To say the room thickened with tension as everyone took me and Roger in would be like saying dry ice is a tad bit cold.

"I think you were right; it's time to go," Remo said, tugging me back to his side and slipping an arm around my shoulders.

"No, don't go, Alena," Yaya pleaded.

My mother glared. "This is a family dinner, and we are all going to sit down and act like a family. Roger, you're here, so why don't you stay?" Why the sudden change of heart? Auntie Janice, no doubt, if her smirk was any indication. Looking to cause trouble. I could just imagine her implying that Mom was less than hospitable. So now Mom would go over and above to prove her wrong.

Why was my family full of a bunch of crazies? How did I get so lucky?

"Are you out of your mind?" I couldn't help it. "You want me to sit down to dinner with my soon-to-be ex, his gold-digging girlfriend"—Barbie shrieked, but I ignored her—"and Dad's side of the family, who isn't exactly human? You have lost your mind, haven't you?"

Mom's face paled. "What do you mean 'isn't exactly human'?"

Tad groaned and then laughed. "Oh, here we go."

There was a soft knock on the door, and a masculine throat cleared. "Have we come at a bad time?"

I spun back to the door and looked past Roger. I was seeing things. I had to be. Because there was no way in heaven or hell that Theseus had shown up for dinner.

I didn't realize I'd said the words out loud until my mom answered me.

"Not Theseus, dear, this is Tim, a new neighbor. He has no family, so I thought it would be nice for him to join us for dinner, to make him feel welcome."

I closed my eyes and leaned into Remo. "We should have left."

"Maybe this will be fun," he murmured.

I blinked up at him. "Fun?"

He gave me a quick wink. "Just watch."

Oh dear Lord, what had I gotten myself into this time?

CHAPTER 15

The dinner table groaned under all the food that Mom, Aunt Janice, and Yaya brought out. Who were they kidding when Mom said there wasn't enough food for a couple of extra bodies? They could have fed three times the amount of people who were there.

Theseus sat at the head of the table, as far away from me as I could get. Beth was with him, her eyes never leaving his face as he spoke of his job as a private investigator.

"Tell us again how you saved Beth," Samantha cooed. I glared at my buxom, doe-eyed cousin. The entire meal had been Mom, Aunt Janice, Beth, Samantha, and Barbie all but falling over themselves to get close to Theseus. Unable to stand it any longer, I pushed my chair back and strode to the front door.

"Cupcakes are there." I pointed at the covered confections on the side table. "Good night, everyone."

Yaya stood as if to follow me, and I waved at her. "Enjoy your dinner, Yaya."

"Alena."

I cut her off as I slammed the door behind me.

Remo caught up to me on the steps and took my hand. My heart pounded like an off-rhythm mixer. I put a hand to my head. "What kind of game is he playing?"

He pulled me into his arms and held me tight. "One he is currently winning. Your family is falling for his lies. You have to be there if you want to show him you aren't to be trifled with."

"I know, but I don't know how." I closed my eyes and breathed him in, letting my anxiety float away for a moment.

Remo tipped my chin up so he could look in my eyes. "He's doing this to make you uncomfortable. To show you he can control your family without even trying. They aren't safe, even now."

I stared at him, my mind racing. "You think I can gain control? That I can play his game and win? All night he's been nothing but sweetness and gentlemanly behavior. It makes me want to vomit."

He tucked a strand of hair behind one of my ears, his fingers lingering at the side of my face. "At least in the conversation you could pull it off. You have insider info; use it against your family to make them leave. They may hate you for what you say now, but it will protect them in the long run. Especially if he sees you treat them poorly. They will not be as valuable to him if they are not valuable to you."

I leaned forward, pressing my head against his chest. "Thank you."

"It's what . . . friends are for." He kissed the top of my head, and it was as sweet as if he'd kissed my lips. Maybe because of the innocence behind the action. As if he truly had feelings for me. Everyone else was wrong; this was not how someone treated a person who was just a weapon for him to use.

I knew in my heart Remo cared for me. I just didn't know if it would be enough to see us through the whole star-crossed species divide we faced. Not to be melodramatic or anything, but it felt at times . . . impossible.

I squared my shoulders and headed back inside, one thought rolling through my mind. To treat everyone as if we, my family and I, were at war. Then again, it wasn't like I got on well with my Dad's side. I knew that Samantha and Everett were angry that our grandparents had left me everything. And that was just one tidbit of ammo I had.

Everyone looked up as I came back in. "Changed my mind."

Theseus all but glowed with pleasure. "So glad you decided to join us again. It wouldn't be the same without your beauty gracing us."

Beth glared at me with an intensity I felt on my skin like a slow burn. I took Remo's hand deliberately, weaving our fingers together. "Remo thought it was silly of me to walk out. Especially when he doesn't know much about the family yet. I mean, other than the fact that I was Grandma and Grandpa Austin's favorite."

Samantha and Everett jerked as if I'd slapped them both. I shrugged. "Don't act surprised, we all know they left everything to me because you two blow through money like it's water in your hands."

Jaws dropped as I sat back down and spread a napkin over my lap. No one argued with me, though. I lifted my eyes to see my mother staring at me with an intensity she reserved for the moments she couldn't yell. Like at a family dinner with guests. I smiled sweetly at her. "Would you pass the salt, please?" I waited until she had the salt partway across to me before I went on. "The souvlaki is seriously lacking in flavor. Did you get it from that cheap restaurant on Abigail Street again?"

Mom dropped the saltshaker, and I caught it in midair. Across from me, Tad gaped, and I gave him a wink. His lips twitched and he cleared his throat, giving me a slow nod. He was a quick study and jumped in with both feet.

"Everett, did you ever finish that degree at community college?" Tad asked, going into our favorite tag-team mode. A funny glow started in my chest.

We all knew Everett had been kicked out for hitting on all the female professors. Everett's lips tightened. "You know I didn't."

"Well, just checking. Staying at home, then?" Tad queried.

Everett stared at his food. "Why are you being a bastard?"

Mom sucked in a breath. "No swearing at this table, young man."

He shot a look at her. "I'm hardly young at twenty-eight."

"That's what I thought when I heard you didn't have a job," Tad said. The table sucked in a collective breath.

I nodded and took a bite of my now oversalted chicken. "Which begs the question as to why you are still at home exactly? Just milking Mom and Dad for all they are worth? That's not very"—here it was, now or never—"human of you."

Except that no one heard that bit. Aunt Janice must have seen it coming, since she stood, flipping her plate over her head to crash into the floor.

"I have never been so insulted in all my life! Your two children have truly turned into *monsters*, Beatrice."

I couldn't help laughing at that one. She had no idea.

At the same time, I decided to make sure Theseus didn't have designs on Sam. We might not have been close, but I couldn't let her just walk away with him. Which, by the way they were trading looks, was a distinct possibility.

"Samantha," I said in an attempt to get her attention. No response, she just kept ogling Theseus. Could he not see she was a goblin under all that makeup? His lips twisted as he looked at her so fast before going back to a smile that I almost missed it. Maybe he knew exactly what she was.

"Alena, pass out your dessert and then you can leave," Mom said, interrupting my attempt to get my cousin's attention. I stood without question, walked to the cupcakes, slid the lid off, and handed them around. Everyone except Yaya, Dahlia, and Remo took one. I lifted an eyebrow at Yaya. "Are you sure?"

"I ate too much sweets yesterday. My guts are killing me. But tell me what they are anyway." She smiled, a funny twinkle in her eye.

"Butter pecan, with a cream cheese icing," I said.

Barbie took a cupcake and fed it to Roger while they stared at each other. I hoped he choked on it. Dad gave me a look that said it all. This whole night was beyond disastrous.

When everyone was served, I sat back down and stared at the little cake in front of me. Remo pressed his thigh against mine. "You aren't done yet."

He was right, I had more ammo. Years of it.

I thumped my hand on the table hard enough to rattle everyone's cutlery. "SAMANTHA."

Okay, now everyone looked at me, including my glowering cousin as she chewed the last of her cupcake. I smiled at her. "Last time you were here you had been struggling to get over that infection you had. Did the doctors finally figure it out?"

Her face flared bright red, and for a split second I saw beneath the veneer of human skin. Wide green eyes and a huge mouth with rows and rows of teeth snarled at me. I had to fight the urge to pull back.

"What are you talking about?" she bit out. "I had no infection."

"Yeah, I remember," Tad said around a mouthful of food. "Something about a burning sensation when you pee."

"I didn't." She choked on the words.

Yaya's shoulders shook, and Samantha shot up from the table, her whole body quaking as she stood and glared at me. "I hate this family."

I spread my hands. "Join the club, Sam. We all hate this family. Roger hates it. You hate it. I hate it. My parents hate me. I mean, what else have we got?"

Yaya grabbed at Samantha and tugged her back into her seat. "Just sit."

Mom's eyes filled with tears, and for just a second I felt bad. But then I recalled exactly how she'd turned from me, all because I wasn't human anymore. Still her daughter, still Alena, but none of that mattered. I leaned back in my chair. "Right, Mom? Isn't that a true testament to being a Firstamentalist? Judge everyone until they feel as though they are as small as a helpless puppy being kicked for being born ugly?"

She stood up, her knuckles on the table, and opened her mouth, then stopped and pressed one hand to her stomach. A loud rumble emanated from her and she belched.

Uncle Robert licked his plate clean of icing as he took a second cupcake. "Tastes a bit like ouzo in this icing. You put liquor in it?"

I shot to my feet, horror flickering through me. Oh no. When Remo had met me at the bakery and kissed me, we'd banged into the table. The thump must have moved the two bowls of icing. I'd been so distracted by his presence I'd not noticed . . . "Oh no," I breathed.

"This is more than 'oh no,' Alena, this is the most atrocious thing you've ever done to this family. Worse than marrying Roger, even," my mother snapped.

"Hey!" Roger protested. "I was a great husband."

"Shut up, Roger!" we yelled in tandem. At least we agreed on one thing.

Mom pointed a finger at me, opened her mouth, then clutched her stomach and vomited to the side, narrowly missing Theseus. He leapt up and backward, knocking his chair over and dragging Beth with him. He couldn't, however, avoid the projectile vomit from Samantha on his other side. She nailed him right in the crotch, chunks of food running down his pants.

My eyes shot to Tad. He was green and gagging. "What the hell did you put in those cupcakes?" he managed to get out.

"Venom." I looked back to Theseus, who'd paled considerably as he swallowed over and over as if that would keep his dinner down.

"You bitch, you poisoned your own family to get at me?"

Everyone who wasn't currently heaving their dinner out in a stream looked at me. So, pretty much Dahlia, Remo, and Yaya. Now or never to convince Theseus my family had no place in my life or my heart. Anything to keep them safe. "What do they mean to me? If I can finish you off and them at the same time, all the better. A whole flock of birds with one single batch of cupcakes."

Cold, that was cold, and I knew it. But if it kept my family safe from Theseus . . . then it was worth it. Remo grabbed me and pulled me back as my dad heaved, the splatter just missing me. My dad reached for me, his eyes pleading. "Alena, don't be like this."

"It's the truth," I snapped, even as my heart broke with the grief in his green eyes. "Why would I care what happens to you? You all turned from me when I needed you most, left me in the hospital to die on my own and acted like I was a leper when I survived." I fought the tears because there was truth in my words.

Dad's shoulders shook, and I didn't think it was from the heaving. I had to look away to stop the tears from pooling. I had to make Theseus believe I truly didn't care.

Speaking of the hero, Theseus pulled a sword from I could only guess where and pointed it at me, the tip wavering as his arm trembled. "Time to end this—"

I held my breath and braced myself. This was it, the battle between Theseus and me. The one that would decide which one of us lived and which one died.

The sword wobbled and his lips twisted. "Monster."

"Summer's Eve," I retorted.

He frowned and Dahlia burst out laughing. "You mean douche?"

"Yes." I didn't take my eyes from Theseus. My experience with Achilles had taught me that heroes were not to be ignored. Beth rose to her feet beside him, vomit splatter down the front of her shirt, but that didn't slow her. "You won't be facing just him; I will not let you hurt him."

"Don't do this, Beth. This is what he wants." I pointed a finger at him. "He's trying to divide us."

"I love him," she said as her whole body heaved.

"Enough!" Theseus roared. "We—"

He bent at the waist and puked all over Samantha, who was down on her knees next to him.

Dahlia guffawed, then gagged. "Oh my God, this is brutal."

As all the people who'd eaten my cupcakes lost their supper and what looked like their last week of meals, the smell of vomit filled the room like some horrible incense. I couldn't take it, my own gorge rising. No need to add to the mess. I scrambled away, Remo, Dahlia, and Yaya right with me as I escaped out the front door to the sounds of retching, crying, and cursing behind us.

Hurrying, I all but ran to Remo's car.

"Alena, stop. Theseus is vulnerable right now," Remo said. I slid to a stop, my fingers wrapped around the door handle of the car.

"What are you saying?"

"Kill him while you have the chance," he said. "He's unable to defend himself. Beth is incapacitated. Though you may not have planned this, the timing is right."

I gripped the handle, the cold metal biting into my fingers. "I can't."

"Why not?" Dahlia asked. "He's right, this is the time to do it. End this before he uses the fennel on you."

Yaya touched the top of my hand, drawing my eyes down to her. "Dahlia and Remo are right. This is war; you can't turn away from this chance. You could save your life right here."

I closed my eyes, hesitating. Fighting with my desire to indeed end things with Theseus, but not like this. Not in cold blood. Not in front of my mom.

That was the real reason. A small part of me still wanted her acceptance. If she saw me kill in cold blood, there would be no hope, no convincing her ever that I wasn't a monster.

I shook my head. "No, I . . . I can't."

Remo sighed and walked to the driver's side, his footsteps fading. "I'll take you home. This will come back to haunt you, Alena. I know. I had my chance to deal with Santos, and I didn't."

I bit my lower lip, a warring mixture of anger and hurt flowing through me at his chastisement. "I have things I need to do. Without you."

His eyes met mine across the space between us, concern thick like molasses in them. "At least keep Dahlia close. Will you do that much?"

I glared at him, and the snake that seemed to live inside of me let out a low hiss. "None of you think I can take care of myself."

Dahlia snorted. "You're getting there, but you aren't there yet, my friend."

"Yaya, I'm taking the Granada." I strode away from Remo's car and headed straight toward the baby-blue clunker Yaya so dearly loved.

"Only if I get to come with you," she chirped. "Not like I'm going back in there"—she jerked a thumb toward the house—"before they get that place cleaned up. Gods, what a mess!"

Ernie floated up in the backseat of Remo's truck, a yawn stretching his face as he rolled the window down. "What did I miss? Anything?"

"Grab the cupcakes, Ernie." I amended, "Please." He disappeared for a split second, then was through the window with my package of wicked cupcakes. One for Merlin, and one for Zeus.

"Got it."

Yaya threw me the keys, and I caught them in midair as a thought rolled through me. Obviously the venom was strong enough to cause issues, but would it be enough to totally incapacitate Merlin? I had no idea how long the puke session was going to last in my parents' house, and I didn't really want to stick around to watch.

Remo and Dahlia pulled away in his car, and for just a split second I wished he'd stayed. That whole wanting him to want to stay, even though I'd told him to leave.

No, that was the old me. The one who wanted a man to help her feel like she was fulfilled. "Yaya, start it up. I left something inside."

I sprinted toward the house, took a deep breath at the door, and plunged back in. The stomach rolling smell of regurgitated food tickled at me even though I held my breath. I grabbed the container with the last few cupcakes and then backed away to the door. Aunt Janice glared at me from the floor where she lay. "Horrid beast," she whispered.

"Coming from a goblin, I'll take it as a compliment," I said, then gagged and backed away. Honey puffs, the smell was beyond atrocious.

Her eyes popped wide and her mouth opened as a slew of pale-green chunk-filled liquid flowed out.

I looked over to where Theseus and Beth had sat. Their places were empty and the back door was open. I put the cupcakes down and scooped up a knife from the table. Just a steak knife, nothing special. But if Theseus was down with the pukes, then it would do the job, and my mom wouldn't see. He'd barely been able to hold his sword up.

I made myself walk to the sliding glass door and out into the backyard. The part of me that was Drakaina approved; Remo was right. Take your enemies out while they were down to minimize casualties.

Out into the backyard I went, steak knife held tight in one hand. My ears strained, listening for the staccato beat that was Beth's heart. The shrieking cry of a bird shattered the night, and I jumped.

A metallic feather buried itself into the ground at my feet where I'd stood only a split second before. I backed up, staring into the sky. A whoosh of wings, another cry, and then the sound of her heart faded. And with her went my chance to end Theseus.

I'd blown it. I bent and scooped up the metallic feather. Gold and silver, it glittered even in the dim light. "You're an idiot." I wasn't 100 percent sure if I was talking to Beth or myself.

Probably both.

Nothing to do now but move on and hope I could get some answers out of Zeus.

CHAPTER 16

Yaya drove us in the direction of Zeus's place. Olympic Drive in the Highlands . . . if Smithy was being straight with us. "Are you sure this is where Zeus lives?" she asked.

I clutched at the container of vomit-inducing cupcakes. "It's where Hephaestus, I mean, Smithy, said he was."

"And he was helping you, why again?" There was a sly tone to her voice that I waved at with one hand, like batting away steam from a pot.

"Yaya, don't go there. The last thing I need is some ex–Greek god deciding to take an interest in me. I mean, look at where that's getting me with Hera. Look at where it got you when you messed around with Zeus. A curse, of all things! I have enough issues as it is."

"You mean like pissing off the rival vampire gang?" Ernie asked.

"That." I nodded.

"And not killing Theseus when you had the chance," Yaya pointed out.

I closed my eyes. "That."

"Ooh, and somehow getting on Aphrodite's bad side? Though that probably ties to Hephaestus, to be fair," Ernie added.

I groaned. "That."

"Anything else you want to tell me about?" Yaya glanced sideways at me, her puffy white hair barely peeking above the steering wheel.

"Keep your eyes on the road," I said. "You make me nervous as it is without looking away."

She snorted and waved a hand at me in a mocking imitation. "I've been driving longer than you've been alive."

"That doesn't exactly comfort me," I grumbled as I leaned back in my seat, the light-blue pleather creaking under me. Ernie shook his head.

"How does one little monster get into so much trouble?"

"Lucky, I guess. And I'm hardly little. Have you seen the size of my snake?" I mumbled.

They burst out laughing, and I shook my head as heat rushed through my face. "You know that's not what I meant."

"Still funny." Ernie chuckled. "Peeeenis humor always is."

"Ernie!" I burst out laughing, giggling uncontrollably.

Yaya reached over and tapped a hand on my leg. "Pay attention. Trouble, our family bloodlines are nothing but trouble. Started long before you, Lena Bean, so don't feel bad. If it weren't drawn to you, it would be drawn to Tad. Not that he seems to be staying out of trouble either. Does he really think things will end well dating a vampire?"

I crumpled in my seat thinking of Remo. Not that we were dating, not at all. But still, she had a point.

"You don't think Dahlia is nice?"

"Not that," Yaya said. "But they aren't known for being monogamous. It's not in their nature any more than being able to stand in the sun is. They are geared to flit between partners in order to satisfy their hunger."

The thought of Remo drinking from different women every night made every part of my body tense. No, it was not my place to judge him. I closed my eyes, but all I could see was Remo with someone who resembled Barbie. As if she would be solely responsible for taking all the men from my life.

"Yaya, what if I can't get this divorce?" I asked softly.

She stared straight ahead through the first rung of the steering wheel. She really needed a phone book or something to sit on.

"I guess you have a choice, then. Either you accept you are no longer attached to Roger and go on with your life. Or believe you are still married and wait for him to die before you move on with your life."

I gaped at her. "Wait for him to die?"

"Well, you could always speed that up. Give him a cupcake with a little more venom in it." She winked at me.

"Yaya!" I couldn't help the laughter that spilled out of me, any more than I could help the shock at Yaya semi-planning Roger's murder. The whole thing was ridiculous. Yet a small, wicked part of me thought maybe it wasn't a bad idea.

"Just a thought." She winked across at me again, then glared into the rearview mirror. "What is it with these idiots and their high beams? Do they not know it's rude to have them on when driving behind someone?"

Traffic was light on the highway with the late hour, so the high beams she spoke of shot through the back window loud and clear as they caught up to us, a little too reminiscent of my previous night for my liking.

The truck attached to the lights roared up behind us and honked its horn as the driver flicked on a second pair of lights attached to its roof as well.

"Oh . . . I got a bad feeling about this," Ernie said.

I twisted around in my seat, and my heart seized up like melted caramel over a block of ice. I recognized the grill on the truck all too well, and the splatter of branches and trees leftover from Dahlia and me running it into said trees.

Which also mean the driver had come to house number thirteen looking for me.

"Asshole," Yaya muttered. "Alena, tell me this isn't more of your trouble coming our way?"

The truck rammed us before I could answer, though I suppose being rear-ended was really answer enough. Ernie splatted into the windshield with a yelp, his limbs sprawling every which direction, wings bent underneath him.

"Yaya, take the next exit," I yelled as the truck behind us revved its engine in preparation for another ram. Yaya jerked the wheel hard at the last second, which sent me sprawling across the bench seat.

The truck roared up beside us, and from the seat I recognized Viking number two. "Oh dear, he doesn't look happy."

Ernie untangled himself. "Crap, Alena, this is really too much, and I was *looking* for excitement."

The Viking twisted his wheel with a grim snarl on his lips. I reached over to help Yaya with the Granada. I pulled her steering wheel to the right, bringing the Granada into contact with the oversized truck for all it was worth. The passenger-side window exploded.

"Insult him!" Yaya said. "If you can make him angry, he'll get sloppy."

I leaned over, took a deep breath, and yelled, "I think the size of your truck is overcompensation."

Yaya barked a laugh. "Call him names!"

"That's not really her forte, Flora." Ernie climbed onto the seat between us.

"I can do it." I leaned over to yell out the window. "Donkey butthole! Dingle nuts! Jerk face!"

The Viking frowned, seeming more confused than angry. Maybe that would be enough.

Yaya rolled down her window and lifted one tiny hand out, a single finger raised. I could easily imagine what she was doing.

"Your father was weak as a little girl, and he wore his hair in pig-tails!" she yelled.

The Viking's face hardened into a snarl, and he slammed the truck into us again. Apparently she'd touched a sore spot. Yaya gripped the steering wheel with both hands and wrestled with the car. I grabbed the steering wheel to help again, but I was too late; the car tires screeched as we were pushed off the road.

"Hang on, this is going to hurt!" Yaya yelped as we were shoved sideways along the road, dirt and gravel spitting all around us, tinging off the metal.

The truck pulled away only to hit us again.

I was thrown sideways and slammed into the passenger door, which decided at that moment to give way.

A scream hovered on my lips as I fell out of the door, barely stop-ping my tumble by grabbing the edge of the car. I dug my fingers in, the metal crumpled, and I hung on for all I was worth. Legs in and upper body hanging out, I stared up at the undercarriage of the big truck. I scrambled with my feet to hook them into something, anything, that would keep me from falling out and under the tires. Sure, I might sur-vive, but I didn't want to add being run over by a rather large truck to my most memorable memories.

All I could imagine was my head being squashed like an overripe watermelon, exploding under the weight and pressure of the truck. Though it was a guess, I suspected even I wouldn't survive my head exploding.

The Viking laughed; I could hear it over the engine roaring and the tires of the Granada screeching.

"I've got you, Lena," Ernie yelled, and a tiny pair of hands wrapped around my ankles. Maybe I could sit up in time to miss being hit.

Then again, maybe not.

The truck swerved toward me, and I had to let go of the side of the car or have my hand trapped. Though I suspected my hand being pinned was about to be the least of my worries. I hung there, on my back, Ernie sitting on my legs in the Granada, watching as the truck ripped toward me. I held my breath. Yaya was right, this was going to hurt.

The two vehicles slammed together . . . and no pain cut through me. I blinked and found myself staring up into the undercarriage of the truck.

"You are one lucky snake." Ernie yelled at me, and I didn't understand at first. Then I got it. The height difference between the two vehicles had created a pocket that had kept me from being flattened.

Mind you, I couldn't move; I was still pinned between the two vehicles.

"Got you now, bitch!" he roared. He was right; he'd pinned me good.

"Alena!" Yaya yelled.

"I'm on it!" I yelled back, not knowing if she could hear me. Or if I had this at all.

I reached up and grabbed whatever bits and pieces I could in the undercarriage and started yanking at a pace akin to hand-whipping cream. Faster and faster I pulled pipes and plastic off the undercarriage of the truck until the engine above me choked and spluttered. Oil and fuel sprayed around me, the fumes gagging me.

The truck jerked, and the two vehicles unhooked, drifting apart. I sat up, my butt on the edge of the passenger seat. I looked over my shoulder, my hair streaming around my face, making it difficult to see. Making me wonder if what I was seeing was what I was seeing.

Remo's car shot up between our slowing Granada and the truck, the slick muscle car moving like a bat out of hell.

"Oh dear, this isn't going to go well for the Viking." I looked back at Yaya. "Are you okay?"

"Yes, now go kick his ass, he wrecked my car!" She lifted a fisted hand and shook it in his general direction.

The Granada bumped into a cement barrier and came to a stop. I jumped out and ran across the road. We'd slid all the way down the off-ramp and were on a quiet side road. Kinda. Cars had stopped in either direction, their headlights streaming through the dark and lighting up the scene like some medieval arena. Humans crowded close, whispers of "What happened?" and "Is everyone all right?" floating on the air.

Remo was already out of his car and had pulled the Viking out. "Sven, I warned you."

Sven. Well at least I was close with the nationality. I shook my head and kept moving. Dahlia got out of Remo's car and grabbed me before I could get closer.

"Don't. He has to do this, or he'll look weak," she said.

"Has to do what?"

I looked past her.

The two vampires circled around one another, like two large cats hunched and prepped to leap. Leap they did, and at the same time, their bodies slammed into one another. They hit so hard and fast, their limbs were a blur of movement. They smashed into the ground, illuminated by the headlights. The humans around us drew near, as did the sounds of sirens. "Poopsicles, Remo can't be taken in again," I said. Maybe it was selfish. Okay, it totally was. I didn't want to think he'd be tossed into jail when it was obvious even to a newbie like me that my fight with Theseus was coming and I was going to need all the help I could get, no matter how badly I wanted to prove I could do things on my own.

Then there was the even more pressing issue of Santos and his gang, seeing as that was more of Remo's arena.

Dahlia nodded. "But he *has* to do this. Believe me, Alena. This isn't a choice at this point." Almost the same words as before. Remo had to fight Sven? Maybe it was a vampire thing, a show of force. I was close in my musing, but I had no idea how close.

"Remo, cops are coming. Hurry it up," Dahlia shouted.

He grunted, or I think he grunted, and he stood up. He had Sven's neck gripped in his left hand, and he put his right hand on top of it. Sven's red beard covered Remo's hands.

Sven's eyes bugged out, and it looked like he tried to shake his head, his feet kicked out, and then his whole body jerked once, stiffened, jerked again, and then was still.

The Viking's head rolled to one side as Remo flipped Sven's body in the other direction.

Dahlia sucked in a sharp breath. "Shit, I didn't think that was possible."

Possible? The world went fuzzy, and for the first time I saw how deadly Remo truly was. He'd ripped another vampire's head off. Without any compunction, with what looked like very little effort. The fight with Achilles came back to me, how Remo had been trying to get his hands around the hero's neck, how Achilles kept dodging him. Remo had been trying to rip Achilles's head off.

My stomach heaved, and I took a step back, swallowing hard, but I couldn't take my eyes from the scene in front of me. Remo had tossed the head across the road, backlit by vehicles. He strode toward me.

I recoiled from him, taking several steps back before I could stop my feet. My heart raced, and all I could think was that this was the man I'd kissed, that I'd wanted to kiss. This man I saw when I closed my eyes to sleep at night had just removed another man's head without so much as a "How do you do?"

No. No. That wasn't fair. This was vampire turf wars, and they were bound to be violent and fatal.

My mind was a jumble of thoughts and emotions I couldn't keep track of, bouncing from horror to straight-out anger. On one hand, I was grateful he'd come, that he'd stood up for me. On the other hand, it was the same thing again. Like I couldn't take care of myself. And while things might not have been going well, I was managing. I could have handled Sven. I was sure of it.

"Alena, are you all right?" Remo took my hand and turned my arm over. My skin had been peeled back at some point, and my scales glittered through in the garish light.

I pulled away from him. "Yeah, I'm good. Thanks." I turned away and strode back toward the beaten-up Granada, doing my best to banish the image of Remo yanking off Sven's head. I had killed people, other monsters. It wasn't fair of me to judge Remo for protecting me in the same way. "Yaya, will the car start?"

Her eyes looked past my shoulder, and I made myself keep walking. Away from him. "Yaya?"

She cleared her throat. "We're stuck on the median."

Without thinking, I made my way around to the other side of the car. In a flash, Remo and Dahlia were there with me. Before I could ask, they pushed the car off the median and back onto the road. I frowned, said nothing. Again. As if I couldn't have lifted it on my own; I knew in every fiber of my being I could have.

Dahlia grabbed my arm. "Aren't you going to thank us?"

The snake in me uncoiled, and I knew it was seconds from bursting free. "Let go of me."

She dropped my arm as if I were a hot pan fresh out of the oven. "What is wrong with you?"

I walked away, my throat tight and the words trapped. Mostly because I didn't want to say things that I would regret later. Words that would hurt or even destroy friendships. "Please don't follow me" was all I managed to say.

Dahlia made a move, and from the corner of my eye I saw Remo grab her. "No, we've overstepped. I've overstepped. Let her go. She'll get ahold of us if she needs to."

Gratitude flowed through me, and I managed to give him a smile. I mouthed, *Thank you*, and he gave me a wink.

Yaya started the car, and we were once more away, headed to find Zeus whether he wanted to be found or not.

"What are you all teary eyed about?" Ernie flicked a tear from my cheek. Yaya glanced at me and nodded. She understood. Remo understood. I had to find ways to make it as a monster, to find my own path without other people trying to save me at every turn. I needed to be able to stand on my own two feet, tail, whatever. That would be the only way I'd ever truly learn to survive in my new reality.

I buckled my seat belt and tucked my chin to my chest. "I don't want to try and explain right now."

Ernie dropped back to the seat between us, cupcake platter firmly held between his hands. How it had managed to stay in one piece was beyond me.

"Well, fine. But are we still going to Zeus now?" He pointed at the cupcakes.

I nodded. "Yeah, more than ever I'm going to get to the bottom of this."

"You going to question him between bouts of puke?" Yaya's eyes sparkled, like she wanted to see Zeus green and on his knees.

I clutched at my seat belt as the cold air swirled in around us. "Something like that."

Really, I was hoping he would answer my questions without the cupcake. But I'd dealt with Zeus, and I knew how he was. An avoider of epic Greek proportions.

CHAPTER 17

Before we went all the way out to Olympic Drive in the Highlands, I pulled over and used Yaya's cell phone to call the Blue Box Store Zeus worked at. I kept the phone on speaker. "Store manager, please," I said.

"He's not available, would you like to leave a voice message?" a raspy voice answered.

Yaya nodded.

I cleared my throat. "Yes, I'd like to leave a message."

"Hold, please, I'll forward you to his voice mail."

I waited, the line buzzed and clicked, then an automated voice came on.

"You have reached the voice mail of—"

"Zeus Olympia," Zeus said, then back to the automated voice.

"The voice mail box for this party is full."

It clicked off, and I handed the phone back to Yaya. She cursed the phone like somehow it was the cell phone's fault. I had to agree; there was nothing more irritating than trying to leave a message for someone only to be told their voice mail was full. Who didn't check their messages at least once a day?

Psychos, that's who. All that meant was I really had no choice; we were off to Zeus's abode.

Number one (yes, Zeus's house was number one) Olympic Drive was a mansion. I mean, like a literal mansion built into a hillside, set way apart from any other houses. The fence was fifteen feet high, the gate solid, and the only reason I knew it was the right place was the seal in the middle of the gate with an oversized lightning bolt through it.

"Subtle," I mumbled under my breath.

Yaya leaned over and pushed the intercom button. It buzzed and clicked before a high-pitched, whispery voice floated through. "Hello, are you here for the party?"

"Of course we are, you idiot. We brought the dessert," Yaya snapped.

"Ohhh! Dessert! I can't wait!" The high-pitched voice cooed and giggled. I couldn't decide if it was male or female. I glanced at Ernie, and he shrugged as if he didn't know either. More like it didn't matter, and I had to agree. If it wasn't Zeus, it didn't matter.

The gate in front of us slowly slid inward, and Yaya drove us through. Okay, the Granada limped through, if I was being honest, but at least it was still moving.

"That was far easier than I thought it was going to be," I said.

Ernie tapped on the dashboard, leaning forward on his elbows. "Yeah, that is making me nervous. If he's just letting people in, either this is a monstrous big party or he's expecting you."

"Why would either of those be bad?" I asked.

Yaya and Ernie exchanged a glance I didn't like. "A *monstrous* party, Alena," Ernie repeated.

"Oh dear. You mean, like me?"

Ernie nodded. "And possibly some of the other pantheon. They all have their pets they bring with them for the entertainment."

I shrunk in my seat. "You mean like . . . Theseus and Beth could be here?" As much as I knew it was coming, I didn't want to face him. Not yet.

Ernie shrugged and tugged on one wing, straightening the feathers. "Possible, but I mean, more like your new boyfriend Smithy, and maybe his wife?"

Spiked snickerdoodles, this was bad. "Then we'll just sneak in. Ernie, you can scout it out, right?"

"Too late," Yaya said. "They've seen us."

We were being waved up to a large covered area right in front of the doors. I looked up at the twisted white marble columns that held the roof, which was easily thirty feet high. I hoped it wasn't a sign of what kind of monsters would be waiting for us. I mean, I was big when I shifted, but there was no reason to believe that all the monsters were like me in size. I hoped.

I grabbed the container of cupcakes and did a quick count. I had sixteen left. I pointed at the two separate ones I'd originally done up for Merlin and Zeus. "Hide them under the seat, Ernie."

He saluted me, and I took the fourteen remaining cupcakes with me.

"You aren't really going to bring them all, are you?" Ernie whispered.

"Yaya told them we were bringing dessert. What do you want me to do?"

We stepped out of the broken-down car. I found myself looking into the most gorgeous brown eyes I'd ever seen.

"Hello."

My mouth dropped and no sound came out. Okay, a squeak came out.

Ernie floated around so I could see him behind the youth. "This is Narcissus. Good looking, ain't he?"

I blushed and Narcissus smiled. "I can take these cupcakes for you."

I tightened my hold on the container. "No, no, I'll personally deliver them to Zeus."

"He's not here," Narcissus said, a slight frown only heightening that perfect beauty. Good grief, I couldn't stop staring.

I made myself look over his shoulder so I only really saw half his face and Ernie's wide grin. It helped, but only a little. "I was told he was at home, and so I made this dessert to his specifications."

Narcissus shrugged. "He's not here. He opened his house up for the party and then left. Said he had business he had to handle. Actually, you only missed him by ten minutes."

I looked at Yaya. She frowned and shook her head. "If he had a police scanner, he would have heard all about the wreck. It's on the only road that leads here."

In other words, Zeus had run the second he'd realized I was headed his way. Was he scared of me? Or was he just avoiding the fact that I would hold him responsible? I was betting on the latter. What a jerk face.

My chest tightened with a sudden bout of anxiety I couldn't tamp down. What the heck did I do now? If he had business, he could be anywhere. "Is Hermes here?"

"Last I saw, he was out by the pool with the rest of the guests. He was given the day off."

"Who gave him the day off?" Ernie swept between me and Narcissus.

"Hera," the young man said.

I took several steps back, the youth's beauty no longer dazzling me. "Is . . . Hera here?"

"Oh, goddess no! There's only a few gods here. Hephaestus, Hermes, and Achilles."

"Achilles isn't a god," I pointed out, even as I realized that him being here wasn't any better, really, than Theseus.

Ernie swept around to me. "Hey, Narcy, back off a second."

Narcissus did as he was asked, a sweet smile plastered on his face. Ernie grabbed my cheeks and turned me to him.

"Look, this is your chance."

"Chance for what? I was hoping to get info on Theseus from Zeus. Like a weakness I could exploit, you know, his Achilles' heel?"

"Ha-ha." Ernie rolled his eyes. "But he isn't here. So use your charms on Hephaestus and get him to spill about Theseus."

"But I don't want to use my charms on him," I squeaked out. "That is the last thing I want to do. You said it yourself that Aphrodite is upset—"

"That is an understatement, but she's already upset. You might as well make the upset worth it." His eyes were serious, no longer teasing.

"You really think encouraging his interest is a good idea?" I grabbed Ernie's hands and pulled him so we were nose to nose. "I do not need more Greek goddesses trying to remove my head from my shoulders. I'm deep enough in pig slop as it is."

Ernie pressed his nose to mine. "Here's the thing. Theseus worked for Hephaestus for years, learning the craft of blacksmithing. If anyone can give up the goods on your rival, it's going to be him. Things happen for a reason, Alena. Take this and run with it."

I let him go, my mind racing with possibilities. "Yaya, what do you think?"

She grabbed my hand and marched us forward. "I think you're overdressed for the occasion."

Narcissus's eyes widened as Yaya dragged me forward. She waved a free hand at him. "Flora, priestess of Zeus, we need to get cleaned up."

He bowed. "I didn't realize. You've aged since I saw you last, Flora."

She swatted him on the butt as we hurried past him into the house. "That's enough out of you, boy."

We stepped into the mansion, me gripping the cupcakes and Yaya gripping me. Ernie floated at my shoulder. "I think the extra clothes are this way."

"Wait, extra clothes?"

"Well, with all the orgies he has, there's always clothing left behind," Ernie said as though he were telling me about the weather.

"Good grief, you want me to wear something that someone else cast off in the middle of an orgy?" I gripped the cupcake holder hard enough that the plastic creaked. I made myself ease off. "Why can't I just talk to Hephaestus and ask him my questions?"

"Because you want him so stunned by your beauty he doesn't realize what secrets he's giving up," Yaya said. She pulled me up the double-wide staircase. At the top she turned to the left. As if she knew where she was going.

"Yaya, when were you here last?"

She didn't turn around. "After the Blue Box Store incident. I came to talk to Zeus, to try and get him to help you with Hera. He gave me the grand tour."

Ernie snickered. "Is that so? The *grandma* tour?"

Yaya whipped around and smacked him on the cheek so fast I was shocked.

Ernie squawked and flew up to the ceiling. Yaya pointed a finger at him. "Don't you imply that I slept with Zeus. Bad enough I was a fool as a young priestess. I'm not that child anymore."

I kept my mouth shut. Tad had been smacked more than once for mouthing off at Yaya, and I'd seen her handprint on his cheek. She had an arm on her. Ernie stared with big eyes.

"Won't happen again." He floated down, but not within reach.

"Here, this room." She pushed a door on our right open and flicked on a light. The room lit up, revealing a glittering array of different materials and even some jewelry. I put the cupcakes down. "Put this on." She tossed me something that looked like an oversized thong. The outfit, if that's what it was, was all strings with the odd patch of material holding it together.

"Yaya, you're out of your mind if you think I'm going to wear this." I flung it back at her.

She caught it, turned it around, and held it up. "It's a bathing suit, Alena. A stringy, flimsy one, but you need a bathing suit for a pool party. And you want Hephaestus blinded. That much is true."

Reluctantly, I held up the supposed bathing suit. "Ernie, go see who is here."

He saluted me and sped out of the room. I shut the door, stripped, and slid the bathing suit on. The patches of material covered, barely, my breasts and bottom. The strings of material attaching the three small pieces were hardly what I'd call coverage.

"Yaya, I feel like a streetwalker." And there it was. I didn't want to use whatever beauty I had to force people to do what I wanted. I didn't want my siren abilities to come into play, not with someone I was beginning to think of as a friend.

I stripped the bathing suit off and put my own clothes back on. "I'm doing this my way, Yaya. No matter what happens."

A soft smile touched her lips. "All right, my girl. All right."

I paused, a thought hitting me hard. "Wait, Yaya, why did you ask if I was sure this was where Zeus lived when you've been here? And why didn't you tell me?"

Her eyes closed and a shudder rippled through her. "I am his priestess, Alena. Even now. And he forbade me from telling you anything about his whereabouts."

"Yaya, that's awful that he can control you like that," I whispered, wanting nothing more than to cut the ties between her and Zeus.

"It's been my life for many years, Alena. I will be all right." She winked at me, and a smile crossed her face. "Go on now, we don't have a lot of time to get this done. It feels like the timer is about to go off on our oven."

I knew what she meant. The feeling that I raced some unseen opponent pushed me. I scooped up the cupcakes and hurried back down the way we'd come, Yaya trailing me now. The sound of laughter and splashing drew me through the house. I tried not to freak out, tried not to think about how badly this could go. But what else did I have? Theseus was playing a game that I wasn't sure I could match. He was slowly taking my friends and pitting them against me in a chess match where I couldn't see all the pieces. He had Beth and Sandy. It was apparent he was working with Santos, so it stood to reason Theseus was behind the vampire attacks on me. Not to mention the fennel oil that he'd had made specially for me and that was no doubt in his stupid hands even now. There wasn't a doubt in my mind that Beth had given the oil back to him.

I stepped through a pair of French doors and into the backyard. Though "backyard" might have been the wrong descriptor. The pool was Olympic size, if a rather irregular shape, and all around it were lounges with different species in them. I saw satyrs, nymphs, flitting fairies that dodged between hands swatting at them, more than a few deer that were talking, and a pair of werewolves in the nude and getting rather amorous, and then there were some that looked like your average people in bathing suits, though I doubted they were just humans. Another sweep of the area showed me that the majority of the attendants were nude, actually. Or at least topless. I shouldn't have been surprised.

Flowering trees, bushes, and exotic plants scented the warm air . . . warm? I drew a breath in, filling my lungs. The air was warm enough that I'd have said it was high summer and not the end of January. A fountain of Zeus stood over the pool, the water flowing from his . . . I blushed and looked at Yaya. "Who would want to play in a pool that was being filled from that?"

She laughed and shook her head. "Oh, Alena. You make me smile. Go on now. Hephaestus has seen you." She gave me a gentle push, and I stumbled going from the stone patio to the lush grass.

A big pair of hands caught me before I could go to my knees. I looked up, and Smithy looked down. The ice in his eyes wasn't as severe as I'd seen it. Though he didn't look happy to see me there.

"Alena."

"Smithy." I pulled myself up and away from him. "I was hoping to talk to Zeus, but he seems to be missing."

"Probably at the store."

I shook my head. "No, he's taken a leave. Pretty much as soon as he knew I was headed this way."

His eyebrows shot up, and it was then I noticed he was wearing nothing but a pair of swim trunks. What drew my eye, though, was the large scar that ran down his right leg, from midthigh to midcalf. It was raised as though the scarring was relatively new.

"Thanks to Zeus." His hand brushed the top of the scar. "And thanks to medical advances, it rarely bothers me now."

I nodded and looked up and to the right, over his shoulder, but it was too late. The image of a smooth chest with the barest dusting of hair that trailed between a six-pack into the top of his shorts was burned in my mind. Though I didn't feel anything for him, I wasn't blind or immune to the sight of a well-chiseled body.

"What do you need Zeus for?" he asked, tipping his head so he was within my line of vision again. I kept my eyes on his, trying to ignore the fact that he was pretty much naked. Maybe I'd been wrong, maybe I should have worn the bathing suit.

I closed my eyes and drew in a breath, but that didn't help. Eyes closed, I could still too easily see his body, and the deep breath drew his unique scent into my mouth: basil and mint. I fought not to roll the smells around my tongue.

"I am trying to get information on Theseus. I don't suppose"—I opened my eyes finally—"you could help me?"

His blue eyes narrowed. "No offer?"

"What?"

"You aren't going to offer yourself to me in exchange? I see you didn't even bother to dress yourself for seduction." He brushed a hand over the bottom edge of my shirt, which drew my eyes down. And once more I was staring at his waistline. I squeaked and tipped my head back so I stared at the sky.

"Look, I don't have anything to offer you. Even if I wasn't married, I'm not that kind of girl. I thought we were friends. I thought . . . I thought you would help me. I guess not." I shoved the cupcakes at him. "Here. Enjoy." I turned and took a step, but a hand settled on my forearm.

"Stop. I'll tell you what I can."

I spun around, and Smithy was already walking away, the cupcake container in one hand. "Really?"

"Yes."

That was him, all straight to the point. I hurried after him, stepping around the lounging people and creatures that were sprawled at the water's edge. A woman popped up out of the pool, huge blue eyes blinking up at me, and a tail flipping out behind her. A mermaid. I wondered if she was one of the ones Merlin had turned. It had been an option for me.

I shook my head and almost stumbled on a blond satyr. "Sorry . . . Damara?"

The healer turned my way, a pair of sunglasses covering her strange eyes. "Alena, I wondered if you'd come." She wasn't wearing much, really just a pair of bikini bottoms, her furred goat legs stretched out to one side of her, and nothing else. Her two boyfriends, Tim and Gavin, were wearing less than her and obviously rather happy about it. I flushed and kept my eyes on hers. "Thanks again for the other day."

She gave me two thumbs up. "Anytime, Alena. You know that."

Smithy cleared his throat, and I hurried after him, waving back at Damara.

He led me to the far side of the pool, where a small covering was set up, like a sheik's tent, open on only one side. He stepped into the shadows, and I glanced back, looking for Yaya. She wasn't even watching me. She'd found a young faun and was chatting away with him as she dangled her feet in the water.

"I think she misses the life," Smithy said, drawing my attention back to him. I made myself step under the covering.

"Why would you say that?"

He shook his head, a half smile twisting his lips. "Because she seems determined to find a way to put you in the middle of things with Zeus and Hera. Think about it, before the changes in the world, she was a priestess of the most powerful god around. Lightning and thunder and controlling the world. She was one of his last to leave his side all those years ago. He sent her away, actually, if I recall. She didn't go willingly."

I sat on a footstool, unable to wipe the frown from my face. "She's human. But you say all that like she's been around for longer than normal."

Smithy laughed and shook his head. "You don't know much about your family, do you?"

A chill swept through me. "No, I don't."

He leaned forward, muscles bunching, and I realized he was doing it on purpose. Trying to draw me in the way Yaya had wanted me to do to him.

That was all it took for me to steel myself against the lovely view. "Tell me what you know about her. About my family. About Theseus."

He raised an eyebrow. "Sounds like you wanted to say 'or else' at the end of that sentence."

I raised an eyebrow right back at him. "Or else I'll tell your wife you were showing skin at the pool party."

He barked a laugh. "You think she'll care?"

"She will if I tell her you were throwing yourself at all the women."
His smile fell. "That's dirty pool."

I shrugged. "Apparently it's all you and the other pantheon know. I came in here, thinking I was talking to a friend, and you just jump all over the fact that you're half naked and try to use it against me."

"I can't help it if you like what you see." His eyes shot to mine, and I glared at him.

"I am otherwise attached." I bit the words out.

"Your husband doesn't think so. You don't think so."

I drew myself up, feeling the shift of power, feeling the shift of everything I believed shimmer in front of me. "I meant to Remo."

CHAPTER 18

Smithy's eyebrows shot up, and he leaned back in his chair. "To the vampire? I never would have pegged you for liking the bad boys, Alena. That's disappointing, I'd thought better of you."

His disapproval shouldn't have stung, but old habits died hard. I made myself push through the sudden shame and ask my questions.

"You were going to tell me about my grandmother and Theseus. Are you going to help me, or should I just go?"

He tapped a finger on the top of the cupcake container, his eyes thoughtful. "Your grandmother is human. But Zeus favored her with a longer than normal life. That doesn't make her supernatural." Smithy leaned back on a lounger and stretched his legs out in front of him. A tiny dryad covered in green leaves and blooming white flowers stepped into the hut carrying a platter of drinks. Smithy took one and motioned for me to do the same.

"Juice?" I asked, and the dryad nodded, a flower drifting from her face to land in one of the cups.

"Of course."

She hurried away, and I took a sip of the juice. It was sweet, but I couldn't peg the flavor, which was unusual for me. I took another sip and rolled it around my mouth before going on with my questions.

"So, how long lived?"

"Oh, longer than you might imagine. I'd say at least a few hundred years. Probably more." He took a big gulp from his cup.

My jaw unhinged, and that is saying something. Smithy's eyes widened and he looked away. "Keep forgetting about that part of you."

I snapped my mouth shut. "Okay, so what do you know about my dad?"

"Your father?" He seemed surprised by the question. "I don't know anything about him."

"He's a supernatural," I murmured. "I've been trying to find out what kind."

"Why?"

I shrugged. "It seems important."

Smithy sighed. "Probably not. He might not even realize he's supernatural. The bloodlines can be thin and still affect the children. That's the way it goes."

"Right." I sighed. "And Theseus? Ernie said he worked with you for a time."

He scrubbed a hand over his face. "Yeah, he did. It was a favor to one of his fathers, Poseidon."

I blinked several times, not sure I'd heard right. "*One* of his fathers?"

"Yeah, the other he's not so proud of. The tales make it sound like Aegeus was this great king, but he was really something of a tool. A goat man who was horny as hell but couldn't get it up. He needed an heir, at least in his mind, and convinced Poseidon to help him."

I tipped my drink and gulped back a mouthful. The image of a goat man, like Damara's two boyfriends, not being able to get it up was amusing. I giggled and then slapped a hand over my mouth. "What kind of juice again?"

Smithy arched an eyebrow. "Nectar of the gods."

"That doesn't tell me much, smarty-pants," I slurred out. Slurred. Oh, that was not going to be good. But why, again? I tipped the cup back and emptied it. "That's gooooood."

Smithy rolled his eyes. "Cheap drunk, eh? Listen to me. Theseus is not going to be easy to kill. He doesn't have an obvious weakness like Achilles. He's all about control, about learning his prey and then going after it, in this case you, with a sudden thrust that comes from a direction you won't expect."

"Thrust." I giggled again, and Smithy leaned forward and grabbed my arms.

"Pay attention, I won't say this again. He wasn't killed by a monster, he just faded away from mankind, and that was how he was 'killed.' He faded like so many of the minor gods. He needs people to believe in him, to support him to keep him powerful."

"So." I pursed my lips and leaned toward him so we were close enough to kiss. Not that I wanted to, but by the way his gaze dipped, he was thinking about it. "There is nothing you can tell me that will actually help, then?"

"He's stealing your friends," he murmured, "and he will make you fight them first. Make you kill them to protect yourself, and then he will take you out. He knows your weakness, Alena. He knows you care too much. You aren't like the other monsters. You aren't selfish like them."

I wobbled in my seat, and he helped steady me. I rolled my head forward until it rested on his shoulder. "I think I'm going to be sick."

A screech from behind us snapped along my spine, shooting me upright, even while I swayed and the world wobbled. I twisted my head around. At the far side of the pool, a woman wearing a bright-white strappy bikini that looked a lot like the one I'd tried on stared at us. A part of my brain screamed that I was in trouble. Like serious trouble, because I recognized her. Or the Drakaina in me did anyway. The long, curling strawberry-blond hair, the pristine blue-green eyes, the perfect body, high cheekbones, lush lips, great big boobies that defied gravity, all could belong to only one woman.

Aphrodite.

"I can see why you married her," I stage-whispered. I mean, I was trying to whisper, but it was really loud. "I mean, she is super-duper hot."

"Shit," Smithy grunted, letting go of me as if I'd flashed my fangs at him.

I wobbled and fell to the ground of the hut, giggling.

I lay there and stared up at the ceiling of the hut. "I think she's mad at you, Smithy."

Those blue-green eyes were suddenly looking down at me. "I'm going to kill you, Drakaina."

"Ohh, wait. That's what Achilles said. You should ask him how that worked out. I think he's here somewhere. You've got great boobs, by the way. From here, it's a good look on you." I laughed up at her, unable to stop the bubbling mirth. I'd never been drunk before, was this really how it happened? I felt great. As if I were on top of the world, when I should have been freaking out.

Smithy's hands were on his wife, and they were arguing as he tried to push her away from me. "She's one of the inmates I have to deal with."

"Looked like far more than that to me. She was holding on to you!" she screamed, and I cringed.

"Too loud!" I grumbled, rolling to my feet. "And I was just bringing dessert." The thought of Aphrodite in her perfect body eating one of my cupcakes made me giggle again. "You should eat several, you could stand to gain a few pounds, you're too skinny."

She gasped, Smithy groaned, and I crawled out of the hut. The water looked so lovely I didn't even think about it, I just slid over the edge of the pool as the sounds of screaming and yelling continued on the surface side of the water, now muffled.

Someone tugged on my hand, and I opened my eyes. The mermaid smiled at me, row upon row of sharklike teeth flashing at me. I wasn't afraid, though. I just smiled back, my fangs dropping down. Bubbles rolled up out of her mouth, and I knew she was laughing. I clasped her hand with my own, and she swam with me across the length of the pool.

With a shove, she heaved me out of the water and onto the deck at my yaya's feet.

"Time to go, Alena. I think you've done enough here today."

"Enjoy the cupcakes!" I yelled over my shoulder. The crowd gave a tiny cheer, and Achilles waved and blew me a kiss. I waved back and even blew him a kiss back like we were grand friends. Like he hadn't tried to kill Tad and I hadn't cut his legs.

With Ernie on one side of me and Yaya on the other, I wobbled out through the house, dripping water and giggling. Narcissus met us at the door. "I hope you enjoyed your visit."

"Oh, totally! Oh my God, you are so hot." I slapped his ass the way Yaya had, and he yelped, his eyes bugging wide.

I fell into the car—it wasn't like there was a door to open anymore anyway—and strapped myself in.

Ernie and Yaya were talking, their voices flowing over me in a smooth dialogue that sounded like Chinese to me.

"Merlin's house. I want to give him a cupcake!" I yelled at the top of my lungs.

"Holy shit, she's drunk as a skunk," Ernie said. "Yes. We're going there right now."

"Good." I flopped my head back and closed my eyes. I must have slept, because what felt like seconds later we were stopping again.

"Here we are," Yaya said. "Alena. Are you feeling better?"

I swallowed once and ran my tongue around the inside of my mouth. "Feels like I've got cotton candy stuck to the inside of my mouth."

"Yes, but how is your thinking? Are you going to break into giggles when someone says 'penis'?" she asked.

I stared at her, shocked. "Why would Merlin say 'penis' exactly?"

She rolled her eyes. "Look, I wanted to see how drunk you were. The nectar is working out of your system, so go ahead. Take him his cupcake."

I scooped up the final venom cupcakes, undid my seat belt, and stumbled out of the car. My clothes were still damp, my hair was a mess, and I could feel the alcohol on my breath, hot and uncomfortable.

I hurried up the steps to Merlin's house. He'd fixed the door I'd kicked in and replaced it with one made of steel. I had a feeling it wouldn't stop me if I really wanted in. I rapped my knuckles on the door twice.

"Who is it?" came a muffled reply.

"Alena. I want to talk. I want to apologize."

The door opened and Merlin stood there, wearing nothing but a pair of black silk pajama pants. His hair was slicked back as always, and his eyes roved over me slowly.

What was it with all these shirtless dudes? I mean, if I was going to see anyone shirtless, I wanted it to be Remo. Not Merlin. Not Smithy (no matter how nice he might have looked).

"You came to apologize at five in the morning?"

"I don't sleep much when I have someone trying to kill me."

He snorted and made a motion with one hand for me to come in. I stepped through the doorway, surprised to see that the main room was empty. Every time I'd gone to see him, there had been a gaggle of Super Dupers playing poker or hanging out with him.

"Why are you really here, Alena?"

I stopped next to the table and set the cupcake down. "I heard a rumor you were going to work for my husband as a lawyer tomorrow; I guess that's today, now," I said. "I'm hoping that's wrong. That you wouldn't . . ."

He smiled at me. "He's paying me very well, Alena. You understand it's not personal."

I clenched my hands, fighting the urge to reach over and strangle him. "I would think you'd want me to win. To gain rights back for all Super Dupers."

He laughed and slid into a chair. "You don't understand, and I don't expect you to. You still see everything as black and white. Most of the world does. Us against them, but the truth is, Alena, they need us to be dangerous. They and we both need them to be prey. I want the Wall down, but other than that, I don't want things to change. Fear works in my favor, you see." He pulled the lid off the cupcake container and swiped a finger through the icing.

I held my breath as he popped his finger in his mouth.

"I see." I turned my back and headed for the door.

"What, no threats? Not even going to try and beg?"

I kept walking. "No. What's the point? You've made up your mind, and I've made up mine."

His laughter followed me out the door. "You are going to lose everything tomorrow, Alena. Or I should say today. If you'd behaved yourself, I would have helped you. But you just had to go and be difficult. You must get that from your mother's side."

I spun at the door, gripping the edge of the new steel. "If I had behaved myself, I'd be dead."

He winked. "Exactly, and then I could have made you into something else."

With a flex of muscles, I ripped the steel door from the hinges and flung it across the room. As if I'd been doing it all my life. He ducked, the door missed him, and I turned away.

"Next time, I'm going to defend myself, and then we'll see who is stronger," he snarled at me.

I pointed a finger at him, my confidence soaring. Maybe it was the leftover nectar, but I didn't think so. "Bring it. I'm not the doormat you think I am."

I walked down the steps and away from the Granada. House number thirteen wasn't that far away. Yaya had the car rolling next to me, though, in a matter of seconds. "Didn't go as planned, did it?"

"What made you think that? The flying steel door or Merlin threatening me as I left?"

"Well, both." She laughed, though there wasn't a single mean note in it. "What are you going to do now?"

"Sleep and get ready for my hearing."

"You're still going to go?"

I gave her a smile as I walked. "He was already eating the cupcake before I left. I'm hoping both him and Roger are so sick they don't show up. If nothing else, that will buy me time."

She slapped her hand on the steering wheel, laughing. "Good. I hope he pukes his guts out, the jerk."

I reached the house at the same time Yaya pulled in. She hustled me inside. "Go get cleaned up. I'll make us breakfast, and then you can sleep for a bit."

I tried to argue, but she was firm and she was Yaya. "No, you need your strength."

I slogged upstairs, showered, and dressed in sweatpants and a loose T-shirt before heading back down. The smell of bacon and eggs and pancakes filled the air. A classic Yaya breakfast.

I stepped into the kitchen and froze. "Tad, how are you eating?"

My brother sat with a full plate in front of him and a fork partway to his mouth. "I puked until I was empty, and then I was all done. Now I'm hungry."

I did a quick count of the hours. "Oh no, it might not be long enough!" I shot a look at Yaya, who waved at me with a spatula to sit down.

"You don't know that; he's a Supe, it might be harder on a human," Yaya said.

Ernie sat beside me as he poured straight corn syrup over a stack of four pancakes. "Probably the Supes burn through the venom faster. Roger won't show today."

Tad stopped chewing. "What do you mean, venom?"

I grimaced. "It was an accident. I put some of my venom in the icing. It was only meant for—"

"Wait!" Tad stood up. "You really did poison us? What the hell is wrong with you?"

"Tad, it wasn't like that, I didn't mean for any—"

"You could have warned me." He slammed the fork down and stalked out of the kitchen.

I stood and hurried after him. "Tad, I didn't know! I only made it for Merlin, and I got mixed up when I was icing the cupcakes for the family."

"I don't know who you are anymore. You know Aunt Janice had to go to the hospital?" He glared at me, and I rolled my eyes.

"Tad, she's not even human."

He shook his head. "Neither are you."

"I know."

"Maybe Beth is right. Maybe you aren't the person you were before you were turned." He stepped out the door and slammed it behind him. I stared, unable to comprehend what had just happened.

Yaya came up behind me and slipped her arms around my waist. "It's not his fault. Theseus is behind this, I'm sure of it."

I shrugged out of her hold. "Maybe you'd better go too. Maybe he's right and I'm not the Alena you remember." I sniffed and headed for the stairs. Yaya grabbed my hand, spun me around, and smacked my face with her other hand.

I clamped a hand over my burning cheek. "What did I do? I was trying to keep you safe!"

"You can stop the pity party right now. You know that Theseus is trying to separate you from your friends. They are what made it possible for you to defeat Achilles."

208

I slowly nodded, her words sinking in. "Ernie, is he really that strong in compulsion? I mean, I know you said he could charm . . . but my own brother?"

Ernie frowned. "You're right, someone like Tad who loves you as much as he does wouldn't be able to just be charmed. I mean, even look at Beth; he used one of my arrows on her because that's how much it took to turn her against you."

The answer came to me slowly. "Tad has been letting Dahlia feed off him; she said it would make him more vulnerable to suggestions, so they had to be careful. That other vampires could use it against him."

Yaya nodded. "And the other vampires are?"

"Santos and his gang." I slapped a hand over my eyes, seeing the chessboard more clearly than ever, and it was weighted for Theseus. On his side he had Santos and his gang, both Beth and Sandy, and now Tad, which meant Dahlia would be with him too. If nothing else, to protect him. "Yaya, I have a terrible feeling about today. I feel like death is stalking us."

"Then it is time to eat and sleep while you can. You barely survived dealing with Achilles. You need everything you can get on your side."

I followed her back into the kitchen and sat down. I ate everything she put in front of me, not really tasting it. My mind went around and around like a possessed stand mixer.

Everything I'd learned about Theseus didn't come up to much. He was smart and liked games. He'd stolen my friends and now my brother from me. He was more than just a dumb jock hero like Achilles; he was a demigod who was manipulating the game at every turn. I stood, went to the door that led to the basement, and headed down on the off chance I was wrong. "Dahlia?"

I stopped at the door to her bedroom. I knocked once and peeked in. There was nobody in the bed. Was she with Tad, protecting him? Or had Theseus somehow taken her and convinced her I was horrible too? A pit in the bottom of my belly opened up and threatened to suck me under.

I climbed back up the stairs and went straight to the phone hanging on the wall by the back door. Remo's number stood out on the single sheet beside it that was pinned to the wall. I dialed and waited.

A sleepy sigh echoed through the line. "Dahlia, I am literally crawling into bed. What do you want?"

"It's not Dahlia," I said. "I . . . just needed to hear your voice. Is Dahlia there with you?"

He sucked in a breath I knew he didn't really need. "Are you hurt?"

"No. Not really. Theseus, he's convinced Tad I'm not myself, and he's turned him against me. And I think . . . maybe he's got Dahlia."

He grunted. "Stay where you are." And hung up on me. Stay where I was? I glanced at the window. There were maybe five minutes before the sun was up, not long enough for him to get from his compound in the valley all the way back into town. What was he thinking?

The front door opened, and a gust of wind brought me cinnamon and honey a split second before Remo strode into the kitchen. Fully clothed, unlike the other men I'd dealt with earlier in the night, much to my horrified disappointment.

I stuttered, "What are you doing here? How did you get here so fast? Is Dahlia okay?"

He grabbed my arm, nodded to Yaya, and all but dragged me toward the door that led to the basement. "I don't have much time. Flora, you'll watch things?"

"Of course. I've still got my lighting rod," she said as she pointed at her purse. As if it would have fit in there. Then again, maybe it was a shrinking and growing lightning rod. Another time, I would have had a giggle fit about that.

I followed him, casting a single glance back at my yaya. She smiled and waved at me with a wooden spoon. "Don't do anything I wouldn't."

This from the woman who had slept with Zeus. Good grief. I flushed as we hurried down the stairs, the sun all but kissing at our heels.

In the basement, Remo pulled me toward the door across from Dahlia's, the second bedroom set up for vampires. I'd not been down in the basement much; I'd been too busy dealing with everything to truly do a walk-through of the house. The door shut behind me, and we were plunged into semidarkness. There was a click, and two side lamps next to an oversized bed flicked on. Remo wrapped his arms around me from behind, his mouth against my shoulder as he spoke. "What happened?"

For a moment, I let myself just breathe. Just . . . exist with someone holding me, someone I trusted. Remo waited without pressuring me to hurry up and spit it out. No demands to get on with whatever I had to say.

I drew a breath and pulled away from him so I could turn and look him in the face. "More of the same. Only this time Tad took off, and I don't know where Dahlia is. Could Theseus use Santos to put people in thrall?"

Remo's face was a careful blank. "Yes, it is possible. But why would he do that if Theseus pulled Beth under on his own?"

I rubbed my face, realizing how much he'd missed out on. "He didn't. He used one of Ernie's arrows to manipulate her. I just . . . Tad wouldn't turn on me. Not like this." A tear slid down my cheek, and I swiped it away with a burst of anger. "He said this was my fault, that I deliberately poisoned our family."

Remo's mouth twitched. "They are all fine, aren't they?"

I nodded. "Yes, they are. But that isn't the point. He is right that I made them sick, even if I didn't mean to."

"Don't fall for this, Alena." He reached out and touched my face with one hand, tracing my jaw. "The doubt will chew you up and bring you to your knees. This is what Theseus wants. To make you believe you are something you aren't. To make you believe you are evil and not worthy of living."

I leaned my head against him. "Remo."

He laughed when I didn't say anything but his name. "Alena."

I wasn't laughing, though. I had to know where we stood, because the more I was around him, the more I felt things I knew were dangerous. Even telling Smithy that I was with Remo . . . that was the truth. It was how I felt. But if Remo didn't feel the same way, I didn't want to make the same mistake I'd made with Roger.

And the whole cross-species taboo . . . was that real, or was it something we could fight? Or was this just a friendship with a few benefits on the side?

"Tell me that you aren't using me, that everyone else is wrong and I'm not a fool for feeling things for you. I know vampires aren't monogamous. I get it, but I can't let my heart go again. Not if this is just a game to you. Not if we're just going to be pulled apart by rules that I don't give two figs about." Even though I hated saying it, I made myself lift my eyes to his. His were closed, and my heart thumped hard against my chest. "Just say it. Please be honest with me; as my friend I would hope you could do that much." Honey puffs, my heart had never seemed so loud in my ears.

His cheek twitched, and he seemed to be struggling with something. "You're right, vampires don't tend to be monogamous. It's too difficult when it comes to feeding if you don't want to drain your donor." His hands slid down my arms. "You . . . I haven't had to feed since I took your blood. I'm not as strong as I was immediately after, but I have had no hunger."

I noticed that he'd said nothing about how he felt, or if he felt anything at all for me other than the usefulness I had to him. So maybe no answer was his answer. I nodded. "That's good. I'll let you sleep." I stepped around him and had my hand on the doorknob before he stopped me, putting his hand over mine.

"Alena, things are not that simple," he said. "You are not a vampire. It would never work in the long run. No matter how much either of us might want it to. They aren't rules without reason."

I stared at the door, trying to not think about how badly I wanted it to be otherwise. I didn't say anything, just pulled the door open and stepped out. "Thank you for coming, and thank you for your honesty." As if I'd asked him to show up and fix my plumbing. I shut the door and hurried up the stairs, through the kitchen, and up the next flight to my bedroom. Yaya followed me, her heartbeat rising along with her steps. She didn't knock, just walked right in and sat down on the bed beside me.

"I'm going to give you some advice, Alena. And you *will* listen to me." She patted my leg, and I buried my face in my pillows as if I were a teenager again, running away from my mom's expectations.

"Yaya, I need to sleep. I have court in a few hours."

"And you're going to listen to me before you go to sleep. Men, no matter what species, will fight you on a relationship. Even if they don't realize it. Don't give up on him. He's being stubborn and pretending it's for your own good."

I rolled onto my back and looked at her. If Smithy was right, she was far older than she looked with her white puffy hair and crinkles around her bright-green eyes. "Yaya, I'm tired."

"Fine, fine. Go to sleep." She stood and then leaned over me. "But I want you to think about something. How did that man get here so fast when you called him? It seems to me that he was waiting close by, letting you do your thing but staying close enough that if you needed him, he could be here in a flash. That isn't the action of a man who doesn't care. Who doesn't hope to defy odds."

She turned and walked out of the room, leaving the door open. I sat up, her words rumbling around inside my head. "Yaya, how did you get to be so smart?"

"Hundreds of years!" she called out from downstairs. "I'm going. I'll see you at the courthouse later."

The front door slammed, and I was alone in the house. Or alone as I was going to be with Remo in the basement.

I was no longer the quiet church mouse Roger and Barbie had accused me of being. I wasn't a woman who gave up on her bakery, even with the odds so stacked against me. I wasn't a Drakaina who lost to Achilles. What the h-e-double-hockey-sticks was wrong with me?

Before I thought better of it, I stood up and ran down the stairs, through the kitchen, and back into the basement. I pounded on the bedroom door. "Seriously? You'd give me up because of some made-up rules that have nothing to do with you and me?"

He swung the door open, his eyes wide. And shirt off. Sweet baby Jesus, that was a beautiful body.

I sucked in a breath and fought to keep my eyes on his and not the body that put Smithy's to shame. "You would just walk away from me?"

He stood there, his throat working. "I've been trying."

"How's that going for you?" I put a hand on my hip and cocked one leg.

His lips twitched. "Not as planned."

"Yeah, well, it looks like I'm breaking all sorts of rules." I reached out, grabbed his face, and pulled him to me. Kissing him for all I was worth. He didn't fight me but wrapped his arms around my waist and picked me up, carrying me backward into the bedroom.

CHAPTER 19

I slid my hands over his bare shoulders and arms, shivering at the feeling of his muscles under my fingertips. His lips were on mine, crushing them, bruising them with the intensity in his kiss. I loved every second of it.

I pulled back as his hands began peeling my shirt up, baring my waist, and I knew I had to stop this while I still could. My body liked his hands, his kisses, the brush of skin on skin so much that in very little time I'd not be able to say no. I'd be so wrapped up in the sensation of Remo next to me I'd forget whatever ability I had to think clearly. To remember that I wasn't truly free to do as I wished. Not yet, anyway.

"I have to sleep," I blurted out.

His eyes slowly rolled up to look into mine. "What?"

"I came to tell you I wasn't giving up on us. On you. But I really need to sleep before the courthouse hearing today."

The sudden and sincere laughter that poured out of him shocked me. "You aren't mad?"

"Alena, you will never stop surprising me, will you?"

"Maybe?" I smiled up at him. "I'm sorry, I didn't mean for this to go this far. I'm scared and I trust you. And I want this, just not until I've dealt with Roger."

His eyes softened as he echoed my words back to me. "I trust you too."

There was something so sweetly intense about the moment that I wanted to hold it to me, cradle it as long as I could, so I could recall it again and again. He tugged me to him. "Stay with me. You'll sleep better if you feel safe."

And that was how I ended up in bed with Remo, his arms around me, and my nose buried in the crook of his neck. Roger had always complained about sleeping face to face, but Remo didn't say a word. I breathed in that subtle spice-and-honey smell that was only his. "You smell like cinnamon."

He grunted softly. "Go to sleep."

I curled tighter around him, as if I could wrap him tight to me.

"Alena?"

"Umm?"

"Ease off, you're squeezing the shit out of me."

Startled, I eased off and pulled away. He tugged me back. "Don't leave. Just don't try to boa constrictor me."

I laid my head back down next to his and closed my eyes. Whatever would come, would come. There was nothing I could do about it for the next few hours, and in a strange way, that gave me some peace.

Sleep claimed me in a matter of seconds, despite the fascination I had with my hand resting on Remo's abs. Sensation faded, and I fell into the dark abyss of dreaming. The best sleep I'd had since the last time he'd held me close, while I'd healed after facing Achilles on the battlefield.

Hours later, I woke up and rolled to look for a clock. Nothing in the room gave off any light; we were in complete darkness. There wasn't a single hint as to what time it was.

I stretched, my hands reaching over my head as I wriggled my toes. "What time is it?"

"Sun just set." Remo yawned, stretching beside me. "So about five."

Horror flashed through me. "Oh no, no, that can't be!" I leapt from the bed and ran out of the room. "The hearing was set for four!"

I couldn't have missed it. Remo had to be wrong. I raced up the stairs and slid to a stop in the kitchen, staring at the clock on the stove. 5:01. It would take me at least two hours to get to the courthouse. By then it would be closed. I slid to my knees, clinging to the counter with my fingertips.

Eyes closed, I fought to breathe through the loss. Everything, everything, was gone, and I'd not even put up a fight. Roger had won without a whimper from me.

I gripped the edge of the counter and yanked up as I stood, pulling the granite off. I flipped it to one side, sending it crashing through the wall as I shook with anger. "I'm an idiot."

I knew without looking that Remo was behind me. "No, you're not." No platitudes like "Don't worry, things happen for a reason" or "You can start again" came out of his mouth, for which I was grateful.

"What do I do now? What would you do?" I turned, and Remo stepped up and pulled me into his arms.

"If you're asking how I would handle it, I'd kill Roger and steal back everything that rightfully belonged to me." He smiled as though giving me his favorite recipe.

I leaned my head against his chest. "That did cross my mind."

Laughing, he held me away from him so he could look me in the eye. "That is not you."

"No, but I can fantasize." I grimaced. "Maybe I can talk to the judge? If I get a lawyer and appeal the decision." But even I knew how fruitless the words were.

Minutes ticked by and I stood there, not knowing what to do. "I'm going to talk to Roger." The thought hit me that he'd be going home, no doubt for a victory party. "Maybe I can convince him . . ." Who was I kidding?

Behind us the phone rang, and I glanced at it. "Probably for you."

Remo nodded and moved to answer it, pressing the receiver to his ear. "What is it?" No "Hello," no "This is Remo." What is it? I made a move to leave him to whatever conversation he needed to have.

He held the phone out for me, his eyes worried. "It's for you."

I walked over and pressed the phone to my ear. "Hello?"

"Alena, this is Judge Watts's court assistant. He's asked me to call you on his behalf."

I frowned. "Yes? Do you need me to sign something?" Probably that was all it was, some silly signature needed so Roger could take everything.

"No, we don't. Not yet. Judge Watts has asked that you please come to the courthouse right away. We were delayed and will be starting your hearing as soon as you arrive. We apologize for any inconvenience."

"Really?" I gasped. "Thank you, thank you! I'll be there as quick as I can."

The other end of the line clicked off and I hung up, excitement coursing through me. "Did you hear that?" This was a miracle, the chance I needed to make things right. I ran upstairs before Remo could answer and gathered up the duplicates of my paperwork. I had a chance. A chance to make things right.

I double-checked my papers, making sure I had everything, including the original bakery deed. I fanned the papers out on the bed, staring at them, doing a quick tally. Yes, I had them all. Hope flared in my chest. This was my last chance, and I knew it. I would not blow it again. I was going to fight for all I was worth to get my bakery and life back. To get my home back.

To make the world see I was worth seeing. I existed, and I was a good person. When I wasn't a giant snake, that is.

Hurrying, I changed into slacks and a nice button-down top, then brushed my hair back from my face.

"You can do this," I whispered to the mirror. "Don't hesitate, don't cringe. You are worth this."

I nodded at myself, then ran back downstairs to find Remo standing where I'd left him, a frown on his face.

He nodded and leaned back against the wall. "Alena, you have to know this is a trap. No courthouse calls someone personally to tell you your hearing has been delayed. Ever. And certainly not that they will wait for you to arrive."

A sour twist developed in my belly, like I'd eaten a whole bushel of crab apples, and the hope that had been growing withered on the vine like a rotten tomato. "A trap."

"Pretty sure." He nodded, picked the phone back up, and dialed out. I listened to the ringing. No one picked up, and he tried another number. And another. After the fourth call going into empty space, he turned and faced me. "Santos has my people."

Chills swept through me, thinking of Beth, Sandy, Tad, and Dahlia on his side. Even Yaya had said she was going to be at the courthouse. "And we know that Theseus has mine." The setup was too perfect; no matter what we wanted to think, we were on our own, unless . . . "There is someone I can talk to. I think he'll help."

Remo raised an eyebrow, but there was no jealousy flashing in his eyes. "Who?"

"Come on, I don't have a number. But I know where he is." I ran upstairs and changed out of my nice clothes, trading them in for jeans and a long-sleeved shirt. I slipped on a pair of running shoes and was once more ready to go. I met Remo at the front door, and he waved me through.

We climbed into his muscle car, and I directed him to the Supernatural Division of Mounted Police. I climbed out and ran to the door, thumping on it. "Smithy, we need to talk."

The door opened, but it wasn't Smithy who grimaced at me. It was Oberfluffel.

"Snake girl. What do you want?"

"I need to speak to Captain Smithy."

"He's been let go of his position." He flipped a picture at me. A picture of me slumped in Smithy's arms at Zeus's pool party. My face flamed bright red.

"Look. It wasn't how it looked. They gave me some sort of juice that made me tipsy. Oberfluffel, where did he go? I need his help."

His face purpled, and tiny veins popped out all over the edges. "OBERFALL. And I don't give a blue harpy's shit where Smithy went. He was fired, his wife is divorcing him because of this"—he shook the picture at me, and Remo took it—"and here you are thinking Smithy would help you?"

I took a step back. "He said he was my friend."

Remo handed the picture back to Oberfluffel, but he spoke to me. "I take it there are no other options?"

My shoulder's drooped. "No."

"Then we go to the courthouse alone." He took my hand and led me back to the car. We drove out the exit of the Wall, and once more the protestors cheered us on. I waved at a few of them; the girl I'd saved from the werewolf was still there. She held up a sign that read, "We Are All the Same."

"Well, that's a crock of pig poo," I muttered. Remo looked across at me and nodded.

"Maybe they need to believe it isn't, though. To believe that fear is just false evidence of something appearing to be real. Humans are funny that way. It's easier for them to pretend they aren't afraid. When deep down they know the truth. That they could be chewed up and spit out by any single Supe out there."

He stared out the windshield, calm as could be.

"You aren't mad about the picture?" I blurted out, unable to wonder any longer.

He laughed. "No. That is the price of being with a beautiful woman. Men will always be drawn to you, try to steal you away from me. And it will happen if I let it get to me, if I don't treat you right."

That seemed far too rational to me. Then again, it wasn't like he was really only thirty years old, even if that was what he looked to be.

"What is your plan when we get there?" he asked, forcing my mind away from him and to the task at hand.

"I need room to maneuver if I'm going to shift. I think . . . I think if I can go in and draw them outside, that would be best."

"And then?"

"I guess I fight whoever is there. There really isn't any other option."

Like it was going to be that easy. I knew it wasn't. Remo knew it wasn't. We had no help; no one was going to stand by us in this. Remo had to get his vampires back, and we had to get my friends back while somehow incapacitating Theseus.

We pulled onto the street where the courthouse stood, and Remo pulled the muscle car over. Scattered here and there were vans and a few trucks. It seemed too busy for a January evening at the courthouse, but what did I know?

From where we sat, the courthouse was lit up like ten thousand candles burning bright, every light in every window on.

"I think I should go in, act like I don't know that there is a trap," I said. I gathered up the papers sitting between us and clasped them to my chest. "If I act dumb, I'll get further."

"I don't like it," Remo said. "I'll hold to the shadows and follow you. But I won't come into the courthouse unless I hear a ruckus." He took my face in his hands and kissed me softly. "Be careful."

I smiled, though it was wobbly, and kissed him back. "You too."

Without another word, I slid from the car and strode toward the courthouse. I strained my ears and picked up nothing. Not a single heartbeat between me and the courthouse. Which did nothing to soothe me. I could be surrounded by vampires and not know it. Breathing through my mouth, I tasted the air and caught a faint hint of blood on it, the coppery tang zinging along the back of my mouth. I clutched the papers harder and hurried my feet.

The front doors of the courthouse beckoned, and I knew that I'd soon be truly on my own. No, that wasn't true; Remo was here. And Yaya had said she would meet me here too. Though it didn't make me feel any better to think of her somehow in the middle of a trap set for me.

The halls of the courthouse were empty, devoid of life on the surface. I listened and picked up several heartbeats at the end of the hall, behind the final set of doors.

I jogged toward them and stopped in front, listening. I leaned close and pressed my ear against the wood paneling.

"I don't really want to kill her, Tim," Beth said. "I just don't want to live with her anymore. I want her to move out so you can move in and we can be together. That's all."

"The only way she is going to leave," Theseus said, enunciating every word, "is if we kill her. She loves me, and I can't keep her away from me. I bet, even now, she's on her way here to stop us."

Beth sucked in a sharp breath. "But she won't. We'll be married, and she won't come between us."

Married? Great gobs of rotten peach pie, this was beyond crazy. Sure, Ernie had said the arrow caused obsession, but to marry Theseus? Fear clutched at me. If Beth was that far under the spell, how was I going to help her escape?

"That's why we have to end her life," Theseus all but cooed.

A laugh rumbled through the air. "She won't survive, boss. Between the fennel oil and my vampires, she won't be leaving here with her skin intact."

The Drakaina in me didn't like that at all, and all the rest of me had to agree. I stepped back, lifted a foot, and booted the door open.

It swung so hard it crashed open, and I got a glimpse of shocked faces before the momentum swung the door back shut with a thud.

"Honey puffs!" I kicked the door again, hard enough this time to blow it off its hinges so it dangled by only a few shattered pieces of metal.

The room held Theseus, Beth and Sandy, Santos, and several vampires I didn't recognize. I didn't see Dahlia or Tad. Or Yaya.

"I like my skin the way it is, dingle nuts," I snapped.

Santos moved like buttered-up lightning. In his hand he held a flask I knew all too well. He unscrewed the cap and flung the contents at me. I backpedaled, scrambling on the floor, hitting the far wall of the hallway with the flat of my back.

Theseus laughed as the oil splattered me in a few spots, my left hand and thigh. Two drops, and within seconds they'd already eaten through my clothes and skin and into the diamond-patterned snakeskin below. The pain was instant, more intense than I remembered, scattering my thoughts like flour blowing in a fan. This was the oil undiluted, and it sent me into sheer survival mode. There was nothing but pain rippling through me and the white noise of my own heart and heavy breathing.

Theseus's voice cut through it all. "Drive her to the main courtroom." My instinct to run screamed at me. If I was going to get back outside, it was now or never. I spun and moved to run back the way I'd come. Beth stood in my way, her blue eyes hard but her bottom lip trembling. She was a nurse, and despite Theseus's spell holding her in its thrall, she was a healer, not a killer.

"Don't make me hurt you, Alena."

"Beth, please, don't do this. I saved you from Merlin," I whispered through the pain. "Please, you're my friend."

For just a second I thought she heard me. Her eyes softened, and a tear gathered in one, then slid down her face. Theseus stepped up next to her and put a hand on the back of her neck, squeezing.

"She lies. Even now she's trying to manipulate you." He kissed her cheek, and her eyes frosted like overchurned ice cream.

"Bullshit, Alena. Merlin turned me for Tim. You aren't my friend." The way her eyes glittered, I could see she believed the warped words.

She didn't shift but instead reached for a sword hanging from one hip, a sword that had Athena's symbol on it. Call it a hunch, but I suspected that sword would cut me. She pointed it at me. "Go on, the other way."

The drops of oil seared my mind, reminding me that I had more than one problem. The Drakaina in me went crazy, writhing and twisting to be released. To fight, to battle our way out, to shift and thrash the building to the ground. But it wasn't time. Not yet. And I couldn't be sure that Yaya and the others weren't in here somewhere. I wasn't going to destroy a building knowing innocent lives could be lost.

I would have only one shot at this, and I knew it. With my mouth pressed in a tight, thin line, I bit back on the whimpers that filled my mouth.

I let Beth drive me down the hall and into the main courtroom with towering ceilings and enough seating for three hundred people. Not that there were that many people in it, but there were enough. Mostly vampires, but I saw Tad and Yaya up at the front, confirming my worst fears. Dahlia sat to one side of Tad, and their eyes . . . they glared at me before looking away. As if I truly were the monster. Shaking, I tried to get their attention, staring hard at them. But they wouldn't meet my eyes.

At the front of the room, Judge Watts sat in his chair, towering over everyone. His face was white, pale with fear, and sweat slid freely down his wobbly cheeks.

Theseus strode to the base of Judge Watts's podium. "Thank you all for coming. I like things to be as fair and judicial as possible. I am not some random hero, some killer that will take to the streets and cause mob justice. No, as you can see by those I've gathered here, I am friend to all those who would be my friend. And enemy to those that would do harm to the world."

What was he doing? I rubbed the back of my left hand on a bench in a vain attempt to get the oil off but only succeeded in spreading it over my hand more. I whimpered, the heat and pain taking my focus off what was happening. I forced myself to look around, to see what I could use, to see if there was anyone who would be on my side. Everyone who was in the room stared at Theseus as though he were indeed a god. Including Tad and Dahlia. Even Roger and Barbie were there, dumbstruck as they stared at Theseus. What surprised me the most, though, was Merlin. He stood to the side, nearest to Roger. He frowned as he watched Theseus speak, his brows drawn low over his hawk nose.

Then there was Yaya. Her eyes were glued to me as she mouthed Remo's name. I shook my head ever so slightly. I didn't know where he was; I mean, he was here somewhere, but that didn't help. The last thing I wanted was for both of us to be trapped.

There was a struggle behind me, the thumping of feet and bodies, a snarl, and then that small hope died. Remo was strung up between four vampires and dragged into the room, then tossed at my feet. I helped him stand up. He was bruised and battered, but he wasn't hurt badly.

"You okay?" he murmured, touching my face gently. I shook my head.

"Oil." I held my hand up, showing him where the oil had sunk in, opening me right up.

He took my hand and raised it to his mouth, suctioning onto the wound, licking the oil off. He grimaced, and I felt him draw some of my blood into his mouth. I gave him the barest of nods to keep going. With my blood racing through his veins, giving him strength and power like no other vampire alive, we might have a chance. Maybe.

We were jerked apart. Theseus pointed at me. "You see, she has him bowing at her feet. She is a siren of the evilest kind, one that preys on men. Even the undead follow her."

I rolled my eyes, fighting the pain in order to speak levelly. "Is this for real? Are you actually presenting a case to the judge to decide if you should try and kill me or not?"

Theseus smiled, his back to the judge. "You wanted the law to claim you exist. If you exist, then you can be judged, you can be tried, and you can be executed."

Anger flared in my gut. "You can't do this!"

Theseus shrugged. "Your Honor, do I have your go-ahead to present my case? Of course, if you disagree, we can always find someone else." The threat was obvious. They would kill Watts if they didn't like his answer.

The judge nodded, his eyes wary and the tension in his shoulders obvious. "Do it. Prove she is guilty."

I took a step back, and my leg with the oil burning through it buckled. I went to one knee as Theseus spoke. "I have witnesses that the Drakaina attempted to poison her family."

One by one my cousins, Samantha and Everett, and Aunt Janice and Uncle Robert stepped through the crowd and up to the base of the podium. They spoke about the sickness I'd caused, that by my own admission I'd claimed it was not an accident at all that my venom had gone into the cupcake frosting. They spoke about my callous words. "She said she didn't give a shit about us," Samantha snapped, her eyes glittering as they landed on me.

"I would never say that! I don't curse!" I yelled back. I mean, it wasn't like this was a real court proceeding. I certainly wasn't going to play by the rules.

Samantha shrugged. "That's what I heard."

The judge wrote something down.

The one that hurt, though, was Tad as he stood up and gave his account, Dahlia clinging to his hand in support. Neither of them would look at me.

"I thought she was my sister still, that being turned hadn't changed her. But the truth of it is, she is a monster. A killer who would prey on anyone weaker than herself. Including her family."

"Those cupcakes weren't for you!" I stood and realized I was about to back myself into a corner.

"Who were they for, then?" Theseus asked, his eyes narrowing.

I struggled with the words. "For Merlin. He . . . was coming to defend Roger." Oh, God, I knew the words were bad.

Remo groaned. "Not the time to be honest, love."

The judge stood up and slammed his gavel on the bench. "Is that all the witnesses?"

Merlin cleared his throat. "I do believe I should have some say in this, since I was the target of Ms. Budrene's *devilishly* good cupcakes."

Remo shifted so he stood just a little bit in front of me. I put a hand on him. "No."

He muscles tensed, but he stepped back. Whatever Merlin had up his sleeve, I would deal with him.

Yaya gave me an encouraging smile.

Merlin gave me a wink. That did not make me feel better after our last conversation.

He strode across the floor, pacing slowly. "I do believe a family feud is something that should be left within families. And while Alena's family was caught in the crosshairs, it should be no skin off your nose, Your Honor, if she hurts other supernaturals. All those speaking today are such. Correct?"

The judge whipped around to stare at my cousins, aunt, and uncle, along with Tad. Slowly, they all nodded.

The judge rolled his eyes. "Good God. I don't want anything to do with supernatural infighting. Go back to your side of the Wall, and what you do there, keep it there. Case dismissed."

Theseus gaped at him, and I took a step back while he spluttered, "But that isn't fair. She's a monster. My case is airtight! I have been planning this for weeks!"

Now that was interesting. Weeks would mean he'd been around before Achilles and I had had our fight. So he'd just let another hero take a fall?

The judge shrugged. "It's a family feud, that much is obvious to me now. Families have a strange way of exaggerating things when they are angry at each other. And while I don't like supernaturals, I can't argue with what he's suggesting." He pointed at Merlin. Who'd essentially saved my bacon.

After I'd poisoned him with a cupcake. Why did that make me nervous? Merlin smiled and blew me a kiss. My stomach fell to my feet.

Theseus pulled a sword. "Then I say we need a new judge." Watts's face went white as Theseus pulled his arm back, prepping to throw the sword. The sword Beth had pointed at me with Athena's crest on it.

I pushed with my good leg and landed in front of Theseus as he swung. I took the blow to my right shoulder, stopping it from hitting Watts. "No, I won't let you kill anyone!"

The blade nicked me, cutting through both human skin and snake-skin, but it was a glancing blow, barely a scratch.

I shoved Theseus hard, sending him flying through the air. I glanced back at Watts. "Go, while you can!" He didn't hesitate, but scrambled away, his black robe flying around him and flashing a pair of bright-orange undies.

I glanced at Remo.

"Run!" he yelled.

I bolted from the courtroom—okay, limped—bowling over several vampires, and then I ran into my Aunt Janice as she attempted to escape.

"Outta my way, brat!" she snapped, shoving a clawed hand into my chest that sent me flying down the hall. Away from the exit. Remo leapt over her and reached for my hand, pulling me to my feet. "We'll find another way out."

The ping of metal slamming into the ground at my feet drew my eyes. A perfectly formed metal feather quivered where it stuck. The screech of a Stymphalian bird snapped my head up. I didn't know which of the girls it was, but a good guess was Beth was the one shooting at me.

I scrambled to my feet, and Remo helped me as we whipped around the corner. Beth was right behind us, slinging feathers like a machine gun. Remo grunted as a feather hit him in his right side, slicing across his ribs.

He healed, though, as fast as the cut appeared. At least my blood was good for something. We raced through the halls, Beth tailing us. Driving us.

"You're going to have to fight her," Remo said as we slid through a door and slammed it behind us. The thud of metallic feathers hitting the door echoed through the room.

Behind us came the shuffle of several sets of feet. I spun around, unsure of exactly what I was looking at. Cameras pointed at me, reporters held microphones toward me, and one brave reporter cleared her voice. "This was a landmark case. How do you feel about losing?"

Hold the powdered sugar, what in the world was going on?

CHAPTER 20

"I didn't . . . lose," I stuttered. Not really. Though I really hadn't won either. The case with Roger wasn't what they meant, of that much I was sure. This whole situation had been all about Theseus proving I was a monster, that I was worth killing. These were his final moves on the chessboard.

I stared at them, beginning to see just how he'd put things in place. "Theseus set you up here?"

The three reporters nodded and pushed their microphones closer. The one who'd spoken tried again, her eyes filled with what could only be fascination. "This is a live feed. Do you have something to say? The entire city is watching."

Several more thumps hit the door, making me jump. Remo pressed a hand to my back and lowered his voice. "Talk to them, and make it juicy."

I glanced at him and then back to the reporter. To the side of her was a sink. I hurried to it, limping. "My name is Alena Budrene, and I contracted the Aegrus virus four weeks ago. I didn't want to die. While I was on my deathbed, my husband left me for another woman. Apparently he'd been boinking her long before I got sick." I took a breath and gripped the faucet handle. With a quick twist, the water was running. I lifted my leg and jammed it under the flow of water as I went on, talking as fast as I could. I only had so long before we would be interrupted. Maybe I would die at Theseus's hand, but at least the world would know something about me.

"So I took a chance and let a warlock turn me into a supernatural; that's the only way to survive the Aegrus virus, you know. But now the courts say my two-timing loser of a husband gets everything. My bakery, Vanilla and Honey. My inheritance from my grandparents. And even the house my grandparents left me." The door behind us shuddered.

The reporter nodded. "Go on."

"I only want it to be fair. I want what is mine, nothing more. I'm not dead; I'm still me. I'm still a person too. Just because I'm different on the outside doesn't mean anything." I stared into the camera, begging. "I want to be acknowledged, no different than anyone else, and be able to say that I fall under the same rules and legislation, not some trumped-up ridiculousness saying that I"—I took my hands out of the water and touched my chest—"don't exist."

The blinking red light on the camera behind the reporter went off, and she nodded at me. "Well, that's going to be quite the piece. Thank you."

Behind us, the door busted open. I was thrown forward with the explosion. The news crews all yelled and ducked. Except for one of the cameramen, who held steady. The red light above the lens came back on, blinking. I stared at the open door but couldn't see through the smoke that filled the space other than the flicker of movement. Shadows that shifted, lurching toward us.

This was what Theseus wanted: an audience—not just the judge and a courtroom full of people, but the world too. He was far more organized than Achilles had been.

Remo looked at me. "Run, you need space to fight him. I'll hold them back."

I nodded and pushed myself up. The window over the sink beckoned. It had worked for me before; no need to change methods. I leapt up and crashed through the window, falling to the cool grass outside.

My leg that had been hit with the fennel oil buckled under me, weak. Above me came the hunting cry of a bird. I ran around the side of the building. Lights blazed to life, blinding me. I threw a hand up to block the lights. More reporters, cameras, and microphones at the ready. In front of them stood Theseus. He had his hands in the air, as if soothing them all. Not a single strand of his hair was out of place. Of course not; he hadn't been fighting me, chasing me. He had Beth and Santos for that. He'd sat back and put his pawns into play.

He spoke to the reporters in a booming voice that echoed with a confidence and power even I felt vibrate along my skin.

"Justice will be served. I will not allow a monster of the Drakaina's size to terrorize anyone a second longer than I must."

Enough of this nonsense. "I am not terrorizing anyone, you dumb jock!" I limped toward them. Theseus held a hand out to me, as if that alone would hold me back, then he swept a sword up into the ready position.

"Stand back," he called over his shoulder. "I'll protect you."

I blinked, at first thinking he was talking to me, then realizing he was talking to the reporters *about* me. My jaw ticked and then I laughed. Because it was beyond ridiculous.

Except that Theseus was a performer, and he knew the game we played far better than I did. One of the Stymphalian girls swept into view, hovering in the air above Theseus. He flicked his sword tip in my direction, and a multitude of metal feathers shot at me. There was no way I'd be able to dodge them all. I tried, though. I threw myself to the side, missing all but two.

They hit me in the hip and right near the oil damage in my thigh. There was no stopping the snake in me this time. She roared up through me, smoke curling around my body as the shift took me.

I blinked and was looking down at the reporters from twenty feet above. My body coiled and twisted as I tried to protect the spots where I'd been hurt. Apparently another monster *could* do damage to me, as

I'd feared, because the feather burrowed under my skin, digging hard as though it actively sought its way into my flesh.

I let out a long, low rumbling hiss and snaked my head toward Theseus. Which happened to be toward the crowd too. I figured it out at the last second and reared back. I flicked my tail around and smacked him in the side with it, sending him flying away from the crowd. The screech of two birds snapped my head up. Beth and Sandy streaked toward me, claws outstretched. I bared my fangs but at the last second ducked, dodging them both.

"Drakaina, come to your death!" Theseus beckoned. I twisted around, my scales glittering in the bright lights. I had no words for him in this form, but someone else did.

Ernie flew up by my head, huffing and puffing. "You have to stop the girls first. Without them, he has nothing. Remo is dealing with the vampires; he'll keep them off you."

I nodded. But I didn't really know what to do. Theseus held back, and I realized Ernie was right. He was waiting for Beth and Sandy to do the work for him. Just like Achilles with his Bull Boys.

I sucked my coils in around me into a tight ball, hiding my injuries. The open wounds were an invitation I didn't need to give.

One of the girls swept past my face and shook her head. Sandy, then. I bobbed my head toward Theseus, begging Sandy with my eyes. *Help me. Help me stop him.*

I could only hope she still had her own mind, that unlike the others she wasn't completely lost under the influence of Theseus.

Slowly she came around in a circle and flew beside me. Our eyes locked. She was close enough that, with a single swipe of her claws, she could blind me if she chose. With a wild screech, she flicked her wings . . . at Theseus. I wanted to cheer. Sandy was with me.

Theseus leapt out of the way of the metallic feathers, barely dodging them. Then again, she'd thrown only two.

From behind us came Beth, screaming. She slammed into Sandy, and they spun through the air, gold and silver glittering under the bright lights in flashes like camera bulbs going off.

Good enough. They would keep each other busy. I opened my mouth and hissed at Theseus.

Ernie floated close by. "You have no choice. Your venom will do the trick; just do it fast."

He was right, I knew it, and I hated it. I shot forward, mouth open. Thinking it would be that easy. More the fool was I for that.

Theseus bolted out of my way and straight back toward the crowd. They fell back from him, but not fast enough. He grabbed a young man with gangly legs and a long, narrow face. He pulled the youth around in front of his body, using him as a shield.

"Now what will you do, monster?" He grinned at me from around the kid.

I pulled back, lowering myself so my jaw was on the ground. Theseus held his sword pointed at me, his other arm around the youth's neck. "What's your name, boy?"

"James."

"Well, James, have you ever seen the inside of a snake?" Theseus laughed the question. The crowd pulled back farther, a rumble going through them. Theseus glanced at them, and I slithered forward again while his eyes were averted. I had an idea of what I was going to do; I just didn't know if it would work. If I could pull it off and still save the boy.

"You think I should not protect myself? That one of your lives is not worth my own?"

His words told me all I needed to know. Ernie was right; Theseus could be killed by me and my venom, or he wouldn't have run. I stared at him, watching sweat curl down one side of his face. I had to be patient, to wait for his confidence to override his common sense.

Theseus glanced over his shoulder at the crowd and opened his mouth. This was my chance.

I shot forward, my mouth clamped shut, as I drove my head between James and Theseus. I shoved Theseus to one side of my body and blocked him from James and the rest of the crowd.

"You think you're so smart," he snarled.

I had only one answer for him. I reared up, pulling more of my body into the air than ever before. I almost doubled my height as I reared above him.

"Monster!" He pointed his weapon at me. "Do your worst. Good will prevail."

I dropped from the sky, my mouth open, eyes closed. I didn't want to see this happen.

Theseus jammed his sword into my mouth as I tried to close it on him. He dug it in, encouraged by my own momentum, digging the blade into the soft palate. I ripped away from him and writhed on the ground, the pain in my mouth blinding me.

Screams rent the air around me, and I tried to still my thrashing.

"Stymphalian bird, pin her," Theseus bellowed. "And for all that you hold dear, do not let go."

A set of claws settled above my head, and a weight held me down. Beth. Had she killed Sandy? My heart clenched at the thought . . . they were best friends. How could she have turned on Sandy?

I rolled my eyes to stare up at Beth. She bent and tried to peck my eyes out. I bucked and writhed and managed to throw her off balance, knocking her with one of my coils. She fell to the side and scrambled up, and I snapped at her, desperate to keep her away, to keep my eyes intact.

Except I underestimated my lunge . . . or maybe my Drakaina knew exactly the distance between us. My fangs buried deep into her flesh, cutting through the metal feathers that covered her like they were made of tinfoil. I jerked away as fast as I could, but even I knew it was too late.

Theseus laughed. "You should finish her off, but you won't. It would make my life easier, one less monster to deal with in the end. So let me do it for you." He flicked his sword hand at Beth's bird form as casually as if he were waving to her.

He cut through her neck, taking off her head as if it were nothing to him. I stared, unable to comprehend what had just happened. Theseus smiled at me. "You see? She was a tool, like all the others. But your venom . . . it would have killed her anyway. This was a mercy I gave her."

I reared up, grief for my friend driving me. It wasn't anger, exactly, but a sense that if I didn't do this, no one would be able to—Theseus wouldn't stop with me, he'd kill Sandy next. And then Tad. And Remo. And Dahlia. He'd clear out the north side of the Wall, killing supernaturals, even as he found ways to make them turn on one another.

I felt it then, a true understanding of who and what I was to the Super Dupers. I could be the one who tipped the scales in our favor. I could not only stop Theseus, I had it in me to be the monster that made the world realize we weren't all evil. We weren't all true monsters, but were of value to the world as we were.

I unleashed my full speed on Theseus, wrapping coil after coil around him and squeezing for all I was worth, but he slipped through.

"You think I don't know how to kill you?" he screamed, the heat of battle driving him. He drove his sword into one of the open wounds, a battle cry on his lips.

I didn't flinch, despite the agony that roared through me. Finally, I wrapped a coil around him, pinning one arm to his body. I squeezed harder, lowering my face so we were eye to eye. I saw now why Hera held him back . . . he was mad with power, with his hero status. Perhaps she saw that.

He laughed at me, eyes wild, breath coming in gasps. "You can't squeeze me to death; I'm a demigod."

I wanted to tell him he would die, that I would kill him. I settled for flicking a single fang out and leaning over him. I let a drop of venom fall, and then another, like adding just enough flavor to a cake. Wouldn't do to waste. He squirmed and thrashed as the venom fell from my fangs, avoiding it at first.

And then a drop landed in his eye. He screeched, his mouth wide open, and a second drop fell into his mouth.

He gulped once, stiffened in my coils, and slumped over. I didn't let him go, but I did pull back, my head cocked to one side, listening closely.

From the group of reporters I heard a single voice speaking, the woman reporter from inside the courthouse. "As you can see, the madman has been dealt with by a powerful guardian. I believe our city is a safer place with the Drakaina looking out for us."

I stared at her, unable to believe what I was hearing. Ernie flew close to my head and whispered softly. "The huntress sides with you. You are gaining allies whether you know it or not."

The huntress. Artemis. The female reporter gave me a slow nod and a salute.

Theseus's heart gave one last beat, then stopped, and I uncoiled from him.

But the night wasn't over. As if an unseen signal had been given, vampires poured out of the courthouse, running every which way.

Dahlia and the rest of Remo's crew drove Santos's people out and away. My heart lurched. Where was Remo? With the adrenaline gone, the reverse shift took me, and I was on the cool grass, buck naked, shivering and unable to stand, my body aching from all quarters, from my mouth and head to my legs and feet. I glanced down. The sword of Theseus had to have been coated in the fennel oil. Even as I thought it, the burn began deep within the sword wound in my side, the power of the oil spreading through my innards. I cried out and fell. I'd stopped him, but at what cost?

Hands caught me up. "We need a healer," Ernie yelled.

A gentle voice spoke, one I didn't know. "I can help with that. She has earned her stripes, protecting her friends. Protecting everyone."

Heat and cold flushed through me, one after another. I gasped and sat up, staring into the face of a woman whose blue eyes made me think of the neon-blue frosting I'd used on a birthday cake once.

"Who are you?"

She smiled. "I am Panacea, healer of the pantheon. Artemis and I . . . we don't agree with what Hera and Aphrodite are doing. They're being stupid again." She brushed her hands on a long, loose skirt that pooled at her bare feet. "While we can't directly help you, we will do what we can. Because until Zeus pulls his head out of his ass, this is going to be harder on you than it needs to be."

She pulled a cloak from her shoulders and swept it around my bare ones. "Heroes come in all shapes and sizes, and are different for every generation. You are the hero now, Alena. Do not forget it." She bent and kissed me on the forehead. Cameras clicked and bright lights seemed to intensify, and then she was gone. Like she'd never been there.

The pain and wounds were gone as suddenly as Panacea, though they were replaced by a bone-deep fatigue. Clutching the cloak closed around me, I stood and looked around. "Remo?"

"I'm here." His voice was fatigue filled, but as he approached I could see he wasn't hurt, at least not badly.

Behind us a muffled cry resounded in the night air. I turned to see Sandy in her human form, on the ground next to Beth's now human body, her head off to one side. Sandy's shoulders shook as she sobbed over her friend. I hurried to her side and folded my legs under me to rest on my knees.

"Sandy, honey, we have to go."

Her eyes were swollen with tears when she looked up at me. "I can't leave her here."

Remo stepped up beside me. "We'll take care of her. We won't let her stay here."

I tucked a hand under her arm. "Come on, let's go home."

She leaned into me, as naked as I was. The curse of a shifter. "Tad," I said, "give her your jacket."

My brother jogged over, his eyes downcast, but he slipped off his long jacket and wrapped it around Sandy's shoulders.

In a matter of minutes, Remo, Dahlia, Tad, Yaya, Sandy, and I walked in a tight group toward the front of the courthouse, where we'd parked. Somehow we managed to exit the building at the same time as Judge Watts. He glanced at me, stopped when he saw my obvious state of undress beneath the cloak. He spluttered once and shook his head. "Your divorce hearing is tomorrow at one in the afternoon. I suggest you be there, Ms. Budrene."

I slumped, defeat finally taking me. "Why, so you can just take it all from me? Pretend I don't really exist, even after I saved your life?"

He pursed his lips. "Perhaps don't argue with the judge who can change things for you, yes?"

I slumped further, turned, and walked away. Yaya caught me around the waist with one arm. "You know, you're getting really good at this ass-kicking business. Perhaps you could charge money for spectators. Like a staged wrestling match."

I smiled but couldn't even manage a laugh. We'd lost someone this time, someone who'd been a friend. I couldn't stop seeing Theseus as he took Beth's head, lopping it off as though she were nothing to him.

Because she was just another monster. And he'd been able to do it only because I'd bitten her. I'd mortally wounded her. Tears tracked down my cheeks as I finally began to process the events of the night.

"Alena."

I stopped, sniffed once, and turned to Merlin. He didn't smile, but there was a light in his eyes. He ran a hand over his slicked-back hair.

"What?"

"I think . . . I think I made a mistake. I need to speak with you."

Why did I think that wasn't going to bode well for me?

CHAPTER 21

We arrived at Merlin's house ahead of him. "Why would he ask us to meet him here?" Dahlia asked.

I had a feeling I knew, but I didn't want to say anything. I didn't want to jinx what was left of the night by saying my thoughts out loud. The last thing we needed was more drama, bloodshed, or fighting. But I expected we were going to get more of that sooner than I wanted.

Merlin pulled up in a slick sports car. He got out, nodded at me, and then flicked his fingers for me to follow. Remo, Yaya, and the others moved with me. Merlin held up his hand. "Alena only."

The others bristled, except for Remo. He shared a look with me and nodded. I could handle myself, we both knew it, and that trust in me gave me renewed energy.

I followed Merlin into his house, and he shut the door behind us. "I think . . . things are not working out the way I'd hoped. I need to come clean."

I folded my arms, holding my cloak tight around me. "Really?"

He went to his dining table and slid down into one of the high-backed chairs. He picked up a red poker chip and danced it across his knuckles. "You see, when I was first approached and asked to start reviving Greek monsters, I thought it would be to the supernatural world's benefit. Hera had a . . . convincing case. And I had my own ideas of what needed to be done. I thought the heroes"—he rolled the chip and then snapped it into the air and grabbed it—"were the answer. That they would be the ones to set our world right. To show the humans that, while they should fear us, we could go back to living the way we had before. Side by side. That they, Achilles, Theseus, and the others, would bring down the Wall."

He sighed and I raised an eyebrow. "Hurry it up, Merlin. It's been a long couple of days."

"So feisty now." He smiled at me. "I did turn you because I thought you weak, and your weakness offended me. I sent your brother to infect you so I could approach you with the offer of being turned." He caught the poker chip, clutching it in his palm. "Then you ousted Achilles." He frowned. "And you rallied the protestors at the Wall, without meaning to. You even displaced the SDMP to some degree, changing how they viewed different Supes."

"So?" I didn't catch what he was rolling out, though it could have been the fatigue.

He leaned back in his chair. "What I saw at the courthouse finally showed me that times have changed. The heroes no longer can function in this world as they once did. They aren't what we need. We need a monster to show us all that there should be no divide between humans and supernaturals." He grinned. "And you are that monster."

"Why are you telling me all this?"

Merlin grimaced, stood, and headed out of the room. Down the long hallway where I knew he kept his newly turned Super Dupers. My skin prickled as we traversed the narrow hall with the single chandelier hanging from the center and the pictures of old bearded men on the walls. I paused at one, thinking he had a familiar face, like I'd seen him before.

"Don't dawdle, Alena." Merlin opened the door at the far end. I walked toward him and stepped through.

A woman lay on the same cot I'd woken up on. Her chest rose and fell, her hair hung in myriad twists of patterned black and blond ringlets, as though she'd had some wild dye job. "You already turned her into a monster, didn't you?"

"Yes."

"Well, she can come with us, then. She can . . ." I trailed off as Merlin put a hand on my arm.

"No, you don't understand. Hera saw that Theseus was going down. She wanted me to create a monster that was bigger and even stronger than you. One she could control. A Hydra to be exact."

"Why?"

"Because if a hero on his own can't kill you and make an example of your death . . ." He stared hard at me, and the pit grew in the bottom of my belly like a burnt-out bread pan.

"Then maybe another monster could help the hero defeat me?" I whispered.

Merlin nodded. "Exactly."

I stood in front of Judge Watts, my hands clutched behind me. I'd given him all the paperwork I had, and he'd silently gone over it. Roger stood ten feet to my right, a smug smile on his stupid face.

To my left, Yaya stood, also smiling.

"How can you possibly be happy about this?" I whispered.

"I have a good feeling," she whispered back.

Judge Watts put the stack of papers down and removed his glasses. "I see everything is in order."

Roger smirked again. "Wonderful, can we move on then?"

Judge Watts frowned. "I hereby award Mrs. Budrene half of the funds in the joint checking account, full ownership of the Kerry Park home, and full ownership of Vanilla and Honey."

Holy crap, what just happened? A shiver of disbelief ran through me. "Your Honor?"

"I further state that Mrs. Budrene is a full citizen of the United States and will no longer be required to live behind the Wall."

Roger flipped out, the crowd went a bit bonkers, and someone cried out from the back. I looked to see if I could identify the screamer. I wasn't sure, but it could have been Barbie or maybe Colleen.

Roger, though, wasn't going down without a fight. "No, no. She doesn't exist! This is not fair! She died; I have her death certificate!"

Judge Watts stared hard at him from his perch. "If she didn't exist, I would not have survived last night. Therefore, she exists, and I must make my decisions based on that simple fact."

The next hour flew by as I signed papers and took my new papers saying I was Alena Budrene. I would change my last name back to my maiden name as soon as I could, but I'd take Budrene for now. I'd earned it. I stepped out of the courthouse, my head still whirling. There was a crowd waiting for me, microphones thrust my way for comments on my landmark case. The protestors from the Wall were there too, chanting my name. Some of them were crying, and they were hugging each other.

The woman I'd saved from the werewolf at the Wall ran up to me. She grabbed my face and kissed me on each cheek. "We are all the same. I knew you would be the one to show the world."

She was pulled away by two police officers, one from the SDMP, one from the Seattle Police Department.

Around us, I could hear a mixture of reactions. The protestors cheered, but there were others that did anything but. I saw them circling around like vultures. Firstamentalists, there to assert their beliefs. They held signs up too. "Monsters Rot in Hell." "The Soulless Shall Destroy the World." "Kill Them All." You know, the usual happy signs they carried. I sighed and turned away, feeling the weight of responsibility on my shoulders. My mom was going to kill me for this.

Ernie high-fived me, snapping me out of my musings, and my yaya kissed my cheek. Everyone was happy. But I could barely keep a smile on my face. I knew Hera wasn't done with me—our battle was far from over. There was a Hydra out there somewhere, working with a new and even deadlier hero in an effort to finally take me down.

Instead of fear, though, determination filled me. I stood straight and stared into the cameras. Words rose up in me, words that felt right and true, even if they were not something I would have ever said before.

"My name is Alena Budrene, and I am a Drakaina. I will protect this city, my family, and my friends from all who would do them harm. Let them come." I smiled and let my fangs slowly drop. "I will stop them."

ACKNOWLEDGMENTS

No book is every complete without thanking those who helped bring it to life. Again I must thank my editorial team, Tegan Tigani, Sara Addicott, and Michelle Hope Anderson. You truly helped this manuscript shine far brighter than if I'd been left on my own polishing away. ☺ To my readers, thank you for continuing to trust me with your escapes from the real world. I love that you take the time to message me and leave reviews, and that you love my characters as much as I do.

Many thanks also to my family, most especially my husband and son. You two put up with my crazy schedule, the early mornings and long nights, the lack of sleep, and the times I daydreamed in the middle of family gatherings. Your love keeps me going.

Thank you.

ABOUT THE AUTHOR

Shannon Mayer is the *USA Today* bestselling author of the Rylee Adamson Novels, the Elemental Series, the Nevermore Trilogy, A Celtic Legacy series, and several contemporary romances. She started writing when she realized she didn't want to grow up not believing in magic. She lives in the southwestern tip of Canada with her husband, son, and numerous animals. To learn more about Shannon and her books, go to www.shannonmayer.com.

Sign up for Shannon Mayer's newsletter:
http://www.shannonmayer.com/tut8.